One Star General

By Al Morgan

NOVELS: The Great Man

Cast of Characters

One Star General

MUSICAL COMEDY: Oh, Captain! (*With José Ferrer*)

DRAMA: The Old Man

One Star General

☆ *A NOVEL BY*

Al Morgan

RINEHART & COMPANY, INC.   New York   Toronto

For
Annie Laurie Williams
and
Bill Raney

All the characters in this novel are purely fictitious.

Contents

La Guardia ☆ 1953   3

Europe ☆ 1944–45   17

La Guardia ☆ 1953   69

Fallview, New York ☆ 1930–32   Margaret   78

La Guardia ☆ 1953   122

Europe ☆ 1944–45   130

La Guardia ☆ 1953   199

New York ☆ 1948   220

La Guardia ☆ 1953   260

La Guardia ☆ 1953

I got to the airport half an hour before the plane was due. Somehow, I always get to airports early. With trains it's different. I've been known to miss trains by a day and a half, but planes and airports are something else again. A very wise bit player I lived with briefly had it all figured out.

"The trouble with you, Harry, is you're afraid to fly and you're ashamed to admit it. So you always get to the airport ahead of time to reassure yourself, to see planes land and take off every couple of minutes. A half hour of that and you've worked up enough confidence to fasten your seat belt, chew on the Chiclet and make like a bird."

That wise bit player is now the undisputed queen of the red, chapped-hands commercials on a TV show that's up among the top ten in the ratings, so you can see she knows what she's talking about.

Another friend of mine, a rewrite man on the *Trib* has another theory. He said I was slowly turning into an alcoholic and was secretly ashamed and afraid of it. So I did my drinking at airport bars where nobody counted the drinks and I was able to pass as a gentleman bound for another city. Killing time before taking off. Why all my friends spent so much of their time analyzing my fears and secret shames is another story.

Anyway . . .

I got to the airport a half hour before the plane was due to arrive. I picked up the early editions of the afternoon papers in the main rotunda and headed for the Kitty Hawk room. I sat at the bar, ordered a double Scotch and watched seven planes make three-point landings or whatever the hell is currently par for the course in DC-7's. I looked through the papers. The General was all over the front pages. The *Journal-American* was running his bio with a red streamer across the top of the page, above the masthead, that read: "Starting Today: The Life Story of General Bronco Bronson." I knew he'd love that. The General had played three football games in his senior year at the Point. In one of them, he'd missed the key tackle and a sports writer covering the game had sarcastically dubbed him "Bronco Bronson." The name was safely buried until a *Time* writer, frantically searching for color on the Old Man for a çover story came across it, carefully got rid of the sarcasm and hung the name around his neck. It was a godsend to headline writers who have a great affection for names like "Ike" "Ave" "Mac" and "Liz." It had the common touch and saved space. The *Post* broke the news with the fewest words: "Bronc Home." As I reached for the *World-Telegram,* I felt a hand on my shoulder and turned around on the bar stool.

"Hi, Harry."

It was Jerry Fessler, a publicity guy for one of the airlines. I didn't remember which, but he'd once picked up the tab for a trip I made to the coast when I was doing that column for the tabloid.

4

"How goes it, Jerry? I see you got another plane through the other day."

"You going, coming or just drinking?"

"I'm a confirmed alcoholic who's afraid to fly."

"I said it to Orville, I said it to Wilbur and I say it to you, that thing will never get off the ground."

For some reason this is a favorite joke with every airline publicity man. . . . I laughed. After all, he *had* picked up that tab for me.

"No kidding," he said. "What are you doing here? Going somewhere?"

"I'm waiting for the General."

"Bronson?"

"Are there any other generals?"

"Not this week. You working for him?"

"Press agent. Official biographer. Historian."

Jerry sat down and ordered a drink for himself. I didn't notice it when he picked up my bar check and put it on top of his.

"How long?"

"How long what?" I asked.

"The job with the General."

"A couple of months officially. We've been friends a long time."

"I thought you were out in Hollywood, Harry. The last time I heard about you, you were doing that big spectacle for Goldwyn——"

"I've been back a couple of months. When the General happened, I figured he was going to need somebody to guide him through the pitfalls. Here I am."

"There must be a buck in it, Harry."

"Look, Jerry, once in a while there's something that's worth doing even without a buck. Even for me."

"Big hero stuff?"

"Something like that."

"Come off it."

"What's the matter? You don't think he's a hero?"

"Sure, he's a hero. What's your angle?"

"Does there always have to be an angle?"

"For you, always. Don't con me, Harry. Why?"

"Why what?"

"Why are you working for him?"

"Who knows? Maybe he just has a couple of empty pages in the back of his scrapbook he wants filled up. Generals have nice orderly minds. You got a scrapbook, the sensible, orderly thing to do is fill it up. I handle his press conferences, write his speeches and I suppose, when he gets around to it, I'll ghost his memoirs."

"You know there's something I can't figure out, Harry."

"What's that?"

"Why's he such a goddamned hero. I know he is. He's plastered all over the papers. He's this year's MacArthur, but I'm not so sure why."

"What's the matter, don't you read *Time* magazine? You subversive, or something?"

"Big deal."

"Look, fly-boy," I said. "I don't give a good goddamn whether you think Bronco Bronson's a hero or not. The whole country thinks so. Take a look out on the apron out there and you'll see what a big deal it really is."

"What're you getting sore about?"

"Listen, I spent four lousy years in a war. I maybe have a better measuring rod than you have. Just don't go around knocking Bronson around me."

"Have another drink."

"You've found the way to my heart."

We ordered two more drinks. What the hell was I

6

getting sore about? Next time I wanted to go out to the coast I'd have to pay my own way. It was about time to mend a few four-engined fences.

"I'm sorry I blew my top at you, Jerry. It's just that I'm fond of the Gen."

"Forget it. I didn't mean nothing by it. You still doing those pieces on interesting occupations?"

"Once in a while."

"We got a school for stewardesses might be worth a look. Anytime you wanna fly out and take a look at it, give me a ring. We can route you so you can stop off anywhere you want to on the way."

"Fine, Jerry. Thanks. Might be something I could use."

"What's he like?"

"He's a general. One star. Those are the best kind."

"What's he going to do now that he's back?"

"What does any GI do when he gets back after two years at the wars? How do I know? Triumphant parade. Address a joint session of Congress. Pin on a couple of new medals and raise blooded horses on his farm in Maryland. And what the hell are blooded horses?"

Jerry finished his drink, slid a bill across the bar and got up.

"Good to see you, Harry. If you ever want to take a plane ride, let me know. We can always work out something for you."

"Thanks. You ever want to meet a general, let me know. I'll walk down with you. I want to check on the newsreel boys."

On the way downstairs, I kept looking at my watch. In twenty minutes the plane would touch down. I wondered if the Gen had any idea of the hoopla that was in store for him? I wondered how he'd feel to have me work-

7

ing for him. I mean, after all, I invited myself in. As soon as the stories out of Korea broke I went to work. I fed the columnists, planted a couple of features with the wire services and got the go-ahead from Margaret Bronson. Not that the General wasn't getting the A treatment. I just gave the whole thing a little goose. Like, setting up the official welcome at City Hall. Maybe they'd have done it anyway, but I wasn't taking the chance that nobody would think of it. I went over the route of the parade and made sure the army held the plane up in San Francisco long enough for it to arrive at La Guardia at eleven in the morning. That way we'd hit lower Broadway at lunchtime when the office buildings empty out. That way the sidewalks would be jammed and it would look great in the pictures and the newsreels. I remembered that from something Grover Whalen told me when we were riding up Broadway together in an official car with some schlumph from some Balkan country. "You can always get a crowd on the sidewalk at noon down here," he said. "And there's nobody alive can tell from a picture in a newspaper whether it's an enthusiastic or just a hungry crowd. . . ." I kept remembering what Jerry had said upstairs at the bar. What was my angle? I didn't have one yet, but it can't do any harm to have the country's official hero grateful to you. It can't do any harm to climb aboard a gravy train. I had a free ride coming to me. He owed me that.

We walked into a room just off the loading ramps that used to be used as a VIP waiting room when the overseas planes were still coming into La Guardia instead of Idlewild. It was pretty "Wild Blue Yonder" with murals of every cumulus cloud between here and Shannon. Forty or fifty reporters were hanging around. The press bar was doing a fine business. The newsreel cameras were set up

8

and a bank of microphones were standing in front of a flagstaff that contained United Nations flags. A fussy little first lieutenant was tugging at them to make their folds a trifle more photogenic. I walked through the room into a back office. Margaret Bronson was sitting at a desk. She was holding a glass.

"I was wondering where you were, Harry," she said.

"I've been checking up on the arrangements."

"And?"

"Everything in order. The color guard is set at the arrival ramp. The cops are in position. NBC has five very good camera angles. I even talked the airport into letting them put a camera up in the tower so America can see the Gen's plane as a blob on a radar screen. How do you feel?"

I leaned over and kissed her on the cheek. She reached up and grabbed my arm and held it for a moment. . . .

"I feel fine," she said.

Margaret Bronson looked pretty good for fifty-one. If you took a quick look. My father used to tell me that was the way to look at women over fifty. Quick. A quick look wouldn't have told you anything about her. The clothes were attractive without being too expensive-looking or too extreme-looking or too stylish. The hair didn't look too blonde. It was touched up very discreetly. She was good casting for the part. Wife of the returning hero. You couldn't tell, for instance, that she was half loaded already and would get progressively drunker as the day wore on. And unless she got really loaded the chances were pretty good that she wouldn't pass out or make a pass at the sergeant who drove the official car.

"I thought we were going to have dinner together last night," she said.

"I called you."

9

"You called the house. You said you didn't want to disturb me and you just left the message that you wouldn't be able to have dinner with me."

"I didn't figure it was the night for us to have dinner, with the Gen coming back today. Besides I was up to my ears in last-minute arrangements."

"You ever been a general's wife, Harry?"

"Not this year."

"Try it sometime. It's great. Get me a refill, will you?"

"How many have you had?"

"None of your business. Don't forget I'm intimately related to the hero. Don't start counting drinks on me, Harry."

I looked at her.

"Don't worry. I'm not going to blow the arrival. I'll be such a great wife they'll revive all the old Myrna Loy movies for me. Come on, Harry. A drink."

I took her glass and mixed her a light Scotch and water. A very light Scotch and water. She sipped it like a little lady.

"You think they'll give him another star?"

"It's already in the works."

"I suppose you fixed that, too."

I smiled. Hell, it was a cinch they were going to pin another star on Bronson's shoulder. Why not take credit for it?

"You know what's so wonderful about Charley's getting another star?"

"The extra pay?"

"I won't have to lose at bridge any more. I threw more goddamned bridge games because I was outranked by the husband of every woman at the bridge table. I was a damned good bridge player, Harry. You know that?

Somehow we always played with the wives of Harry's superiors. I got so sick of throwing bridge games. They ought to put out a manual for army wives, Harry. Maybe you could write one. Just don't forget about the two occupational hazards of being an army wife . . . throwing bridge games and this. . . ."

She held up her glass and twirled it so that the ice made a clinking noise.

"Behave yourself," I said.

"Sure. A regular Myrna Loy. I missed you, Harry."

"I missed you, too."

"What's your angle?" she asked.

She put the glass down and came over to where I was standing. She put her arms around my neck and kissed me. I pulled away.

"For God's sake, Margaret. Somebody might come in."

"You didn't answer my question."

"What question?"

"What's your angle? All of a sudden, after Charley goofed up you turn up at the door telling me what an old friend of his you are and how he needs somebody to handle his public relations."

"What do you mean 'goofed up'?"

"Harry, this is Margaret. Save the hero stories for *them*. I know Charley. He goofed up. Don't make me swallow the hero stuff, too. I know Charley."

I looked her over carefully. In two months I'd gotten to the point where I could tell at a glance how many drinks she'd had. I figured this was probably her fourth. She sipped it slowly. She was cold sober, for Margaret.

"I'm the prize in the Cracker Jack box, is that it, Harry?"

"Margaret, talk sense."

11

"I'm not talking sense? What are we going to do, ask Charley for a divorce so we can get married? Or should I have written him a Dear John letter?"

I kissed her on the cheek.

"Is your aim bad or are we tapering off now that Charley is a blob on a radar screen in every living room in America? I repeat, Harry, what's your angle? You really don't think you can make anything out of Charley, do you? Don't you know he'll goof this hero thing up just the way he's goofed up everything else in his life? What've you got in the back of your head, Harry?"

"Margaret, will you please just behave yourself for a couple of hours?"

"All right, Harry. I'm sorry."

"The suite at the Towers is all squared away," I said. "They gave us the whole top floor."

"Are you staying there with us?"

"Sure. You never know when an emergency might arise."

"How cozy."

"Just think of me like the family doctor . . . around for an emergency."

She put her drink down and lit a cigarette.

"Harry," she said. "You wouldn't tell me what you really think of me, would you? A moment of truth? An honest appraisal?"

"I think you are the adoring wife of General Bronco Bronson. You're the mate for the All American Boy. You haven't seen your husband for two years and if your eyes are misty, it's a mixture of pride, emotion and gratitude. Only now your Charley isn't just your Charley any more. He belongs to all America."

I had the grace to smile when I said all this.

"Two years is a long time, Harry. A lot of bellboys

12

and elevator boys have gone over the dam in two years. . . ."

"You play it tough, don't you, Margaret?"

"Sure."

"Just don't play it tough from here on."

"I told you. Myrna Loy."

"Look, Margaret. I don't give a damn what's between you and the Gen. I don't give a damn how much Scotch you put away in private. I don't care where you get your kicks as long as it's nice and quiet. You got that straight?"

"You talk big for a guy who invited himself in. Suppose I just invite you out?"

"I don't think you'll do that, Margaret. Remember those bridge games. You want to invite me out? O.K. I'm out. Let's see how you can handle this thing yourself. Or maybe you think the Gen can handle it? Don't start threatening me, Margaret. You got a seat on the gravy train, only none of you know how to make the train go. I do. I've spent my whole life puffing people up way out of recognizable size. It's what I do. It doesn't matter to me whether they're fourteen-karat gold or whether your finger turns green after a while. I know how to do it. You behave yourself and let me run the show and we'll do fine."

"All right, Harry. A regular Myrna Loy. What about Charley? Have you thought that he might not go along with you the way I have?"

"Don't worry about that. Once he pokes his nose out of that plane he'll get a good whiff of immortality, and begin to see those old shoulder pads of his in a glass case at the Point."

"Bronco Bronson!"

"Boy hero," I said.

13

"How soon does he get here?"

"What's the matter, Margaret? Getting nervous? Or are you just impatient to see your returning GI?"

"How soon?"

"Twenty minutes, give or take an hour. You all right? I want to go out and check on the crowds."

"Sure, go ahead."

I opened the door. . . .

She came over to me.

"Harry . . ."

"Yeah?"

"I'll behave."

"I know you will. . . ."

"Don't be too long. Come back and wait with me. I promise. No more Scotch."

"I'll be back."

Buddy Evans, the kid I hired as a leg man pushed his way through the door.

"The jet escort picked the plane up over Cleveland. It'll be about a half hour late."

"How are the crowds?" I asked.

"The cops estimate around eighteen thousand."

"The kids arrive?"

"Twelve busloads. I passed out the flags."

"Good."

"Harry, I don't know whether I should bother you with this or not, but Irene Miller wants an interview with Mrs. Bronson."

"Don't worry about bothering me, Buddy. You can bother me with that kind of syndication any time. How about it, Margaret? Are you up to an interview?"

"Sure. It will help pass the time."

"Be careful with Miller. She's a wise guy."

14

"After a couple of months around you, I eat wise guys for breakfast. . . ."

"OK, Buddy, send her in."

"Right, Harry."

Buddy left.

I went over to the table and picked up Margaret's glass. It was still almost half full. When the door opened Irene Miller came in. I was holding the glass and nipping at it.

"The sun isn't over the yardarm yet is it, Harry?" she asked.

"Only in my mind, Irene."

I can't stand Irene Miller. First of all, she looks like a cheap cameo. Second, she always has the needle out for you. But she's syndicated in forty-seven papers and that covers a multitude of snottiness.

"How are you, Harry?"

"Fine. Loved your piece on Sinatra last week."

"Thank you, Harry. That's very nice of you."

"I'm a very lovable guy. This is Mrs. Bronson. Mrs. Bronson, Irene Miller."

Margaret smiled.

"I feel that I know Miss Miller very well. I've read her column for years."

"Thank you, Mrs. Bronson. That's very flattering."

"I'll leave you two alone for a while. I want to check on the General's plane."

"They just picked it up over Cleveland with the jet escort," said Irene. "It'll be a little late getting in."

"So much for my lunchtime crowd on lower Broadway. What the hell, if it's late enough we can catch the midafternoon coffee-break crowd."

I hung around at the door just long enough to hear how these two were getting along. . . .

15

"You must be very excited, Mrs. Bronson."

"Indeed, yes."

"Do you mind if I smoke?"

"Please do. It's a habit I never picked up."

I crossed my fingers and hoped Miller didn't see the lipstick-stained butts in the ash tray.

"Of course I'm very excited," Margaret continued. "You get used to separation if you're an army wife, but somehow these last two years have seemed almost unbearably long." She laughed quietly. "I said I never picked up the habit but as you can see, I've been so nervous I tried smoking a couple of cigarettes to calm my nerves this morning. I'm afraid I can't quite pick up the knack."

Good girl! That little piece of verbal sleight-of-hand over with I felt very secure leaving our Margaret alone with Irene Miller. I circulated among the newspaper guys at the bar, had a fast Scotch and water and headed for the gate the General's plane would taxi to. Three Pentagon colonels were there, checking the color guard. I saw the crowds on the promenade held behind the police lines. Saw the motorcade standing by and traded some wisecracks with the TV cameramen. I felt the paper in my pocket: the Gen's speech of welcome at City Hall and his speech at the banquet in the Waldorf's grand ballroom. Everything was as set as it could be. All we needed was our hero. Right now my whole future was riding on a blob on a radar screen, being escorted in by a squadron of jets.

Europe ☆ 1944-45

I met the General for the first time in a beat-up German town in the winter of 1944–45. I spent most of the winter boozing around Paris, picking up my copy off the big board in the correspondents' briefing room at the Scribe: copy that some poor GI correspondent had filed within small-arms fire of the Krauts. That was a big deal for those of us lucky enough to be covering the war for a wire service that winter. Every morning the PRO guy would tack up the copy, broken down by armies and it was yours for the taking. The GI combat correspondents had it all there—all the tear-jerkers; all the cuties, switches; all the names, ranks, serial numbers and home-towns. It was an easy way to cover a war. You just lifted the copy off the board, rewrote enough of it to give it what you liked to think of as your style and slugged it with your by-line. I always felt a little guilty about it, but the others took it in their stride.

"Screw the GI. He got drafted, didn't he?"

Still, it didn't seem right.

They were up there, getting shot at and we had nothing more hazardous to cope with than a bottle of black-market champagne or smuggling a drunken French broad past the concierge. There were a lot of drunken

17

French broads that winter. And a lot of black-market champagne.

Hemingway was around a lot that winter.

It made you feel big to sit around with him in one of those sidewalk cafés and act like there wasn't any real difference between you. After all, he was covering the same war you were and doing it the same way, drinking the same booze and talking the same talk. Talk was good that winter and nobody was rupturing himself trying to win any Pulitzer Prizes on any barricades. Barricades were a little old-fashioned and a little embarrassing. We drank and talked and each of us filed enough copy to keep the home office off our necks. Some of the guys were faking date lines and making up the stories. Some of them were doing the kind of think pieces you can think up where the women and the booze are good and plentiful. I was just lifting the stuff off the big board in the Scribe. The briefing officer used to call it background material. "It's pretty rough," he'd say. "But it may fill in some of the holes for you." It sure did.

Ernie Pyle passed through on his way home. It's funny, but I didn't talk about the war with Ernie. Correspondents were the greatest war-talkers you ever heard. Put two of them together in any room and the 88's and the burp guns would be louder than they were on Anzio. It was different with Ernie. We talked about the damnedest things. We talked about Nebraska and North Dakota. You figure that's hard? How much can you talk about Nebraska and North Dakota? Ernie knew the damnedest things about both of them. I remembered that, before the war, he used to do a travel column and that was all he wanted to talk about. He wouldn't say a damn thing about the war. When Ernie left, I began to get restless. Or maybe guilty. Anyway, I decided to get up to the lines

again and start filing my own copy. I'd been away from
the shooting war for nine months. Long enough to have
a baby. All I had was a bellyful of butterflies. It's hard to
go back to a war when you've been away from it for nine
months. You keep thinking of excuses to put it off for a
week or ten days. I thought of them all, but one afternoon, in the middle of the first Paris snowstorm of the
season, I caught a troop train out of the Gare du Nord
and headed for Germany.

I kicked my ass, mentally, all the way to the German
border. Who was I trying to impress? In the middle of a
snowstorm I had to head for a war. Couldn't I at least
wait until the sun came out? I got into a crap game that
lasted for three days in the box car that passed for transportation that winter in France. By the time we crossed
from Alsace into the Rhineland, I was flat broke and was
down to grubbing cigarettes from the transportation
officer, who kept "sirring" me all over the place because
he thought I was traveling on the cattle car to do a story
on him personally and the movement of troops in general. He kept trying to break up the crap game, but I
kept telling him to take off or I'd damn well spell his
name wrong in my story. Everytime the train stopped,
which was fifteen times a day, GI's would erupt from all
the box cars to trade their K rations for wine, eggs, or
anything else the countryside might offer. That transportation officer took care of me good. I never ate so
many eggs in my life. The only trouble with him was he
kept talking in autobiography. I knew more about that
guy before we got to the railhead than you'd believe possible. He made sure I could spell his name and knew his
serial number and his address, "In case I wanted to check
any of the facts with him." He even slipped me a bottle
of cognac when I left. The poor bastard must still be

19

reading his local paper every morning for the story about him.

When I got off the troop train, I hitched a ride on a four-by-four up to the press camp. It was in a schoolhouse on the main drag of a pretty big city. I was still pretty far from any shooting, but I put my overseas cap in my musette bag and started wearing a helmet. When you've been in Paris for nine months, even the rear echelon gets you nervous.

I got a big welcome when I walked into the press room.

Yeah.

A big welcome.

Paris Commando was the nicest thing they called me.

I got peeved.

It's easy to get peeved when somebody's telling the truth about you.

At the briefing session next morning, I got a fill-in on the Seventh Army front by the press officer. I'd picked a great war to cover. Nothing was happening.

"The Lines Are Static."

"Regrouping of Forces."

"Consolidation of Gains."

"Preparation for a Major Push."

The copy that was flowing through there was the same collection of cuties, tuggers and malarkey that I used to pull off the big board at the Scribe. The only difference was that I was now a couple of thousand miles from my French broads and my black-market champagne. I spent the next three days finding a decent billet for myself and filing stories on mess sergeants who had adopted local orphans and motor-pool sergeants who built cathedrals out of K-ration boxes. That kind of crap. I began to get restless and at the end of the week I pulled up stakes. One of the divisions had one of those colorful generals. Colorful generals are always good copy. This guy didn't collect pearl-handled revolvers, like Patton, but he was supposed to be bringing his wife home a hand-carved doll from every town his division passed through. How damned colorful can you get? I didn't really believe the doll story. It's the kind of rib one correspondent pulls on another after a couple of bottles of the local white lightning. It's considered very funny the next morning. Particularly if the victim checks out, rides a couple of days on a four-by-four and comes back empty-handed to find his billet gone and no place else to shack up. The truth was I was getting bored with the rear echelon. If nobody's shooting at you, you might just as well be really comfortable back in Paris. To be safe and only half comfortable is very unsatisfactory. I kind of missed the informality and the feeling you get among the line troops when things aren't too rough but somebody chucks in an 88 once in a while just to keep you honest. I hitched a ride on a half-ton headed for a division headquarters seventy-five miles away. I figured I'd go up and look this general over on the off chance that he really was collecting dolls. The papers back in the states were running out of generals for the Sunday supplements and maybe I could even talk him into the doll bit after I got there. My nerves were coming back and I had an itch to cover the war again. I'd heard a lot about this particular general, in addition to the doll story. He was a pro. West Point ought-nine and all that. He came out of the First World War a captain, did a stint in the Philippines, headed up a CCC camp during the depression, was given command of a regiment in a National Guard unit and through the attrition of the first two years of the war wound up with two stars and command of a division. He

21

was supposed to be heavy on the "Spit and Polish." Whenever his division was off the lines he put them on a garrison basis with inspections every morning and surrounding towns off limits. The correspondents had nicknamed him "Corn Cob Corridon." He was that tough. That didn't bother me much. I'd run into a lot of tough generals in my time, but sooner or later they get the itch to see their names in print and dream about a cover story in *The Saturday Evening Post*. Sooner or later it dawns on them that I'm a direct link to that cover. I didn't figure I'd have any trouble with Corn Cob Corridon.

His CP was in a rambling old inn, three blocks from what passed for the main drag in this part of the world. It must have been *Gemütlich* as hell in the old days. An 88 had blown one side of the wall into the river that ran through the town, but it still looked like something out of a Shubert operetta.

Even if you're a civilian, it pays, in the army to go through channels. You don't just go busting in on a general. There's always the chance that his powdered eggs haven't agreed with him that morning. The worst thing that can happen to a correspondent is to get a general on his tail. A correspondent is a real parasite. He's dependent on the army for his rations, a place to sleep and his transportation. Rub a general the wrong way and you find yourself hiking your way out of his area of command. A division front covers a lot of territory. The first thing I did was introduce myself to the boys in the motor pool. I took a lot of notes, a lot of names, serial numbers and home-town addresses. I even planned to write a couple of stories. "Sergeant Joe Nichols of Paducah Kentucky is a veteran of four major campaigns in Europe." I'd file it through regular army press channels, addressed to the guy's hometown paper and in a couple of weeks he'd have

22

a clipping from home and I'd be sure of a jeep anytime I wanted it in that division area. I worked the same routine with the kitchen crew. That took care of my rations. Next in line was the message center. That took care of getting my copy back to press headquarters to the censor for processing to the states. I introduced myself to the division medic and arranged to billet with him if I stuck around the division area. There's always plenty of alcohol around the medics and it doesn't taste too bad mixed with a little of that GI lemon powder. I borrowed a mess kit from the supply sergeant, lined up with the rest of the GI's and had the usual chipped beef on toast. I'd forgotten how bad GI coffee tasted. After lunch I headed for the Inn and looked up the division press officer. I was going through channels. He could fill me in on what the division was doing, what subjects to avoid with the general and the best way to lead up to the doll bit. I got a break. The press officer was an ex CBS radio announcer that I'd known back in the States. It was a touch of Madison Avenue in the middle of Germany. Somehow, in the middle of a war, his uniform looked like something Brooks Brothers had run up for him. He was glad to see me. I think he felt that he'd fallen into a den of squares.

"How are you, Harry?" he said. "God, I'm glad to see you."

"I'm flattered. How come I'm so welcome?"

"You gonna be around long?"

"That depends on what happens around here."

"In that case, you'll be out of here tomorrow morning."

"Nothing doing?"

"The Old Man is talking about drawing up a training schedule, running problems, lectures in how to assemble the M-1 rifle. Can't keep the troops idle, you know."

"I've heard about him."

"You heard right. What the hell are you doing here?"

"Just looking around. I heard he was an interesting character."

"Who in the name of God told you that?"

"A couple of the boys in Paris."

"Paris! It's still there, huh?"

"Still there. Listen, I want to check something with you. I hear the Old Man collects dolls."

"Collects what?"

"Dolls."

"You mean German dames?"

"No. I mean dolls. Wooden dolls. Hand-carved wooden dolls. He's supposed to be collecting one from every town the division passes through. For his wife."

"That's a lulu. Where'd you hear that?"

"From a bottle of Calvados."

"Sounds like it."

"There's nothing to it, Bill?"

"Listen, this guy doesn't collect anything but enemies. On both sides."

"One of those."

"The original one. You didn't hear about old Corn Cob?"

"I figured it was a rib. It doesn't matter, Bill. I wanted to get out of Paris, anyway."

"Are you out of your GI mind? Get out of Paris. You're bucking for a section eight."

"How's it going?"

"It's a long war, Harry. I think maybe I'm going psycho. You know what I dream about at night?"

"Making major?"

"Listen, with Corn Cob I'll make major in World

24

War Seven. No kidding, you know what I dream about at night?"

"French girls?"

"Besides that."

"I give up."

"Soup."

"Soup?"

"Yeah. Soup."

"You're right, Bill. You'll never make major."

"Louis and Armand's soup. Vegetable. Mushroom. Minestrone. Chicken noodle. Pepper Pot. Jellied Madrilène. Potato and Leek. Cream of Tomato."

"Might make a story, Bill. It would be a nice change of pace from all the stories about GI's who are fighting for Mom's apple pie. Maybe what America needs is a GI who's fighting for Louis and Armand's minestrone."

"You going to be around long, Harry?"

"Depends on what I can file."

"There's a GI in one of the line companies who used to write soap operas for CBS. Interest you?"

"Not much."

"A runner in one of the battalions was born in a town about five miles from here. It's still in German hands, but you might want to stick around until we take it. Be a good picture feature. I can assign the division photographer to you."

"That's a possibility. *If* you take the town. *If* you don't bypass it. *If* the GI isn't killed before then. Any idea how long you're going to be sitting on your cans here?"

"You know I can't tell you that, Harry."

"Even if you knew it."

"Which I don't. There's a little action in one of the

25

regiments. They're out on the point of the division front. Patrols and things like that."

"No thanks."

"I'm afraid that's all I can offer you. That doll story would grab a lot of space."

"If it were true."

"Even if it's not. If we could just get Corn Cob to sit still for it."

"What do you think the chances are of that, Bill?"

"About like the chances of their accepting my resignation. I'd sure like to get the division date line in one of your stories, Harry."

"Cause I'm your favorite correspondent."

"Because somewhere in the story you'll be able to drop my name in to remind CBS they got a dulcet-toned crusader that's going to be around Four Eighty-five looking for a job. Listen, Harry, suppose I got one of the brass to sit still for the story? I'd have to clear it with Corn Cob, but he wouldn't have to know it was a phony. There's a Kraut cabinetmaker in town could run up eight or ten dolls for a picture. How about it?"

"It'd be worth it just to see the look on the faces of those bastards back in Paris. They'd drop dead if I came back with a piece about a doll collector."

"What do you want, a GI or an officer?"

"Normally I'd say a GI. Maybe not this time. You hang it on a corporal or a sergeant, he's gonna sound like a fag that got by the psychiatrist at the induction center. This is a brass story. It'll get a bigger play that way. I can blow it up for a big take, maybe a Sunday piece with lots of pictures."

"How big do you want the brass to be?"

"Field grade."

"You wouldn't settle for a captain?"

26

"No."

"Why not?"

"They wouldn't swallow it from a press officer. The story has to have a clean ring to it. I need a colonel, a lieutenant colonel at the very least. I need a nice solid member of the club."

"It was just an idea."

"I'll file a piece on you, Bill. I'll do one of those soldiers-in-grease-paint pieces for *Variety*. That'll do you much more good than any phonied-up doll piece."

"Thanks, Harry. Now I gotta pull out a bird for you. You wouldn't want to hang it on Doc Saunders, the division medic, would you?"

"He's a civilian in uniform. I need a guy with the Point ring."

"I got just the guy for you. Charley Bronson. Lieutenant Colonel Charley Bronson. You'll go for a junior bird, won't you?"

"Depends. You got a dossier on him?"

Bill opened a file drawer and pulled out a folder that was marked with Bronson's name. There wasn't much in it. There were a couple of pictures of him pinning medals on GI's. He looked fine. He had sandy, crewcut hair, a straight jawline and a kind of twinkle in his eyes. There wasn't much in the way of information. Born 1909.

"What's he like, Bill? Will he go along with us on this?"

"I think so."

"Nice guy?"

"Very nice guy. As regimental G-2 he used to get back here to division once in a while. We used to play chess together. I hope he takes better care of his men

27

than he does of his pawns. Pretty good soldier. This is his first command, but I have a hunch he'll do fine."

"O.K. I'll take a chance on him. If you know him so well you might give him a ring and tell him I'm coming. Don't tell him what it's about. Just tell him to extend the courtesy of his command to the most important correspondent in the ETO."

"I'll make you sound like Ernie Pyle."

"I'll settle for Hal Boyle."

He twirled the handle on the field phone, asked for "Tiger Red," the code signal for the regiment and was finally connected with Bronson. He gave me quite a build-up. After he'd finished he put his hand over the mouthpiece of the field phone.

"He wants to know if you play chess."

"Tell him my middle name is Capablanca."

It was all arranged. Bronson would be delighted to put me up for as long as I liked. As far as he was concerned, I was doing a piece on the division and just wanted to look around.

On the jeep ride from division to regiment I began getting the jitters. It was a ridiculous thing. Regimental headquarters is usually as safe as the Stage Door Canteen. But once you get in a combat zone, you begin to think of everything behind you as the rear echelon. The man in the squad who becomes first scout and is sent out in front of his company to draw enemy fire, who is as close to coming face to face with the enemy as it's possible to be, whose life expectancy in combat is twelve seconds, has a right to think of his buddies twenty yards behind him as rear echelon. The men in his squad think of the rest of the platoon that way. The platoon thinks of the rest of the company that way. To a company on the lines, battalion headquarters is as far away and as desirable as

28

paradise. . . . And so on, all the way back across the ocean to the States. Once you set foot on an alien continent, every step forward is a hazard. I kept my eyes peeled all the way to the town regiment was set up in, expecting to hear the ping of a sniper's rifle any minute. I'd have been a pretty funny character to the boys in the line companies.

Sight unseen, I had to say this for Charley Bronson, he had fine taste in CP's. The courtyard we pulled into would have made a pretty good football field back in the States. The house itself was large, Germanic and luxurious, in a castle-villa sort of way. An MP with sidearms and a white helmet checked my credentials and let me into the main gate. Inside I was checked again by another white-helmeted MP. I found out later this "spit and polish" was on the direct order of General Corridon. He'd ordered all MP's to paint their helmets white and had insisted on strict military clearance at all CP's. I began to wonder about good old Charley Bronson, boy chess player. He put me at ease immediately when I met him. He looked younger than his pictures in the dossier at press headquarters at division. He shook hands and offered me a slug from an honest to Dewars Scotch bottle.

"You're the chess player Bill told me about on the phone. I hope you're good," he said.

"Capablanca is my middle name," I said.

"I'm terrible," he said. "But I like to play with good players. You can't learn anything playing with people who know less than you do. That doesn't just go for chess either."

"I admire your taste in refreshments."

"My wife smuggles it over to me. It's against the law to send liquor through the mail. She gets a big loaf of bread, scoops out the center, inserts the bottle in the

29

middle and then glues back the ends of the loaf. She figures that way, risking imprisonment, she's making her contribution to the war effort."

"Beats knitting socks for the Red Cross."

"I think so. Now what can I do for you, Mr. Williams?"

"Just call me Cappy."

"Cappy?"

"For Capablanca."

"Right."

"I've been away from the wars for a while. I guess I just want to get my feet wet again."

"There isn't much doing around here. A little patrol action, but that's about all."

"Good. I don't believe in diving off the diving board. I'm one of those people who prefer to wade in, a bit at a time."

"I hope you'll stay around awhile. We can fill you in here at headquarters, and you can go down to the battalions or the line companies if you'd like."

"Fine."

"Have you been with a line company before, Cappy?"

"Lived with one for three months on Anzio. Made the Southern France invasion with the first wave. Traveled with the Forty-fifth as far as the Belfort Gap."

"I accept your credentials. I just didn't want you going up to the lines and poking your head up at the wrong moment. There's a lot of sniping and an occasional mortar round. It's quiet, but it's not quite rest and rehabilitation."

"How long do you think you'll be hung up here, Colonel?"

"Not too long now. The Siegfried Line is ahead of

us. They're holding because of that. We're not pushing through them yet because we're waiting to build up for an all-out assault on the line. We're just sitting like this by mutual consent."

"This is your first command, isn't it, Colonel?"

"I commanded a line company for a while when I first came over. I was G-2 before I took over the regiment. You know, a minute ago when I was telling you to keep your head down, I couldn't help thinking of my baptism of fire over here. You have to understand that this was my trade, Cappy. Since 1928, when I entered the Point, it was my occupation. I'd spent a lot of years studying it, reading the books and even teaching it, but until I actually got into combat it was all theoretical. God, it was exciting. I damn near got my head blown off. We were pinned down on a hill in that first attack. Everybody else was down in the dirt, digging in, trying to put any hunk of dirt they could find between their butts and the tracers. I was just standing up there looking around. It was amazing, Cappy. It was just like the books. I watched another company take off in a flanking attack and they did it just the way we were teaching it down at Camp Hood. I probably wouldn't be here to tell you about it if a platoon sergeant hadn't brought me down with the neatest tackle you've ever seen. 'Begging your pardon, sir. If you wanna get your ass shot off, that's your business, but you're drawing fire on the rest of us.' You won't make that mistake, will you?"

"I don't think so."

"I learned a big lesson that day," said Bronson. "I learned that if you somehow, through luck or stupidity live through your first battle, you're going to live awhile. You learn things. Instinct takes over and you're able to

31

measure how close a shell is coming and to tell what's coming in and what's going out."

"I remember my first battle on Anzio. You know what impressed me most, Colonel?"

"I haven't the faintest idea."

"The smell. Did you ever notice that a battlefield, in the middle of a battle, smells like celery tonic?"

"Damned if it doesn't."

"It was at dusk and I'll never forget how pretty the tracers looked cutting across the trees. If you could forget how deadly the whole damned thing was, it was a pretty sight."

"You get over that, don't you, Cappy?"

"I'm over it. I'm fresh from Paris. My nerves aren't quite back in the combat zone."

"They'll catch up with you. In a couple of days you'll be bored with sitting around here, safe and comfortable and start hoping something hits the fan."

"I wouldn't bet on that, Colonel."

"Call me Charley. Now where do you want to sack out? Rudy can rassle you up a bedroll and a cot and you can bunk with me if you'd like."

"I don't know," I said. "I thought I might look up the doc and see if——"

"You don't have to do that, Cappy. Margaret's been very busy with the bakers of America. There's plenty of Scotch. Unless you really prefer alcohol and lemon powder."

"You've got a roommate, Charley."

"Fine. You really do play chess, don't you?"

"Capablanca is my middle name."

Bronson took me around and introduced me to his officers and the men in the headquarters. He had the G-2 give me a complete briefing on the situation in the map room. He showed me the situation map with the acetate overlay marked up with grease pencil. There was no crap about this is classified material or "We can't give you the details about that." He laid the whole thing in my lap. This is not standard operating procedure with correspondents. It was a nice gesture of friendship and respect on his part. Bronson's dog-robber was a runty little Puerto Rican kid from East Harlem, named Rudy. He adored Charley and spent most of the day scrounging around the countryside, trading and stealing food. He made a mean stew out of the basic GI five-in-one rations. He called Bronson "Colonel Charley." He dug up an officer's down sleeping bag for me and one of those folding canvas cots. He checked on my cigarette supply and when he found out I was low, came up with— from God knows where—a carton of Lucky Strikes.

The regimental officers ate together in what I assumed must have been the dining hall of the castle. It looked not unlike the Encyclopaedia Britannica illustrations of King Arthur's Round Table. It had some of the same feeling to it. Bronson was obviously the headman and the whole table took its cue from him. There was none of the smutty, dirty talk you usually find around an officers' mess. The officers' orderlies had all dug up some wine from the surrounding countryside and after the table was cleared, a bottle of cognac and a box of cigars were put out. It had an unreal quality to it and yet you had the feeling that they had fallen into it naturally. You didn't feel that after dinner some of the officers were going to get together and laugh at the Old Man's Dining Club. It was a nice civilized note in the middle of a very uncivilized world and I had the feeling the men appreciated the chance to act like the gentlemen Congress had made them. I know I had the best meal I'd had in years. It made that black-market place in Montparnasse look like the Automat.

After dinner, Bronson had a conference with his G-2 and the battalion commanders. He let me sit in on it. There was nothing very exciting or dramatic about the meeting. It was, as a matter of fact, very routine and unimportant. The first Battalion had been out on the point, committed, doing the patrol duty. He moved them back into reserve, which meant simply that they would get a chance to get a change of clothes and a shower from the portable unit that was set up in the regimental town. It meant no duties while they were in reserve and a chance to write letters, catch up on sleep and poker. The second battalion replaced them on the lines and the third battalion went into support. Bronson also requested permission from division headquarters to send men from the reserve battalion on three-day passes to the rest camp set up thirty miles behind the lines. I was very impressed with the way he handled the routine details of his job. I was also impressed and a little worried about the way he passed his Scotch bottle around. I hoped Mrs. Bronson was busy pulling the guts out of lots of loaves of bread back in the states.

After the meeting we sat down to the chessboard. Bronson was wrong. He wasn't terrible. He was a damn fine chess player. I spent four years on the college chess team and most of my life I've had a book of chess problems on my bedside table. Come war, unemployment or love affairs, I've always played at least five games of chess every week and I had a tough time with Bronson. We drew the first game and I began to realize that I was playing somebody that required serious consideration. Chess originally was a war game and Bronson played it that way. To him the pawns were foot soldiers, expendable but vital to your offense and your defense. He used the knights like cavalry, the bishops like artillery and the rooks like tanks. His queen was his air force. I beat him in the second game when I broke through his king side in the middle game. We played one more and I made a stupid move and gave him a stalemate when I had him beaten. I looked at my watch and was amazed to discover it was a quarter to three in the morning. He was perfectly willing to continue until dawn, but I was dead tired and begged off.

"I tried to teach Rudy how to play chess."

"And?"

"He has it confused with a gang war."

"You play very well, Charley."

"I'm out of practice. Nobody else in the regiment plays. One or two of them out of courtesy are willing to let me teach them, but it's dull because they don't really have any interest or any understanding of the game. How about a nightcap?"

"Fine."

He poured two big hookers of cognac and we sat silently sipping it.

"I hope you're going to stay around awhile, Cappy," he said quietly.

"Because I play a good game of chess?"

"That's one of the reasons. To tell you the truth, Cappy, I'm something of a misfit."

"Are you?"

"That's what Margaret keeps telling me."

"What does she base that opinion on?"

"Being married to me. She thinks I'm in the wrong business."

"Oh?"

"Oh" is a very good thing to say when somebody

starts talking about himself. It doesn't interrupt his train of thought and it lets him know that you're still there.

"She doesn't think much of the army. As a career, I mean."

"Do you?"

"A fair question."

"And what's the answer, Charley?"

"It isn't simple enough for me to say yes or no. You think you know something about the army, don't you? You're a correspondent. You've sweated out beachheads, you've made invasions. You've probably had a case of trench foot, you've probably had lice and even had a few moments of pride when you saw a display of just plain guts on the part of soldiers somewhere. But you haven't the faintest idea what the army is like."

"I suppose not."

"I'm talking about the peacetime army. You don't know what it's like to be the low man on the totem pole, a brand-new second lieutenant, fresh out of the Point. You don't know what it's like to have your social life controlled by the system. You pick your friends by rank. And if you're entertained by somebody who outranks you, you have to treat him with the respect usually reserved for your grandfather or a rich uncle. And it's perfectly all right if he's a long-winded, stupid, opinionated bore, who can't hold his liquor and likes to paw your wife. If you're a second lieutenant, you can't win a golf game except against other second lieutenants and even then you have to be careful about date of rank. To make it really unfair you have to play well enough to make it look good. A captain likes to feel he really beat you, even if he knows he didn't. Or couldn't. Does that sound childish?"

"I never make snap decisions, Charley."

36

"I guess I didn't play the game very well. I think I was longer in grade than any other second louie my age and weight in the United States Army. Margaret kept telling me to either play the army game or get out. She's older than I am, Cappy. Did I tell you that?"

"How much older?"

"Seven years older. I don't know why she married me. Maybe it's simple. Maybe it's just because it was the middle of the depression and there was something sort of stable about the army. I think she had the whole thing confused with a Dick Powell movie. Remember those Dick Powell movies. 'Flirtation Walk' and Ruby Keeler and 'The Caissons Go Rolling Along.' . . . She got her eyes opened fast. We moved six times in the first five years of our marriage. That raises hell with a woman—crating up the furniture and moving on, wondering what the commanding officer is going to be like, hoping his wife doesn't play bridge, fighting to get a decent billet, making the same small talk and caring about how long you're in grade and when you can expect a promotion. To any army wife, a promotion is the most important thing in the world. It never was to me. I was bored with the army two years after I got out of the Point. The work was childishly simple. There wasn't any particular challenge or difficulty to it. And I was bored by my fellow officers and their rank-conscious wives. I got sick of their drinking parties and their absurd cocktail parties. They bored me to tears, they were so goddamned stupid. But once in a while I'd stop and think if maybe they all felt the way I did. Looking at myself from the outside, I saw that I'd taken on the protective coloration of my surroundings. How did I know that wasn't true of the rest of them?"

"Was it?"

37

"I never found out. You know who the real casualties of the peacetime army are?"

"No," I said.

"The wives. They drop like flies. We at least had something to do to keep ourselves busy. We played soldier. We had exercises and war games. We went on bivouac. We filled our day. The wives had nothing. How much shopping do you have to do? Maybe that's why there are so many babies born on army posts. It's to give the women something to do. We never had a baby. Oh, sure, the girls used to have hen sessions, afternoon bridge games, quilting parties. Honest to God they had quilting parties. But whatever they did, they drank, and after a couple of years I discovered that Margaret was a little drunk every night. I didn't mind it too much. I was drinking a lot myself in those days. Thank God for the war."

"Would you say that again, Charley?"

"I said thank God for the war. You civilians don't like to hear that, do you? Maybe God has a war every generation to keep the armies of the world from going crazy. Two generations without a war and every soldier in the civilized world would wind up in the booby hatch. At least we're all working at our trade now. At least we're using all the things we learned and were trained for. All of a sudden we get prestige and become important. I'll tell you the truth, Cappy. If the war hadn't come along I'd still be a lousy little first lieutenant with an alcoholic wife. If I hadn't volunteered for an overseas transfer, I'd still be playing boy scout in some submarginal hunk of real estate in the middle of the dust bowl. As it is I made captain only because the division's TO called for a captaincy for a company commander. Then after I stayed alive awhile and was made G-2, I was promoted to major.

Now here I am. A lieutenant colonel. A junior bird. If the war lasts long enough, I might even make brigadier. I think Margaret's even a little proud of me. She figures I've learned how to play the game and when I come back, she'll get a chance to win a couple of bridge games."

"When did you discover you hated it so much?"

"Two years out of the Point."

"How? Did you have a sudden revelation? Did you wake up one morning and say 'I hate the army'?"

"No. There was no one thing. . . . Wait a minute. This doesn't answer your question, but maybe you'll spot a symptom. I used to play the piano pretty well. I had lots of records, a lot of chamber music stuff. Most of the Brahms and Beethoven symphonies. I discovered them all smashed one morning. One of our guests thought it was very amusing to scale them out the window in an excess of drunken zeal. I had to smile and say, 'He's a hell of a funny fellow, isn't he?' He was a major, so he was a hell of a funny fellow instead of being a drunken bastard. That doesn't pin it down for you, does it, Cappy? All right. I got sick of playing ragtime at the officers' club or accompanying drunken quartets in 'Sweet Adeline.' I stopped going to concerts because I was told by my superior officer that it set a bad example for the men to have one of their officers going off post to hear some foreign pansy play that hifalutin music. Honest to God, that's what he said. I used to play chess with one of my platoon sergeants until I was ordered by my commanding officer to discontinue it. 'Officers do not mix socially with noncoms.' I gave him an argument and wound up with a snotty comment on my fitness report. One night I wandered into a bedroom and found a captain making a rather serious pass at Margaret. I poked him in the nose. Nothing was said about it officially, but three weeks later I got a transfer and I was somehow passed over for promotion again."

"Don't you think things like that happen in other businesses?"

"Sure. But you can always quit. I wasn't a kid any more and this was the only trade I knew. It was a little late to come out into the wide civilian world and to go to work as an office boy. Sure it happens in other businesses, but there are competitors. You can always quit and find a job in the same industry with another firm. Where could I go?"

I sneaked a look at my watch. Bronson saw me.

"I know," he said. "It's late. I'm sorry I've bored you with all this."

"I wasn't bored."

"It's good to have you around, Cappy. Stick around awhile, will you?"

"Sure. I have to get even for that stalemate."

We played chess every night after that. Bronson was like a kid in a candy store. He'd have stayed up all night, if I'd agreed. During the day I made the rounds of the battalions, doing color pieces, home-town-paper stories, the usual cuties and tuggers to justify my being with the division. The front didn't move as much as a foot for three weeks. There was talk that Bronson's regiment was going to be relieved and sent into division reserve. That meant rest camps for the GI's, nightly movies and maybe even a visit from the Red Cross doughnut truck and the Red Cross girls.

The night before the relief was due to take place, I set up the chess board as usual after dinner. I put the cognac bottle on the table and bit the end off a cigar and sat down. The colonel was in the G-2 section and when he came back in I motioned him into his usual chair in front of the chess board.

"Not tonight, Cappy."

"Why not? You getting bored with chess, too?"

"Hell no," he said. "I just have something better for us to do."

"Like what?"

"How long do you usually stick around a division area?"

"It depends."

"On what?"

"On all sorts of things."

"All right, Cappy. I'll be specific. How long do you usually stay with one regiment when nothing is happening?"

"It depends on how good the chow is and how the supply of alcohol holds out."

"All right, I'll be very specific. How long do you usually stay around a regimental headquarters—even when the food is good and the liquor plentiful—if there's nothing really happening?"

I smiled. "A day and a half."

"That's what I figured. Thank you very much."

"Don't thank me, Charley. I don't find many good chess partners either."

"I figure you have a bonus coming to you."

"What kind of a bonus?"

"You know we're being relieved tomorrow night. We're running our last patrol at midnight. The men will go out, take cover, listen and return by dawn."

"Yeah?" I said.

"What's the matter, Cappy?"

"Nothing. I'm just afraid I'm way ahead of you."

"We're both going on that patrol tonight."

"We are?"

He looked at me. There was silence for a minute.

"It was just an idea. You don't have to go if you don't want to."

I didn't want to. I couldn't tell him that.

"I'd love to," I said.

"I thought it might be a dividend for you. A kind of bonus. You could do a story on it, reduce the war to seven men going through the enemy lines."

"That's fine, Charley, but what are you going along for?"

"That's what I get paid for."

"You don't get paid to go out on seven-man patrols."

"I like to keep my hand in. It keeps me from getting too scared."

"Scared?"

"You said it when you came up here, remember? You said your nerves weren't quite in a combat zone yet. I get the same thing sitting in my CP when things are the way they've been for the past month. After a while you get frightened to death when an eighty-eight comes zooming in. You're out of condition. You get careful and frightened. This way, going on a patrol once in a while keeps it from being a terrible shock to you when the war starts up again. And it will. Don't kid yourself about that. You know what happens to a fighter who stays out of the gym too long?"

"He doesn't get his nose broken."

"Cappy, a patrol like this is routine. You take a route that keeps you under cover all the way, you infiltrate through the outer defenses and you sit down and listen. You just take a long walk to see if you hear any special activity like trucks bringing reinforcements in,

42

or tanks moving up. You just sit on your tail for a couple of hours and then walk back before dawn."

"Just like that?"

"Most of the time. Oh, sure, once in a while you run into a Kraut patrol on its way to do the same thing to you and you have a little fire fight. Once in a while one of your men gets a fit of coughing or sneezing and gives away the position and you have to fight your way back. But only once in a while."

"And what makes you think this won't be one of those once in a whiles?"

"Nothing. That's what makes it an interesting change from the chessboard."

"O.K., Charley. You sold me."

"There's one other thing, Cappy, I haven't told you."

"Go ahead," I said.

"You can't carry a gun."

"Great!"

"You're a noncombatant. If we're captured, it'll be rough on you if you're carrying a gun. Without a gun you're a legitimate observer."

"And the Germans don't shoot at legitimate observers?"

"I guarantee it."

"That's good enough for me, Charley. Now just get it in writing from the German commander. Listen, seriously, aren't you afraid I'll louse the whole thing up on you? I'm a pretty clumsy clown of a guy. I don't want to be responsible for six dead members of a patrol."

"Seven counting you."

"They don't kill observers. Seriously, Charley. You think I can do it?"

"I can do it. Why can't you? You'd be surprised what you can do if they're shooting real bullets."

"O.K."

All the way up to the line company in Bronson's jeep I was trying to think of some face-saving way of getting out of it. What the hell was I doing playing commando? I'd probably be bounced right out of the Newspaper Guild. I'd been in tough spots before, but until now I'd just been a target. This time I was really doing something aggressive against the Germans. I mean, hell, I'd have made a lousy infantryman. I'd have worked on the theory that as long as I didn't fire my gun at them, they wouldn't fire at me.

We covered the last five hundred yards to the company position on foot. It was rough going. Most of it was up hill through a deep woods. The only thing that kept me from falling flat on my face a couple of times was the moon, which was full and shone bright and clear through the trees. We were challenged by a guard in a foxhole when we got to our destination. Bronson gave the countersign and was directed to the company CP. It was a hole in the ground. You could tell, even in the moonlight that the company had been there for a long time. The top of the hole was covered with tree trunks, sandbags, sod and dirt. Two GI blankets and a shelter half covered the small hole that served as the entrance.

"Coming in," said Bronson.

He waited a minute until we heard a voice from inside.

"O.K., come ahead, the light's out."

Charley pulled aside the shelter half and the blankets and dropped into the hole. I followed him. It was deeper than I thought. You could stand up inside. After I'd put the blankets and the shelter half over the hole, I looked around. There were nine of us in the hole. It was kind of cozy and reminded me of the underground apartments we'd dug on Anzio. The walls were covered with blankets, there was a table made out of a K-ration crate and two kerosene lamps hung from the ceiling.

Bronson introduced me to the company commander, a pink-faced captain named Wylie. He introduced me to the platoon sergeant and the four other men who were going on the patrol with us. The ninth man was the chaplain. He was sitting against the wall censoring mail and every once in a while he'd laugh out loud at something in one of the letters.

The sergeant didn't like the idea of my going along on the patrol. I couldn't blame him.

"Look, Colonel," he said. "We been running these patrols for the past five weeks. We all know each other and trust each other. It ain't nothing against Mr. Williams here, but patrols can be rough enough without having somebody along who ain't never been on one before."

"Didn't you go on your first patrol once, Sergeant?" asked Bronson.

"Yeah. But I had basic training. I'd been in combat. I knew my way around."

"Mr. Williams sweated out three months on Anzio. He made the invasion in Southern France in the first wave. He lived with a line company in the Forty-fifth all the way through France. He knows his way around."

"O.K., Colonel, if you say so."

"I say so, Sergeant. And while we're at it, do you have any objection to *my* going along?"

"It's your regiment, Colonel."

"It's your skin if I louse it up. How about it? Any objections?"

Nobody said anything.

"Good. All right, Paul, suppose you brief us."

The captain put a map on the table. We all gathered around it.

"It's the same patrol we've been running for the past week and a half, Mr. Williams," he said.

"Make it Harry," I said.

Bronson looked at me quizzically.

"The purpose of it, Harry," said the captain, "is to tell us if there's any change in the Kraut plans. We're not out there to get in a fight. If an outfit is preparing for an offensive or preparing to move out, they have to make preparations for it. That means trucks coming in, reinforcements moving up, things like that. It makes noise. And that's what we're out there for, to listen and see if there's any unusual noise or any unusual movement. All the men on this patrol, with the exception, of course, of you and the colonel, speak German. Sometimes a patrol can pick up information by listening around the enemy's foxholes."

"You get that close?" I asked.

"We get that close," said the sergeant.

"Bud here," said the captain, nodding toward the sergeant, "has been on this patrol every night. He can fill you in on the route."

Bud leaned over the map and put a finger on it.

"This is where we are. We go out through our outposts here." He traced the route with his fingers. "We have cover most of the way. About four hundred yards in front of our lines we come out into the open. We go across the open spot one at a time. You stay in the bushes here until the patrol leader gives you the word and then you haul ass across the opening as fast and as low as you can go. The German outpost is right here."

46

He pointed it out on the map.

Bronson broke in before he could finish. "I want to mention, Sergeant, that you are the patrol leader tonight. I'm just another member, under your control. When you yell go, I'll haul ass like the rest of you."

The sergeant laughed. I had the feeling he was beginning to enjoy himself.

"We haven't had any trouble getting through the German outposts so far," he continued. "I think the Krauts out there are goofing off. Anyway, we go through, one at a time. We reorganize here. From here on it's gotta be really quiet. The Krauts have their heavies set up here and their defense perimeter runs along here. There's some cover right here and that's where we sit. We spread out, fifty yards between us. And nobody takes along rations this time. Last night it sounded like a popcorn box in a movie. The Krauts may be dumb, but they ain't deaf. You got all that so far, Mr. Williams?"

"Harry," I said.

"You got it?" he repeated.

"Got it," I said.

"Pete here is the getaway man," he continued. "That means, Mr. Williams, if we get into a fire fight, he takes off to get back here with whatever information we pick up. That means we cover him, and when he's free, we pull back, one at a time, on my order while the others keep up a covering fire. Colonel, you'll carry the B.A.R. and pull back after the rest of us open up from a new position."

"Right," said Bronson, and you'd have never known from his tone of voice that the sergeant was giving him the finger, handing him the dirtiest and most dangerous job. Even I knew that.

"This is a Jolson job," said the sergeant. "That

47

means, Mr. Williams, that we black our faces and hands. That's on account of the moon. And if a flare goes off just stand still and close your eyes so the whites won't pick up the reflection. We strip down. That means all jewelry off, no rings or watches. No cartridge belt or canteen. No helmet. Nothing that's going to make noise as you go through the underbrush. Every man carries a knife in his shoetop. A knife, Mr. Williams, doesn't make any noise and it doesn't give away your position. Sometimes you have to use it on a nervous sentry."

"Ours or theirs, Sergeant?" I asked.

"If we do run into a Kraut patrol, we will try to avoid a fight. Remember, our job is to get through the lines, not kill Krauts. If we're fired on, we try to disengage and get away. If we're forced to return the fire and get into a fight, the patrol is off and we pull back, with the B.A.R. man covering the final withdrawal. Everybody clear on it? Any questions?"

I had several. Like, "What the hell am I doing here?" I somehow didn't think the sergeant would give me a very civil answer, so I just nodded my head.

The sergeant folded the map and put it back on the table.

"Now let's go out to the outpost and I'll point out our route on the ground. And then I suggest you all get a couple of hours' sleep. It's nine fifteen. We meet here at the CP at eleven forty-five."

"You mean twenty-three forty-five, don't you, Sergeant?" I asked.

"Look, Mr. Williams, stop needling."

"You're right," I said. "I'm sorry."

The captain was smiling. So was Charley Bronson. I felt a little silly, like the smart aleck at school who got clipped across the mouth.

48

The six of us who were going on the patrol followed the sergeant out of the CP and stood with him in the two foxholes on the ridge that formed the outpost of our lines.

He showed us the route we were going to take. It looked awfully goddamned bright and exposed to me . . . a little like a fly trying to walk across a billiard table without being noticed.

When we got back to the CP, Bronson and the captain took off to inspect the positions and discuss the relief that was due the next night. The chaplain was still sitting in the corner censoring mail. He looked up when Bronson and the captain left.

"We were never really introduced," he said. "I'm Father Barry, the Catholic chaplain."

"I'm Harry Williams."

"I know. You're going to earn your hot cakes the hard way tonight."

"How's that, Father?"

"I don't know why, but hot cakes have become a kind of symbol to the line companies. Before they go on the lines, their last hot meal is hot cakes. From then on they're on K's. Their first hot meal when they get off the lines is hot cakes. The GI's live from hot cakes to hot cakes. When you're going on the lines, they stick in your throat and you can't swallow them. When you get off the lines, they taste like filet mignon. The boys are talking about them tonight."

"You don't usually travel with the line companies, do you, Father?"

"I'm like the hot cakes. I come up with them the first night in a new position. I come up the night before they're relieved. I run a mass both times for them. If they see Father Barry around, they know the rumors about being relieved are true."

"That's a nice thing to be, Father, a symbol."

"I deal in symbols a great deal, Mr. Williams."

"I know. I saw you laughing before. Funny mail?"

"That's another tradition with this company. Usually their own officers censor their mail and the boys are, I think, understandably shy about what they write. When I'm up here, I censor the mail, so they let themselves go. Some of it's very funny. Some of it's rather pathetic."

"Like what?"

"Well . . . there's one boy in one of the platoons that's trying to embarrass me. He writes very graphic descriptions of his homecoming to his wife."

"And are you embarrassed, Father?"

"Mr. Williams, after twenty-two years in a confessional, there isn't much the human race can do that embarrasses a priest."

"That's the way I feel about the ten years I spent covering police headquarters back in New York."

"There's one soldier who never fails to impress me. His powers of invention are monumental."

"Making a hero out of himself?"

"Quite the opposite," said Father Barry.

"What do you mean, Father?"

"This boy's mother is evidently very ill. He feels that if she knew he was in the infantry or in a line company, it would kill her. So he's been writing her letters about what a wonderful, easy time he's been having overseas. He goes into great detail about all the USO shows he's seeing, all the sight-seeing he's doing and the easy desk job he has. It's amazing the things he writes about."

50

"Doesn't the address tip her off that he's in a line company?"

"Evidently she doesn't understand the significance of it. Of course, I haven't seen her letters to him, but from his letters, he's still getting away with it. When his company goes into relief or is in a static position, like it is now, he spends most of his free time stock-piling letters for the times when he's on the lines and can't write. He gives them to me, thirty or forty of them at a time to hold and mail off one at a time. That way she gets a letter from him every day."

"That's amazing," I said. "I don't suppose you'd like to tell me his name, would you?"

"I'm afraid I can't do that, Mr. Williams. I'd be violating a confidence. And even if that didn't enter into it, the story would be bound to come to her attention. I don't think you'd want that on your conscience, would you?"

"No, I guess not."

The colonel and the captain called from outside and I put out the lamps. They dropped into the hole and I lit the lamps again.

Bronson threw a can about the size of a can of shoe polish into my lap.

"Time to put your make-up on, Cappy," he said.

"What is it?" I asked.

"Shoe impregnator."

"Shoe what?". .

"Impregnator. Makes GI shoes waterproof."

"Any chance it'll make me bulletproof?"

"Very little. Of course, if they can't see you, they can't hit you. It'll help that way."

I dug my hands into the goo and spread it on my face. I covered myself from the hairline down to the

51

end of my neck. I rubbed it on my hands and up my arms to the elbow.

"You missed the inside of your ears," said the captain.

"Inside my ears?"

"That's right. You have very shiny ears, Cappy," said Bronson.

"Father," I said, "when I get back to Paris, I'd like to send that GI the best guidebook I can find. If I send it to you, will you see that he gets it?"

"Of course," said Father Barry. "That would be a very thoughtful gift."

"What are you two talking about?" asked Bronson.

"The GI tour of Europe," I said. "All expenses paid."

Bronson had finished putting the goo on his face.

"How do we look, Father?" he asked.

"Like Amos and Andy."

"How about a quickie?" Bronson asked me. He pulled a traveling chess set out of his pocket.

"Fine," I said.

"Unless you'd rather sleep."

"I don't think so," I said. "I'm a hard man to wake up. I wouldn't want to go out on this jaunt tonight, half asleep."

"Good. Your move."

We played two games before the sergeant turned up and yelled, "Coming in," outside the hole.

We put the light out and he slid through the entrance. When we put the light on again, he looked our make-up over carefully. We passed the inspection with flying colors. I think he was a little disappointed that we'd done it so well.

"O.K.," he said. "It's time to take off. You can leave your jewelry here with Father Barry."

He said the word "jewelry" with great contempt and scorn. I took off my wrist watch and my class ring and handed them to the chaplain.

We met the other members of the patrol on the top of the hill. The whole thing had an eerie quality to it. We were all bareheaded and blacked up. The sergeant was whispering and I got a tic in my eye.

"All right," said the sergeant. "Let's go over it once more. That's the path we take down there. We turn to the right when we hit that line of trees. I'll be leading. When we leave here there'll be no talking under any circumstances. That means whispering, too. Got it? O.K. We start out with a ten-yard interval. When we hit the tree line, keep visual contact with the man in front of you. But don't go climbing up his back. Visual contact, but don't get less than ten yards behind him. Remember, if we're fired on, hit the ground and don't open up except on orders from me. If anything happens to me, Robbie takes over as patrol leader. Any questions? Mr. Williams?"

"None, Sergeant."

"Colonel?"

"None."

"Fine. Move out."

In spite of myself, I was excited. I was scared silly, but I was excited, too. Just before we started, the colonel tapped me on the shoulder. I turned around. He handed me a forty-five.

"Merry Christmas," he said in a low voice.

I checked to make sure the safety catch was on and stuck it in my pocket. I felt much better.

The sergeant moved out first. I was fifth. The

53

colonel was behind me. Pete, the getaway man, was last. The outpost had been alerted by phone that we were on our way, so we were not challenged. I heard a clink behind me. It was the colonel shifting the B.A.R. to his other shoulder. The Browning Automatic Rifle may be a handy little device to have along on a patrol, but it's not the lightest weapon in the world. I felt sorry for him but was damned glad that a war correspondent goes into battle with nothing heavier than a smuggled .45 in his pocket.

We were remarkably quiet.

I could just make out the form of the sergeant ahead of us. He was just reaching the tree line. Even though I knew we were still only a couple of hundred yards in front of our own lines, I kept expecting somebody to open fire on us. It had turned chilly and I put up the collar of my combat jacket and wished I'd remembered to wear the o.d. knit cap. Suddenly I saw the figure in front of me turn and disappear. I turned instinctively and could just barely make him out ahead of me through the trees. I increased my pace, stumbled over a root and fell on my face. I picked myself up and picked my way carefully through the trees until I could see somebody in front of me again. The woods thinned out a couple of hundred yards in and I came to a stream of water about eight feet wide. There was no way of telling how deep it was, but, since there didn't seem to be any way around it and since the man ahead of me had presumably made it, I waded in. It was ice-cold and knee-deep. When I got across, I'd lost sight of the fourth man again. I had no idea which way to go. I remembered that the last time I'd seen anyone in front of me the moon had also been directly in front of me over the top of the trees. I sighted on the treetop and the moon and moved forward. I wasn't worrying too much about the noise now. What I was interested in was speed and the welcome sight of another GI. I must have traveled two hundred and fifty yards. I came to the end of the woods. Ahead of me was an open plain. I stopped and sat down on the spot. Suddenly a hand grabbed me by the ankles. I started to open my mouth and I started to jump up when another hand went around my face and the fingers clasped themselves over my mouth. I turned my eyes, expecting any minute to feel a knife blade across my throat. Instead I saw the white teeth of the sergeant shining in his blackened face. Behind him I could make out the forms of three other GI's. Evidently we'd reached the spot where we had to make a run for it individually. I nodded my head and the sergeant took his hand from around my mouth. He motioned me into the shadows and I sprawled out behind a bush to get back my breath and my courage. I didn't remember having been this frightened in my life. My heart was pounding so hard that I was sure the Germans could hear it and zero in on it.

My teeth started chattering. I wanted a cigarette desperately.

Bronson arrived a couple of minutes later, followed by Pete a few minutes after that. The party was complete. The sergeant got up and took a few steps out into the clearing and stood stock-still. He remained there and then turned around and came back to us. He motioned the second man forward. He held his hand over his head and the GI sprinted from under cover, crouched low and ran fast and true across the open plain. The third and fourth man followed him on signal and suddenly it was my turn. I saw the hand drop and ran. God! How I ran! Even though the other three had gotten across, I expected to hear a bullet go whizzing by any second.

55

Nothing happened and when I reached the tree line on the other side, I fell down and vomited quietly. The others ignored me. We were joined almost immediately by Bronson, Pete and the sergeant. After the seven of us were together, we moved out again with the sergeant taking the lead, the rest of us ten yards apart, in visual contact with each other. I had no idea how long we'd been out. It seemed like hours. I got very careful from there on. We were certainly close to the German lines and I fought a desire to giggle. I reached into my pocket, took out the .45 and clicked off the safety catch. It made an amazingly loud noise in the dark. I felt better with the gun in my hand. From there on, we went slower and closer together. There was no problem about keeping visual contact. It had turned very cold. About twenty minutes later, the man in front of me stopped. So did I. My feet were freezing and my teeth were still chattering. The figure in front of me came walking back to where I was standing. He put his mouth against my ear and whispered, "The German outpost is right ahead of us. Get under cover quietly and wait there until the sergeant comes and tells you what to do. Pass it on."

He went forward again and disappeared into the shrubbery on his right. I walked back until I came to the colonel. I whispered the message to him and went back to where I thought my standing position had been, found a clump of bushes and sprawled out.

I must have fallen asleep. Suddenly I was wide awake and curiously frightened. I looked up and saw a figure standing over me. The hand with the gun jerked up automatically. It stopped in mid-air. The figure bending over me was the sergeant.

"You O.K.?" he whispered.

"Fine," I whispered back.

"You're doing fine. The other three have already gone through into the German lines. Go straight ahead. Sight yourself on that big tree on the skyline. About seventy-five yards from here, you'll see a big boulder. Take thirty steps past that, take ten steps to the right and find some cover and stay there. And don't fall asleep. We have about two hours before we have to start back. Got it?"

"Right," I whispered.

"O.K. take off."

I took off. I spotted the large tree and headed straight for it. I remembered something I'd learned on Anzio. When you don't want to make any noise, you put your heel down first, carefully and then kind of roll the rest of your foot onto the ground. Then you lift the other foot, put the heel down and then roll the rest of the foot down. I was about ten paces from the boulder when I heard a loud noise on my right. I froze. I put my head down, clamped my lips together so my teeth wouldn't shine, closed my eyes to a slit and listened. The noise got louder and closer. Suddenly, six or seven yards on my right I saw a figure, wearing a German uniform and carrying a rifle. I was afraid I was going to giggle. Fear affects me that way. The figure stopped ten yards or so from me and stood still. Had he heard something, too? Was he listening and looking into the darkness? Then I really wanted to laugh. I heard a wonderful sound . . . the sound of water. He was out there for a much more basic and much more important reason than spotting a GI patrol. He turned and disappeared into the darkness of the trees. I heard him for another couple of seconds and then there was silence. I waited for what I estimated was five minutes and moved forward again. I was really careful now. I knew I was inside the German lines and I wanted to be damned sure I didn't go tumbling into any Kraut foxholes in the dark. I turned right at the boulder, walked thirty steps beyond it, counted off ten paces and crawled into the underbrush. I was ringing wet and after a while, when the sweat dried on my body, I felt very cold.

It was a long two hours.

I didn't hear a damned thing that remotely came under the heading of military information. Or is there a significance in the fact that one of the outpost soldiers relieved himself four times during the night? That gave me a rough time for a while. There's something about that noise in the middle of the night that evokes a sympathetic response. I bit my teeth and told myself stories, tried to solve equations in my head and tried to remember the lyrics of popular songs. By the time I worked my way through the scores of all the old Bing Crosby movies, it was time to head back. The sergeant motioned me forward and signaled for me to follow him. I came to the boulder, headed down over the hill and without waiting for any signal, sprinted across the open plain. At the stream, I found the others waiting for me. I waded across and joined them. We sat in the under-brush and when the colonel and Pete arrived we went farther back into the bushes. The sergeant went from man to man and they whispered what information they'd picked up. Robbie had heard two Kraut soldiers in a foxhole talking about being relieved in three days. That was important. That meant that if they were relieving these troops, there were no plans to either attack or withdraw. That one overheard conversation justified the patrol. I didn't think the sergeant was interested in the lyrics of "I'd Like To Be a Bee in Your Boudoir," or the fact that Y plus 304 X = 2Y (X + 4Y) + 397. Or

58

whatever the hell the equation was. I told him I hadn't heard a thing except one Kraut who'd obviously had too many liquids to drink. All the information was passed on to Pete and we started back in the same formation as we'd assumed coming out. I had the feeling the trees looked familiar and I felt almost lighthearted. It's amazing how suddenly those holes in the ground in the company position began to take on all the nostalgia and beauty of My Old Kentucky Home. Suddenly all hell broke loose in front of me. I couldn't see a thing and I stopped dead in my tracks. The colonel dropped the B.A.R. and high-tailed it past me. I followed him. I stumbled over a body and stopped. It was the GI who'd been in front of me all through the patrol. He had a knife in his back. A little farther on I found another body—the second man in our patrol. The noise was still going on and suddenly I came upon the source of it. The sergeant was on his back on the ground. On top of him was a German. I caught the glint of a knife in the moonlight. But it was only momentary. Suddenly the colonel threw himself on top of the German. I saw another knife flash and heard a scream and the colonel kicked the German over on his back. He was dead.

The sergeant was still on the ground. I bent over him. He was moaning. "Under the ribs," he said.

I put my hand where he was pointing. It came away wet and sticky.

"The son of a bitch jumped Robbie and Don," he said. "They never heard or saw a thing. He came up behind me and jumped me. He had his forearm across my throat and I couldn't do a goddamned thing. He must have flanked us."

"Shut up," said the colonel.

"There'll be more around," said the sergeant.

59

"I've been on patrols before, Sergeant," said Bronson. "Now just shut up."

Pete and the man behind me joined us.

"How are the others?" I whispered.

"They're dead," said Pete.

"How far are we from our lines?" I asked.

The sergeant started to answer me.

"We're about ——"

"Shut up, Sergeant," said the colonel. "We're about a thousand yards from our outpost. I don't think the boy with the knife was alone. That means they have us spotted and are setting up an ambush. Robbie or Don or both must have stumbled into him and he had to get them fast. You're sure they're dead?"

"They're dead," said Pete.

"Cappy," said Bronson. "I'm going to give you a dirty job."

"Fine," I said.

"You heard the information passed around at the stream?"

"I heard it."

"O.K. You're the getaway man. You stay here with the sergeant. You still got the forty-five I gave you?"

"Still have it."

"Good. Now listen carefully. Stay here under cover. The three of us will take off to the left and try to lead them away from you. We'll open up when we get a couple of hundred yards away. As soon as you hear me firing, hoist the sergeant on your back and take off like a big-assed bird for the lines."

"For Chrissakes, leave me here," said the sergeant. "They won't find me. You can come and get me at daylight."

"Shut up, Sergeant," said Bronson. "I'm pulling

60

rank on you. Normally, Cappy, we'd just bull our way through this close to our lines, but with a wounded man you lose a certain amount of mobility. Now where the hell is my B.A.R.?"

"Here it is, Colonel," said Pete. "I picked it up where you dropped it when you high-tailed it up forward."

"A soldier never drops his weapon in combat," said the colonel.

"I forgive you, Sir," said the sergeant.

"O.K., let's move out." He shook hands with me and then formally shook hands with the sergeant.

How goddamned "Journey's End," I thought.

"Good luck," he said.

"You, too," I said.

The colonel and the two others left.

"Do you know the fireman's carry?" asked the sergeant.

"I come from a long line of firemen," I said.

"I'm sorry about the blood," he said.

"Shut up, Sergeant. How does it feel?"

"It hurts like hell."

"Isn't a soldier always supposed to carry a first-aid pouch with sulfa powder?"

"Sure. It makes too much noise on patrol."

I suppose we shouldn't have been talking. It didn't seem to me that it made much difference. If the Krauts were looking for us, they weren't going to have any trouble finding us. An overage war correspondent with a .45 he could just barely shoot and a seriously wounded noncom weren't going to be much of a challenge. The talking made me feel better. The sergeant lying there on his side bleeding and the dead Kraut staring up into the trees were a little too much to bear in silence.

61

Suddenly the B.A.R. opened up on our left flank. A german zip gun returned the fire. Bronson had found his fight. Two M-1's opened up with him. That meant all three were accounted for. I hoped the Germans weren't counting. I hoisted the sergeant up on my shoulders and started back. I don't know how far it was or how long it took me to get back inside our own lines. The sergeant kept up a steady monologue that broke off every now and then when the pain got to be too much for him. The blood from his wound had soaked through my jacket and felt wet, sticky and strangely cold against my skin. The sound of firing was almost continual and I wondered when the colonel was going to run out of ammunition for the B.A.R. I tried to remember how many clips he had with him and couldn't. I asked the sergeant.

"I been going on patrols all my life," he said. "All my GI life. Who'd think I'd get knifed like that . . . ?"

"How many clips, Sergeant?"

"I didn't hear a thing. He had his forearm against my Adam's apple. I didn't have a chance. That dirty, lousy . . ."

Suddenly two figures jumped up in front of me. I turned and started to run back the way I'd come. The figures came after me. With the sergeant on my back, I didn't have a chance to dodge them. They grabbed me.

"For chrissakes, Mack, where are you running to, the Kraut lines?"

"What happened to Bud?"

It was the GI's on our outpost. I'd forgotten they'd be expecting us back before dawn and would be on the lookout for us. The firing in front of them alerted them that something had happened. They helped me carry the sergeant to their foxholes, called back on the phone and within ten minutes two medics turned up with a litter.

62

As they rolled the sergeant on, he turned for a minute and looked up at me. "Thanks, Harry," he said. "Spell my name right, willya?"

"Sure," I said. "Take care of yourself."

"Tell the colonel thanks, too. I'm sorry I gave you both such a hard time."

They took him away and I went back to the CP and reported in to the captain. I passed along the information and we sat there, with Father Barry still censoring mail, sweating out the return of Bronson and the other two members of the patrol.

"Corn Cob will really ream me out good," said the captain. "He'll break me to yardbird for letting Bronson go on the patrol."

"How is it you're just thinking of that now, captain?" I asked.

"You've been with Bronson, Williams. Do you think I could have kept him off that patrol—even if he didn't pull rank on me?"

"I suppose not."

"You're damned right not. I mean, what the hell, patrols are nothing to a line company. They're as routine and as much a part of your life as rations. So . . . the Old Man wants to go on a patrol. He wants to keep his hand in, make like a GI. . . . O.K. What's the harm? Patrols go out all the time. Nothing ever happens on patrols. Except once in a while. Except every so often. And it has to be this patrol. Who'da told Corn Cob that Bronson went on a patrol if everything worked fine? Now, I gotta report him missing in action. 'How did a regimental commander come to be missing, Captain?' he'll ask. And I'll say 'I don't know—we just kinda lost him.' He'll ream me out good."

"Aren't you giving up a little soon, Captain?"

63

"Listen, he had six clips for the B.A.R. at the most. You heard the firing. He was luring them away from you and Bud. He had no firepower to get out with. He had to try to outsmart them. Sometimes they don't get outsmarted."

"What do you think is the deadline?"

"If they're not back by noon, you can start writing the obits."

"Why noon?"

"Because the Krauts pull back their patrols at dawn. If they're not back at noon, it's because they're not around to come back."

"Maybe they were captured."

"Patrols don't take prisoners unless that's their purpose. Once in a while we send a patrol out with that as a mission. If, for instance, we think a new unit has moved in against us and we want to find out what it is, we pick up a couple of prisoners. Normally a patrol has to stay mobile and prisoners slow it down."

"Like overage war correspondents and wounded sergeants."

"Something like that."

"What do we do, just sit and wait?"

"If they're not back by nine o'clock, I'll send a two-man daylight patrol out to look for them."

They were still not back by nine, so the patrol went out. I also pointed out the position of the two dead men on the captain's map and a graves registration unit went out and picked them up. The patrol came back at one. They hadn't found any evidence of the colonel or the men. The patrol had gone as far as the stream and fanned out left and right on the flanks.

"Well," said the captain. "At least they didn't find any bodies. That's something."

64

"Not much," I said.

"No. Not much. But something."

At four o'clock Father Barry held mass and served communion. Just after dusk the company commander and the noncoms of the relieving company moved up and were shown around the positions. The relief was scheduled for ten o'clock.

At nine thirty, when the three of us, the captain, Father Barry and I were sitting around the CP, we heard a voice outside. "Coming in."

It was Bronson's voice!

We put the light out, the covering over the entrance pulled back and Bronson fell into the hole. We put the light on.

He was grinning.

"I hope you didn't wait up for me," he said. "I got detained."

"You sunuvabitch," said the captain.

"Is that any way to talk to your regimental commander?"

"How are you, Charley?" I asked.

"I'm fine," he said. "How's Bud?"

"Pretty bad. They evacuated him this afternoon. What about you? What happened?"

"We ran out of ammunition. There were twelve of them in the patrol, not counting the one I killed. We didn't have a chance of getting around them. Pete was all for making a break for it. He said they don't take prisoners."

"They don't," said the captain.

"In this case they did," said Bronson.

"What?"

"That's right. I took my insignia off before we left, but I had the oak leaves in my pocket. I just pinned them

65

on my collar and waited. You should have seen their faces when they found us. We didn't put our hands up or surrender. We just sat on the ground looking at them. One of them was ready to let us have it, but the leader of the patrol spotted my oak leaves and called him off. I guess a lieutenant colonel was a prize for them. At least I hoped so. Pete tells me there was a long debate about what to do with us. They'd already found the dead member of their patrol, so they weren't feeling too friendly toward us. The noncom kept telling them he had to deliver us to the company commander. I think he was as surprised as Corn Cob would have been to find me on the patrol. For a while it was touch and go. Then I saw Pete turn pale. He told me they'd decided to bring in the officer but to kill the men. The noncom talked them out of it. He felt that if he was bringing in one prisoner he might as well bring in three. The whole thing evidently confused hell out of him, and he wasn't sure that the GI's weren't as important as I was. So they took us back."

"And?" I asked.

"We escaped."

"Just like that?"

"Almost," said Bronson. "We got back to their lines just before dawn. They took me to the company CP and their CO was pretty confused to find himself facing a junior bird. I told him we had been on our way back from a USO dance and our jeep had broken down. He asked me if I normally carried a B.A.R. to USO dances. I told him, I normally did. Anyway, he called headquarters on the field phone and was told to send us back. They loaded us on a ration truck with four guards and we started back to their headquarters. A couple of miles behind the lines I nodded to Pete and the other guy and we jumped the guards."

"Just like that?"

"Almost," said Bronson. "I kicked one in the groin and got his rifle and hit him in the jaw with the butt. Pete took care of two of them fine. The other kid was kicked in the face."

"Carlyle," said the captain.

"What?" asked Bronson.

"Carlyle. That was the kid's name."

"We had to leave him. Pete and I got off the truck and headed into the woods. We ran like hell and finally dug into the side of an old abandoned foxhole until dark. Then we just infiltrated our way back and here I am."

"Just like that," I repeated.

"Exactly," said Bronson. "I don't see any reason to mention this whole thing to General Corridon, do you?"

"No reason at all," said the captain.

"Good."

He looked at me.

"Where'd you get the shirt, Cappy?"

"I borrowed it from Father Barry. Mine got a little mussed up. Didn't the German commander want to know if you always went to dances with your face blackened?"

"Funny, he never mentioned it."

"Showed a lot of tact."

"I thought so," said the colonel. "Listen, we have about twenty minutes before the relief arrives. How about a quickie?"

He beat me. I guess my mind wasn't on the chessboard.

We got back to regimental headquarters around

midnight and I did a long piece on the patrol while it was still fresh in my mind. Maybe you read it. Most of the papers used it on the front page. You'll find it in a lot of anthologies of war pieces.

I hung around with Bronson for another three days and then took off to cover an artillery battalion. After that I moved in with a tank unit. I didn't see Charley Bronson again for a long time. The next time I saw him he was a full-fledged colonel. . . .

La Guardia ☆ 1953

I went into the temporary headquarters the army had set up just off the main rotunda. The colonel who was running the show nodded to me.

"They'll be about forty minutes late, it looks like, Harry," he said.

"Maybe you shoulda flown him in here on a commercial plane," I said.

"Very funny."

I figured it was about time to look in on Margaret again. She was still talking to Irene Miller.

"We were married three weeks after Charley graduated from the Point," she said.

"You'd known each other a long time?" asked Irene.

"All our lives. Charley's father was in the army and like any army family they moved around a great deal but their roots were in Fallview and after he was killed in the First World War, Charley's mother moved back to Fallview to live. They lived three houses away from us. Charley's grandmother and grandfather lived in Fallview, too."

"You went to school together?" asked Irene.

"I suppose you could say we did. I was older than Charley so we were never in the same class. Actually,

Charley and my sister Helen were classmates all through high school."

"Oh."

"They were about the same age."

I figured it was about time to break it up.

"I'm sorry, Irene," I said. "But I'm going to have to borrow Mrs. Bronson for a while."

"That's all right, Harry. Thank you for giving me this time with her."

I wasn't sure Margaret was going to like being talked about like a toothbrush somebody'd borrowed.

"Thank you, Mrs. Bronson," said Irene.

"You're quite welcome. I enjoyed it."

"You must be very proud," said Irene.

"And very impatient," said Margaret.

Two points for her!

Miller left and we were alone again.

"It'll be another half hour at least," I said.

"Charley's goofing up again."

"Margaret," I said. "Did Charley ever tell you about a patrol we went on together?"

"You mean that one you did the story about? . . . He showed me the clipping. So?"

"So. I didn't notice him goofing up that time."

"Seven of you went out on the patrol. Three of you came back."

"Four, counting the sergeant."

"He died later, didn't he?"

"Yes. He did."

"Every time Charley's involved in something, people die. It's like that all the time. I wouldn't be surprised if that plane he's on crashed."

"You're a real loving wife, aren't you?"

"What do you know about it?"

"I know, Margaret. Tell me about the bridge games."

"I could tell you. Plenty. Don't forget it. We'd see how proud you are of your goddamned Gen then."

"I don't think I ever thanked you for the loaves of bread."

"What loaves of bread?"

"You've forgotten your criminal past, Margaret. Don't you remember the way you used to hide the bottles of Scotch inside the loaves of bread?"

She smiled. "I remember."

"You remember what you're supposed to do when the plane lands?"

"Smile. And be proud. And put my arms around him. And look up at him while the flash bulbs are going off and the newsreel cameras are grinding. It would help if I cried a little, wouldn't it? Quietly. Ladylike tears."

"Like you said, Margaret, Myrna Loy."

"What happens now, Harry?"

"What do you mean by now?"

"I mean after all the hoopla is over."

"He gets another star. He retires."

"Where? To Fallview? So he can make the Fourth of July Speech in Grant Park every year? Or address Rotary and the Lions once a year? Or be elected commander of the American Legion Post?"

"Or maybe he writes his memoirs."

"Which you write for him. Is that your angle? You're not doing it for a lousy little book of memoirs. There must be more than that to it, Harry."

"Or maybe some university that needs the publicity offers him the presidency."

"That sounds just dandy."

"Or maybe he gets to be chairman of the board of

some nice big fat corporation with defense contracts that isn't opposed to having a gold-plated two-star hero with contacts at the Pentagon working for them. There are lots of opportunities for retired generals these days. The ones who have ticker-tape parades and address Congress have a particularly high market value."

"And what happens when they get wise to Charley?"

"Why should they get wise to Charley?"

"You know what's wrong with him, Harry?"

"No. Tell me."

"He hates it. He hates the whole thing. He's in the wrong business. He's a snob . . . If being intolerant of the army is snobbery. If hating the caste system is snobbery. If refusing to play the old Army Game is snobbery. If being bored to tears with the whole thing is snobbery. He doesn't hide it very well."

"How did you do with Miller?"

"Fine. I told her exactly what she wanted me to tell her. I told her all about our whirlwind courtship. It sounded very romantic. I'da curled that kinky hair of hers if I really told her the story of the courtship of Charley Bronson—Boy Hero."

"I'm glad you restrained yourself."

"You think I'm a grade-A government issue bitch, don't you, Harry?"

"I wouldn't quite put it that way."

"You had me pegged the first night you saw me. Remember, Harry, when you came to the house after they filled the papers with all that guff about Charley? 'I'm an old friend of your husband's, Mrs. Bronson,' you said. 'I thought I might be some help to both of you now that the story has broken out of Korea.' You had me pegged right away, didn't you?"

"You want the truth, Margaret?"

"Sure. Why not? A little truth is always welcome. Just a little, Harry. Not too much."

"Sure. I had you pegged. Remember I'd heard something about you from Charley."

"That must have been an earful."

"It was."

"Well? What about that little truth, Harry?"

"All right. You drank too much. That was obvious right away."

"Occupational disease. What else?"

"You were on the make. I detected a slight touch of nympho."

"And there's nothing worse than an aging nympho?"

"There are a couple of things worse, Margaret."

"All right. A drunk and aging nympho."

"I didn't say that. I said you drank too much. I said I detected a slight touch of nympho."

"How delicate of you. How fair. What a fine sense of proportion you have, Mr. Williams. And why didn't this apprentice nympho score, Mr. Williams? Had you taken a vow of celibacy? Or was it because of your close relationship to my husband? Was it that inherent sense of decency that marks the true gentleman?"

"I don't know why, Margaret. I honest to God don't. With me it's always open season on nymphos. As far as the Gen is concerned, I only saw him three times in my life. The first time was that patrol you know about. I saw him once more in Europe and I ran into him quite accidentally one night in a bar on West Forty-eighth Street after the war was over."

"Then it must have been me? I just didn't attract you."

"Since we're having our moment of truth, that isn't

73

it, either. You were made to order. A mature woman, married, no hooks, no strings, no designs."

"You did very well for Charley."

"I didn't do as much as I'll take credit for, Margaret. He was a legit hero. Most of it would have happened anyway. I just greased the skids a little, made it happen faster and easier."

"And here we are waiting for him to come home to a hero's welcome: his official best friend who beats a loud drum and his loving wife who happens to be an overage tramp."

"That's a little harsh, isn't it, Margaret?"

"On which one of us?"

"On both of us. I don't know what turned you into whatever you are, but I'm probably the world's greatest expert on me."

"What makes you think I turned into anything. I was always this way."

"Nobody's always any way. You asked me before what my angle is. I honest to God don't know. I'm without an angle to my name. Maybe for the first time in my life. Sure, there are obvious angles. Sure, I can ghost his memoirs and split the take from *Life*. And it's nice to have a seat in the Cadillac with the guy sitting up on the hood waving to the adoring millions. But that isn't really an angle. Maybe I think the Gen deserves a little applause and a little appreciation for a change. Maybe it's that simple."

"Maybe," she said. "Look, Harry, if the plane's gonna be late, can I have another drink?"

"What do you think?"

"No?"

"It's up to you, Margaret. How many have you had this morning?"

74

"Four. No, five, counting the one you took away from me when you brought Irene Miller in."

"Let's say four and a half."

"O.K. No drink."

"Look, Margaret, I'm not your nursemaid. You ought to know whether you can have a drink or not. You ought to know what your capacity is. You ought to know how many you can get away with."

"You want to know something, Harry? I'm scared."

"Of what?"

"Of Charley. Isn't that silly? At my age to be afraid of Charley. I think it's the first time in my life I've ever been afraid of him. You like him, don't you?"

"Yes. I like him a lot."

"It's funny. Everybody does. One time . . . well . . . never mind."

"No. What was it?"

"Well Charley walked in on me one time, at a party at our house. It was a kinda drunken brawl, I guess. Anyway he walked into a bedroom and found me with a captain on the post. We were both blind. He socked the captain."

"Yeah."

"That's all."

"What do you mean, that's all? He got transferred, didn't he? He wound up with a derogatory remark on his fitness report, didn't he?"

"You know about it? He told you about it?"

"He told me there'd been a fight at a party."

"They lowered the boom on him. They had to. It was the Army Game. You don't go around hitting captains even if you find them in bed with your wife at a party. And yet, Harry, even when they did it to him, even when they wrote that fitness report and transferred him,

75

they liked him. They really transferred him out of kindness. I was an embarrassment to him and, I guess, to them."

"So transferring him solved the whole thing?"

"Don't bet on it, Harry. There is no grapevine in the world like the grapevine that operates in the United States Army in peacetime. Two days after you're at a new post, they know all about you. They know that Mrs. Bronson puts away Scotch like there's no tomorrow and that, given the opportunity and enough liquid lubrication, she's a pushover."

"That must have been great for him."

"You think there was something so unique about me? I just got caught once. Once is enough. The army, Harry is the point of no return. There's no such thing on an army post as an ex-lush or an ex-nympho. Once they peg you, brother, you're pegged. That's it."

"Wasn't there ever anything between the two of you?"

"Me and Charley? We got married, didn't we? There musta been something. You'd say that, wouldn't you, Harry? You'd say, 'They got married, so there musta been something, sometime, between them,' wouldn't you?"

"Yeah."

"You'd be wrong, Harry. You shoulda heard my story to Irene Miller about the courtship of General and Mrs. Bronson. There'll be a lot of horse laughs in a lot of army posts when that little piece of syndicated fiction turns up in the papers. How come Charley never told you about that, Harry? Or did he?"

"No, he didn't tell me."

"You're itching to hear about it, aren't you? You have a neat mind, Harry. You like to put all the pieces together. Everything has to have a beginning, a middle

76

and an end, like a good news story, doesn't it? Who? What? Where? When? Why? And How? Isn't that what they teach you in journalism school? The five W's and the H, the answer to everything. Form, and neatness. Order."

"All right, Margaret. What are the five W's and the H?"

"Who? Me and Charley. What? Our marriage. Where? Fallview, New York, ancestral home of America's number one Hero . . . this year. When? Nineteen thirty-two. The why and how aren't that easy to answer, Harry. You're itching, aren't you?"

"I couldn't stop you now if I wanted to, could I?"

"Not if you wanted to, Harry. Maybe you'd better grab yourself a drink. It's a story that goes better with a drink. I found that out."

Fallview, New York ☆ 1930-32
Margaret

I don't know how to tell you about Fallview, if you've never been there. God, I've been in a lot of towns like it since. And yet none of them were Fallview. I suppose I had what you call a happy childhood. That makes me suspect right there, doesn't it? I have no hook to hang my neuroses on. How easy it would be if I had a father that was a drunkard or beat me or chased girls! How I could justify things if I was the poor girl in class or lisped or hated my mother! My father never drank anything in his life but an occasional glass of beer on a Sunday afternoon. As Fallview families went, we were pretty well off. My father was the office manager of a furniture factory. I dressed just like all the other girls in the elementary school and later in Fallview High School. I not only didn't lisp, I was the best female debater Fallview High ever had. As far as chasing girls was concerned, my father was much too fat and much too contented to chase anything. You see? A psychiatrist couldn't hit pay dirt in my childhood. I never had a dog that died; I never felt inferior and—forgive me for sounding so old-fashioned—I liked my parents.

Fallview. I started to tell you what it was like. Well

. . . it was like every other big, small town in America. Let's see.

We were very proud that our ball team never finished worse than third. Going to a baseball game in Fallview was a little like athletic bingo. Every score card had a number on it and between innings they used to call out what they called "Lucky" numbers and the prize was a free dry-cleaning job or a bag of groceries. Every time one of the players hit a home run he got a free meal in a Fallview restaurant. Most of the ball players looked like they needed it.

What else?

Well, every male child wanted to grow up and join Rotary, the Elks, the Woodmen of America, The Optimists Club or the Lions. You just did, and the more clubs you belonged to the more prestige you had. A lot of the social life of Fallview revolved around the clubs. The women belonged to the Order of the Eastern Star, the Ladies' Auxiliary of the American Legion, the D.A.R. or the Woman's Club. Everybody in town who'd spent any time in the army in any war belonged to the American Legion. They were great joiners in Fallview.

What else?

Once a year Billy Sunday used to come through Fallview and play to a full house. People went to church every Sunday. I don't think they were religious about it. They just went to church. It was something you did. Nobody would think of sleeping after nine o'clock on a Sunday morning.

I don't think I ever saw a woman smoke on the street in Fallview. Women smoked, but indoors. Somehow, smoking on the street was indecent. I suppose it makes sense. There are a lot of things you can do indoors that

79

would be considered indecent if you did them on the street.

There were two movie houses in Fallview when I was growing up and they didn't convert to talkies until 1930. Fallview was pay dirt country for *The Saturday Evening Post*, *The Literary Digest* and later the Book-of-the-Month Club and *Time* magazine. The principal industry of the town was the manufacture of furniture and most of the workers in the factories were Swedes and French-Canadians. They lived in a part of town called "Swede's Hill" and I always wondered how the Canucks felt living on "Swede's Hill." There were occasional fights between them but most of the time everybody got along fine together. My father used to say the Swedes and the Canucks were crackerjack workers. That was one of his favorite words—"crackerjack." My mother didn't think much of the French-Canadians. She thought the Swedes were the cleanest people in the world. Her favorite expression about Swede's Hill where she served as a volunteer social worker was: "Their kitchen floor was so clean you could have eaten off it." The Park Avenue of Fallview was a very attractive, wide, tree-bordered street called Lakefront Avenue. It was an optimistic name. The nearest lake was five miles away but a Lakefront Avenue address was a mark of caste. Your social position in the town was rated on how close you lived to Lakefront Avenue. Its four blocks contained beautiful houses with white pillars and broad sweeping lawns. Most of the Old Guard, the social leaders, the elderly widows who clipped coupons and voted Republican and the owners and directors of the factories and banks lived there.

We lived in one of the side streets just off Lakefront. My father was always talking about moving around the corner and when he said it, it sounded like somebody talking about someday getting into Heaven. He never made it. I wasn't aware then of a social caste system in Fallview. It was there, under the surface, but the reins were held in a loose hand. The children of the Lakefront Avenue families went to the local elementary schools, but they never went to Fallview High School. The girls went to junior colleges downstate and the boys went to prep school. Most of the boys and girls of Fallview went on to college.

Fifteen miles outside town was "The Lake." It was always called that—"The Lake"—in capital letters and with quotation marks around it. You know I don't even remember the full name of the lake. We just never called it by name.

It was Fallview all over again. The Lakefront Avenue crowd had the big houses on the lakefront and the rest of us huddled around them in little houses that I suppose you'd call bungalows—except that we never would. The summers were wonderful. The kids who had gone off to prep school or junior college would be back and we'd spend most of our time on the lake. We had a rowboat with an outboard motor, but you could always get an invitation to crew on somebody's sailboat. The big social events of the season were the weekly dances at the yacht club, the annual formal dance at the country club and the Fourth of July fireworks. Everybody who owned lakefront property set flares along their shore line and lit them after dark. The residents chipped in for the kind of fireworks you see only at amusement parks now— the kind that make a lot of noise, whirl around and spell things. The fireworks always ended with a huge blaze of color that shook every window in the neighborhood and turned into an American flag. Most of the boys had cars their senior year in high school and we used to go on picnics a lot. The boys used to chip in and buy the steaks and the girls brought along the rest of the fixings for the meals. There was always one girl in every picnic crowd that brought a casserole of scalloped potatoes. Every time I have scallopped potatoes now I think of Fallview and those picnics on the lake.

Let's see.

I know something interesting. I was growing up in the early, wild twenties. We were supposed to be the flaming youth, but I don't ever remember anybody bringing along anything to drink on any of those picnics. It just wasn't done. I don't mean we didn't drink or that the boys didn't carry hip flasks to dances. Sure they did, but none of us really liked drinking very much. We used to do it because I think we thought we should, we thought it was expected of us. Like the fact that there was one speakeasy in Fallview. Only it wasn't a speakeasy. It was the best restaurant in town. Only it was called a club and members were given a key to the front door. The door was never locked, but you got a key anyway and everybody in town, it seemed to me, belonged to the club and had the key. There was never any trouble with the police all during Prohibition and, as a matter of fact, most nights you could find Herman Wallman, the chief of police, at the bar.

I guess there was the usual amount of necking but nothing really serious. We were a great generation for pairing off and through most of my senior year at high school and on vacation when I came home from college, Bobby Skinner and I were going steady. "Going steady" in those days meant necking privileges. I'm not saying that there wasn't an occasional scandal, an occasional quick marriage followed by a premature baby, or an occasional fast trip to Europe for an unscheduled vacation for one of the Lakefront Avenue girls, but for the most part we were a surprisingly moral group of kids. Once in a while a couple would go out on a moonlight sail and get becalmed and return the next morning. Everybody assumed that nothing had happened. Nothing serious, that is. I can vouch for it. Bobby Skinner and I were becalmed one night. Nothing happened. Nothing serious, that is. . . .

I know. What about Charley Bronson?

O.K. The Bronsons lived a couple of houses away from us. Mrs. Bronson was a very thin, very quiet woman, who was "Old Fallview." That was the term used for anyone whose great grandfather, at best, and grandfather, at least, had lived in Fallview. Of course, when she married Charley's father, she had to move, but after he was killed in World War One, she moved back. Of course, she had to do something to support Charley, so she took a job as telephone operator at the hotel. Nobody thought it was strange or unusual, and it had no effect on her social standing in the community. She was still "Old Fallview" and as such was invited everywhere and included in everything. Of course, they didn't have baby sitters in those days and Mrs. Bronson couldn't afford a nursemaid or a governess for Charley, even if she could have found one in Fallview, so Charley just sort of ran loose during the day while she was working. He spent most of his time at our house. He was there all the time. He was in the same class as my sister Helen and from the first day the Bronsons moved to Fallview, they were inseparable. He was really like a member of the family. During the summer he used to come up and spend a lot of time at the lake. He was always included in every family outing or picnic. He and Helen fished and swam, had secret code words, secret hiding places, climbed trees, were equally happy playing with dolls or playing war. Everybody thought of them as a team. Somehow, Helen's girl friends accepted Charley as a member of *their* group and the boys treated Helen the same when Charley brought her around—which was most of the time. By the time they were in high school together, everybody in Fallview knew that Helen was Charley's girl. Nobody would have thought of asking either one of them for a date. They teamed up in doubles at tennis, were elected president and vice president of the senior class and always crewed together on the same sailboat. It was just taken for granted by everybody, including the two families, that Charley and Helen would get married. They didn't have to get engaged. They'd been engaged since they were ten years old. Another thing that was taken for granted was that Charley was going to West Point, like his father. His mother couldn't afford to send him to a prep school, but he worked hard at Fallview High and was always on the honor roll, always at the head of his class and when he graduated, he was valedictorian.

Now let's get back to me for a minute. The last time we saw me I was becalmed with Bobby Skinner. Did we get married and live happily ever after? Well . . . Bobby went off to college and today is the best dentist Fallview ever had. He is also well on the way to having the largest family. Last time I counted he had nine children. By the time I finished college, I was getting itchy. In my senior year, I came home for my vacation and suddenly Fallview seemed smaller and dirtier and duller. I had the feeling I knew what everyone was going to say before he said it. I found that sailing bored me and I was sick of Bobby Skinner trying to slip his hand under my sweater. It was a very dull vacation and when I went back to school, Bobby Skinner and Fallview had both had it as

84

far as I was concerned. I taught school for two years in a town twenty-five miles from Fallview and used to come home on weekends occasionally. Then I quit the teaching job and moved to Buffalo. I got a job in an architect's office. That lasted a little over a year. I fell madly in love with my boss, who just happened to have a wife and two children. We were both very sane and intelligent about the whole thing and I came limping back to Fallview. Just to have something to do, another girl and I opened a nursery school. For some reason it caught on. Now that I look back on it, I wouldn't be surprised that most of the mothers sent their children to us because that poor Margaret Davis needs something to take her mind off that married man she was in love with. You didn't suppose Fallview didn't know all about it, did you?

Anyway, there I was in 1930 back home in the bosom of my family. I know there was a depression but somehow it hadn't hit Fallview yet. The factories in town were cutting down, but that had happened before and there was nothing particularly unique or frightening. I suppose there was a little less coupon clipping on Lakefront Avenue, but the only thing I was aware of that year was that I was considered by the townspeople to be right on the edge of being an old maid. I must admit I was beginning to worry about it a little myself. Most of my contemporaries were married. The only available young men were either too young or out of the question. But I was enjoying myself with the nursery school and after all I was only twenty-seven.

Helen was nineteen and in her second year at junior college. Charley was a yearling at the Point and having survived the horrors of the plebe's life was looking forward to the three-month summer furlough. He and Helen had every minute planned and I must admit by the

85

time school was out, I was almost as much in a tizzy about the summer as she was. Helen was the most infectious person I've ever known. If she was sad, it was impossible not to cry with her. If she was happy, you found yourself laughing out loud with her. She and Charley wrote to each other every day. God knows what they found to write about! And her whole life was pointed to the time his train arrived at Fallview station. It's funny, isn't it, how you never notice your sister when she's growing up? I remember really looking at her one morning and thinking to myself: She's beautiful. Why didn't I notice that before? She had a way of smiling that turned her whole face into something you had to label "happiness." Every once in a while I had the feeling I wanted to keep going around snapping still pictures of her, so I'd remember this expression or that one. She was something! She was also a walking encyclopedia of West Point slang. She never washed the dishes. She "policed the table." Food, around our house was called "Slum." She signed all her letters to Charley OAO which is cadet slang for "best girl." It means "One And Only" I think. She memorized all the ridiculous things they make plebes memorize at West Point and she used to spout them at the damndest times. I remember some of them: "How many lights in Cullum Hall? Three hundred and forty lights, Sir. How many gallons of water in Lusk Reservoir? Ninety-two and two-tenths million gallons, Sir, when the water is flowing over the spillway. How many names on the battle monument? Two thousand two hundred and forty names, Sir. How is the cow? Sir, she walks, she talks, she's full of chalk, the lacteal fluid extracted from the female of the bovine species is highly prolific to the nth degree." She was impossible to have around. And yet it was kind of sweet and wonderful. I don't think I ever saw anybody

86

as much in love as Helen was. I think it was more than that. There had never been any question in Helen's mind about what she was going to do with her life. From ten on, she knew that she was going to marry Charley and have his children and, since Charley was going to be an army officer, she studied the army the way you'd study for an exam. I honestly think she knew more about the army and army life than Douglas MacArthur. She knew which posts were good posts and which weren't. She had opinions on the relative values of the various branches. She talked learnedly about "Diamond formations" and "Skirmish lines." She sweated out Charley's plebe year at the Point because she knew that it was hell on wheels, and I think she wasn't quite sure that Charley would be able to take the calculated cruelty and humiliation that the army considers character training for its new cadets. When Charley finally made it, she breathed a sigh of relief. "Thank God," she said. "We're not a beast anymore."

During Charley's second year at the Point she was up there every time he was allowed to have visitors. It was like going home to her. She knew every inch of the Point from her reading and she couldn't wait for Charley to take her on Flirtation Walk for the first time. I guess you'd have to say that Helen was more than just in love with Charley. He was her way of life and the army came in the package. Plebes aren't allowed off the post during the summer vacation, so Helen was looking forward to that summer of 1930. Yearlings are given a three-month summer furlough and all her letters home to us from college ended with the number of days until vacation. We all took for granted that to Helen, this year, vacation was a synonym for Charley.

They had a wonderful summer. They were off by

themselves more than usual. Once in a while they'd include me in on a date. I sailed with them a couple of times, and went to the amusement park on the lake, but most of the time they were alone. I was surprised at the way Charley had matured. He'd grown taller, filled out and seemed more sure of himself. God, he was a good-looking boy.

I felt very old that summer. I had occasional dates. I was very big with the young doctors just setting up their practice or the boys out of law school, who were working on the routine things like wills and contracts in their fathers' offices. The torch I'd been carrying had just about flickered out and the dominant emotion in my life was boredom. You won't believe this, but I actually started painting to give myself something to do. I spent a lot of time that summer sitting on the shore line of the lake with my easel set up, capturing the passing scene. If you know anybody wants to buy a collection of gobby paintings of water-skiing, lake at sunset, lake at dawn or just plain lake, my mother's attic is full of them.

I think my mother had given up on me. She just had me figured for an old maid and accepted it. I thought of applying for a job as a teacher at Fallview High, but decided to give the nursery school one more year.

I read a lot. *A Farewell to Arms, Dodsworth, Look Homeward, Angel* and *All Quiet on the Western Front* were new. I remember I used to sit in a lounge chair outside the bungalow reading and listening to Amos and Andy. I remember the songs we used to sing. Even now when I hear one of them it brings that whole summer back to me. Until the night of the country-club dance it was just another summer and would have merged in my mind with summers just like it I'd spent when I came home from college. But just let some orchestra some-

88

where start playing "Just A Gigolo" or "Betty Coed" or "Beyond the Blue Horizon" or "Three Little Words" and I'm right back there on the lakefront in 1930.

Talking about it this way, it sounds like a terrible summer, doesn't it? Actually it wasn't. It was pleasant, in a negative kind of way—easy and lazy. If there wasn't anything exciting in my life, at least there wasn't anything that bothered me.

Now let me tell you about the country club dance that year. In every town there's one big social event of the year. In Fallview it was the annual Labor Day weekend dance at the country club. It officially marked the end of summer, and there was something very special about it. Most of the young people of Fallview had gotten engaged at the country-club dance. It was the kind of an event that you took your best girl to. Young girls used to sweat out invitations and the final humiliation was not to get a bid to the dance. The social implications of not being invited even affected me. I breathed a sigh of relief when Eddie Price, a young lawyer who was high on anybody's list of dullards, asked me to go with him. I drove to Buffalo to buy a dress.

Of course, Charley and Helen went together.

It was a beautiful night. The club is smack at the east end of the lake and the sun deck, which extended out over the lake, was used for dancing. They hired one of the name orchestras that was on a series of one-night stands in that section of the country. Could it have been Hal Kemp? I think so. Anyway, Eddie and I drove up to the club in Eddie's car with two other couples. People usually doubled up in cars going to the country-club dances. It was assumed that there was going to be some drinking and with three couples in a car the chances were that when it was over there'd be at least one member of the group sober enough to drive. Helen and Charley drove alone in a beat-up jalopy that his mother had given him for Christmas the year before. "We might want to leave early," Helen said. "This way we're on our own and won't inconvenience anyone else."

The moon, or the liquor or the tradition of the occasion must have gotten to my young lawyer date. About halfway through his hip flask he proposed. "I don't want you to think there is anything impetuous about this," he said. "I've given it careful thought, talked it over with my father and decided to ask you to marry me," he said. You know, I considered it, for a fast ten minutes. What the hell, I was obviously going to stay in Fallview for the rest of my life. I was old enough to know that there were certain biological needs that don't get satisfied in a town like Fallview without getting married, and Eddie was a nice, sober young man, who would inevitably inherit his father's practice and might even wind up with a house on Lakefront Avenue. Why not? I told Eddie I would think it over. As a clincher he told me how much he was apt to inherit when his father died and gave me a rundown on the state of his father's health to show that there was the chance in the immediate future that we'd be probating a will together. You have to admit it was pretty romantic. I think that was the first time I remember having too much to drink. One of the other girls drove the car home. Eddie, acting on the principle that we were almost engaged, pawed me, in a methodical way all the way home in the back of the car. There was nothing passionate or romantic about his pawing. It was a little like he was taking inventory of something he's just offered to buy.

Anyway I got home just before dawn, got out of my clothes very fast and climbed into bed without shower-

90

ing, brushing my teeth, putting on a nightgown or any of the other things well-brought-up girls are supposed to do before getting into bed. I don't know whether it was the effect of the pawing in the car on the way home, the liquor I'd consumed or the strangely exciting feel of the sheets against my nude body, but I had wild, exciting, erotic dreams.

I woke up suddenly to find my father standing over me, shaking me by the shoulders.

"Wake up, Margaret," he said. "Wake up."

I sat up in bed, remembered suddenly that I didn't have anything on and pulled the sheet up around my neck.

"What is it, Pa?" I asked.

"There's been an accident. They just called from the hospital."

"An accident?"

"Helen and Charley. They had a crack-up coming home from the dance. They don't know when it happened. They found the car after daybreak. They're both in the hospital. Will you go down and stay with your mother? I have to go to the hospital. I don't think she should go and I don't want to leave her here alone. I'll wait until you get dressed."

"How bad is it?" I asked.

"I don't know. They're both still alive. I think it's pretty bad, Maggie."

He hadn't called me Maggie since I was a child.

"I didn't want to tell your mother, but it looks like Helen was hurt much worse than Charley. He was thrown out of the car. She was pinned inside. I think it's very serious, but she's still alive."

"How's Mom?"

"She's all right now. I gave her a shot of whiskey.

91

Mrs. Evans is with her now. Get dressed fast, will you, dear?"

He left the room and I jumped out of bed and got into my clothes.

When I got downstairs, my father had already left for the hospital. I kissed Mother, something I hadn't done in years. Mrs. Evans left and I went out and made some coffee. Mother and I sat there sipping the coffee and not saying a word to each other. We both kept looking at the phone and the clock, waiting for something to happen.

The phone rang about an hour later.

I answered it.

"Hello," I said.

"Hello, Maggie," my father said and he started to cry. He cried for a full minute. "She's gone," he said and hung up.

"It was Dad," I said. "He'll be right home."

"She's dead. Isn't she, Margaret? She's dead."

I couldn't say it.

"He'll be right home," I said.

"I should have gone with him," said my mother. "I should have been there. I shouldn't have let him talk me into staying here. I should have been there."

I got the details later from the state trooper who had found the wreck. The car had gone off the road on a lonely stretch about four miles from the country club. His guess was that it had been going very fast and had suddenly swerved and gone over an embankment. The car had turned over, pinning Helen inside. Charley had been thrown clear, had his arm broken and was suffering from shock. They hadn't told him about Helen's death. Since there was no guardrail on the road at the point of the accident, nobody realized it had happened until the patrol car, on its routine morning check had found it. The trooper told me that they always checked the roads carefully the morning after the country-club dance. He said there was some possibility of a formal manslaughter charge against Charley.

They wanted to perform an autopsy on Helen's body, but my mother refused. She also refused to allow them to file charges against Charley.

"What difference does it make?" she asked. "Of course they were drinking. People do at the country-club dance. I'm not going to have you perform an autopsy to find that out. We admit it. I don't want anything to happen to Charley. It's over with and nothing you do can bring her back."

Mother, once she got over the initial shock, behaved beautifully. I didn't. I kept remembering things and bursting into tears. I'm afraid I made it very difficult for them. My father handled the funeral arrangements, went to see Mrs. Bronson to sympathize with her and let her know that we felt no hatred against Charley because of what had happened. He wanted to see Charley at the hospital but the doctor advised against it. They hadn't told him about the death. He wasn't seriously hurt, but he had crying spells and for three days he was unable to talk. The doctor said this kind of a shock reaction wasn't too unusual.

Helen was put in a closed coffin. Father told me that her face and head had been badly bruised.

I talked to some of the other couples who had been to the dance and they said that Charley hadn't seemed to be drinking too much. He and Helen had left shortly after two in the morning. That was very early to leave a country-club dance. They hadn't had an argument and they'd gone out arm in arm. Nobody thought it was unusual for them to leave so early. Helen and Charley were always going off from the group on their own.

A week after the accident the doctor called. He said that they had told Charley about Helen's death and the doctor thought it would be a good idea if some member of the family went to see him in the hospital. Mother wanted to go.

"I don't blame Charley. Really I don't. It's one of those things that happen. He must be going through the tortures of the damned. I'll go see him."

Father vetoed the idea. It's funny, for a man who had been pushed around all his life, in a loving way, by my mother, he could take a really firm stand about something when he considered it important. He considered this important.

"I don't think Charley is ready to face you yet," he told Mother. "I can imagine the shock he's going through. I know the feelings of guilt he must have. Seeing you now would be too much for him. I don't know about the rest of you," said my father. "But I look at it this way. It was a terrible thing to have happened. Nobody denies that or evades it. But I always felt we had two children in that car. There's a time when you have to be thankful for small favors, small measures of mercy. I'm thankful that one of our children came out of it alive. I hope someday Charley can realize we feel that way. I don't think he's ready to yet. And this is the most important period of his life. His whole life can be destroyed right now by thoughtlessness. I don't think he's ready to see either one of us. I think Margaret should go to the hospital."

"I do too, Dad," I said.

It's strange. I wanted to and at the same time the thought of doing it—of walking into that hospital room and facing Charley—terrified me. I wasn't worried about

94

my reaction or my feelings or my behavior. I was worried about Charley and what he would say and what he would feel, seeing me.

I almost pulled two boners before I left the house. I put on a black dress. As I opened the front door, I suddenly realized what the sight of me wearing black would mean to Charley. I went back and changed. I also carried a copy of *A Farewell to Arms* with me. I remembered in time and left it home.

When I walked into the hospital room, I was afraid for a minute I was going to cry. Charley was sitting up in bed staring out the window. He didn't hear me and I stood on the threshold looking at him. He looked so whipped and so much like a little boy. He also started me thinking about Helen again. I think everybody had that reaction for a while. Charley was a kind of walking reminder of Helen. Everybody was so used to seeing them together that when you saw him alone, you looked around for Helen before you remembered the accident.

"Hello, Charley," I said.

He turned his head and looked at me.

"Hello, Margaret."

His arm was in a cast and there was still a discoloration under one eye. I walked over to the bed and for some ridiculous reason shook hands with him. He looked up at me and started to cry. Suddenly I had my arms around him and he was sobbing against my chest. He pulled back after a minute, took a handkerchief from the bedside table and blew his nose.

I sat down in the chair by the bed. "How is your arm?" I asked.

"It was a clean break. It will be all right."

We were both silent for a minute.

"God, Margaret, it's good to see you."

"It's good to see you, Charley."

"Do you mind if we don't talk about it? Not right away, anyway."

"Sure, Charley. What about the Point?"

"Mother's taking care of it. I'm due back Monday. She called them. I'll be out of here in a couple of days. It's all arranged for me to be late. Mother doesn't want me to bother about it now."

"Sure, Charley. You shouldn't bother about it now."

"I have to go back, don't I, Margaret?"

"Don't you?"

"Yeah. I have to go back, I guess." He stopped talking and turned his head and looked out the window. When he turned back, there were tears in his eyes again.

"I do have to go back, goddamnit. God damn it to hell."

I didn't stay long that first day. I came back the next day and brought him two mystery stories and a batch of magazines. I screened them first to make sure there were no pictures of automobile wrecks or girls who looked like Helen. He was sitting up in bed. He'd been waiting for me. I walked over to the bed and kissed him on the cheek.

"Mother just left," he said. "She came up on her lunch hour. It's all squared away with the Academy. They're sending me a study course that will keep me up with my classes."

"Fine," I said. "I brought you some magazines."

"Good."

We were silent again.

"Margaret?"

"Yes?"

"How do your mother and father feel? God! That's

a stupid damned question, isn't it? How do they feel . . .
I mean . . . about me?"

"They love you, Charley."

"Now?"

"They didn't come to see you, Charley, because
they thought it might be easier for you at first that way.
That's why I came instead."

"You can tell me, Margaret. Honest to God, it's all
right. You can tell me."

"You know what my father said? He said two of their
children were in that car and they thank God that one
of them was spared to them."

"He said that?"

"Yes, Charley. He said that."

"I'm sorry I'm acting like such a damned fool, crying like this. He really said that?"

"Charley darling, that's the way we all feel."

Charley looked up at me.

"Sir, my cranium consisting of Vermont marble,
volcanic lava and African ivory, covered with a thick
layer of case-hardened steel, forms an impenetrable bar-
rier to all that seeks to impress itself upon the ashen
tissues of my brain. Hence the effulgent and ostentati-
ously effervescent phrases just now directed and reiter-
ated for my comprehension have failed to penetrate and
permeate the soniferous forces of my atrocious intelligence. In other words, I am very, very dumb and I do
not understand, Sir."

He recited it fast, crying all the time he said the
ridiculous words.

"You know what that is, Margaret?"

"One of those things the plebes have to say at West
Point?"

"Yes. They told me the lessons of my plebe year

would come in handy sometime. I can't think of anything else to say after what your father said."

"You don't have to say anything, Charley. I told you about it because I think it's something you should know and remember. I don't think this is the time to talk about it anyway, Charley."

"I'd like to, Margaret."

"I don't think you should."

"Let me ask you something else."

"What?"

"I've got to talk to somebody, somebody who knows me, understands me and loves me. Can I talk to you, Margaret?"

"Of course you can, Charley."

"I mean . . . you know . . . I've always been the young kid around your house, sort of like your younger brother. Can you forget that for a couple of minutes and let me talk to you as an equal—as if we were the same age?"

"I've never thought of you that way, Charley. Not as the younger brother."

"I don't want to go back to the Point, Margaret. I hate it."

"Charley, that's a natural reaction. It'll pass. You have to start thinking of your life again. You have to go back to what you've always done."

"I don't think you understand what I'm saying, Margaret. I hate it. I've always hated it. You don't believe that, do you?"

"I don't know, Charley. It's a new idea. It takes a little getting used to."

"You've seen my house. It's like a shrine to my father. Everything that's hanging on the wall has something to do with him and the army. Every picture on every piece of furniture is a picture of him in uniform.

98

Ever since I was old enough to understand it's been drummed into my head that I was going to West Point, that I was going to be an army officer, like my father. I just took it for granted. Everybody did. Charley Bronson was going to West Point. Charley Bronson was going to be an officer like his father. Look, I know how hard it's been for my mother. I know how she's worked her tail off to keep me in high school when other kids my age were out working. I know what a sacrifice it is to her to keep me at the Point. But dammit, Margaret, I'm the sacrifice. I'm the final shrine to my father. I don't want to be my father all over again. I don't want to go into the army because he was in the army. I don't want my life laid out for me because that's the way somebody wants it to be. A man should be given a choice. At least he should be consulted. He shouldn't grow up with the obligation to do something or be somebody when some other person doesn't even know if he can. Does that sound hysterical to you, Margaret?"

"No, Charley."

"It surprises you, doesn't it? You always thought I was little soldier boy Charley Bronson, didn't you?"

"Did Helen know you felt this way about it?"

"I didn't know it myself until a while ago. I wrote her about it. We talked about it this summer. She thought I was dramatizing myself a little."

"Aren't you?"

"A little, I suppose."

The nurse came in and told me that visiting hours were over.

"Come back tomorrow, will you, Margaret?" Charley asked, when I got up to go.

"Of course I will, Charley. And thank you for telling me what you told me."

99

"I never told anybody else. Except . . ."

As I got to the door he called to me.

"You won't forget about coming tomorrow, will you? There's something I have to tell you."

"I'll be here, Charley."

"Good. Good night, Margaret, and thank you."

The next day he was sitting up in the easy chair in his room. He was wearing a robe and slippers and smoking a pipe.

"I've been rehearsing how to tell you what I have to tell you, Margaret."

"Why don't you just say it?"

"All right."

He paused and drew on his pipe. I didn't know what he was about to say, but it must have been something very important and very difficult because he was preparing himself to blurt it out.

"I killed her," he said.

"That's ridiculous, Charley."

"Is it?"

"Isn't it?"

"How do you know, Margaret? You haven't heard about it. How do you know it's ridiculous?"

"Charley, everybody who's been through a shock like you have feels that way. You were driving so, of course, you feel guilty about it. It was an accident."

"Was it?"

He looked at me.

"What makes you so sure it was an accident, Margaret?"

"I talked to the state trooper."

"What could he tell you? How fast we were going, where the car went off the road and what he thinks must have happened? Margaret, just sit and listen to me.

100

Don't interrupt me because I have to go through it from the beginning. All right?"

"All right, Charley."

"Before I start let me tell you something else. You don't know what it meant to me yesterday when you told me what your father said. I think you know how I feel about all of you. You were the only real family I ever had. I don't mean anything against my mother. She did everything she could, but there was no love in her after my father was killed. I wasn't really her son any more. I was a replacement for him. You and your father and mother and—Helen—were the only family I ever had. I loved all of you very much. Did you know that?"

"Yes, Charley. I think I must have known it."

"All right. Now let me start at the beginning. Dammit, I don't know how to start. The first thing I have to tell you is a shocking thing to say to you like this in a hospital room in broad daylight."

"Go ahead and say it, Charley."

"Helen was pregnant."

"Oh."

It was the only thing I could think of to say.

"Does that shock you terribly, Margaret?"

"No, I don't think it shocks me, Charley. Just give me a minute. It's quite a surprise. It takes a little getting used to."

"It happened at the beginning of the summer. For Christ's sake, Margaret. We loved each other. We'd loved each other since we were ten years old. I wanted to marry her when I got out of Fallview High. A cadet can't have a horse, a wife or a mustache. And I had to be a cadet, remember? I wanted to quit after my plebe year and marry her. She talked me out of it. She told me we had our whole lives together and that I had to graduate

101

from the Point. So . . . this summer it happened. Can you understand that it had to happen, Margaret? Because if you can't, there's no point in going on with this. . . ."

"I can understand it, Charley. Are you sure? You know girls sometimes . . ."

"We were sure. She went to see a doctor. Oh, not in Fallview. We drove over to Doverville one afternoon and saw a doctor there. We stopped at the five and dime and I bought her a wedding ring to wear in the doctor's office and I sat in the car outside. We were sure.

"You know something? I was delighted. Now she'd have to marry me. It was going to be rough on my mother, but she'd just have to get used to the idea. But Helen wouldn't marry me. Do you know she actually talked about an abortion? Can you imagine that dirty word on Helen's lips? I told her that was out of the question, that she had to marry me. I wanted to tell all of you immediately. I knew that if I did, you'd be on my side and make Helen marry me. This is a real switch on the old shotgun wedding story, isn't it?"

"What did she think you were going to do?"

"I don't know. At first, I think she felt that it wasn't really true, that if we just ignored it, it would go away. Then she talked about how people have miscarriages all the time. You remember how she was always out on water skis this summer? How she was always crewing with me on somebody's sailboat? Remember how much tennis she played. Apparently she thought that, if she exercised a lot, she might have a miscarriage. I couldn't do anything about it. She wouldn't even discuss our getting married or my not going back to the Point. Finally . . . the night of the country-club dance . . . we talked the whole thing out. She just refused to marry

102

me. I loved her so much, Margaret. Can you understand how my hands were tied?"

"Of course I can, Charley. Why didn't you come and talk to me?"

"How could I? We were a couple of kids to you. I suggested it once to Helen and she could never talk to you about it."

"What did she think she was going to do about it?"

"We came to a decision the night of the country-club dance. We sat in the car in the parking lot before we went into the club. She was going to tell your mother and father. She was going to go away and stay with your aunt in Topeka until the baby was born. She had it all figured out. She'd stay with them and after I got out of the Point and got my first assignment, I'd introduce her as a young widow with a small baby. Six months after that we'd get married."

"You agreed to that?"

"Not really. It accomplished one thing. She was going to tell your father and mother. I was sure they'd side with me. I was sure they'd talk sense into her and talk her into marrying me."

"Do you think they could have?"

"I don't know. It was the only chance I had. I couldn't go to them on my own against her wishes. She'd have gone away from me, if I did. I was sure of that. The whole thing was that goddamned United States Military Academy. My goddamned father, who didn't have the decency to dodge a bullet at Château-Thierry. Anyway . . . we went to the dance. We left early. We didn't have too much to drink. I swear to God, Margaret, I was not drunk."

"I know that."

"I don't think we were going more than thirty miles

103

an hour. It was a warm night, remember? We had the top down. Helen was sitting very close to me with her head on my shoulder. She told me that she had tried to lose the baby. 'What did you say?' I asked her. 'Not like that,' she said. 'I didn't do anything like that, but why do you think I was doing so much water-skiing and playing so much tennis? Sometimes exercise like that brings the baby on. It didn't work.' We drove in silence for a while and then she said something terrible. 'Wouldn't it be wonderful,' she said, 'if we had an accident? You know, Charley, just a little one—maybe a broken leg or something. That would take care of it, wouldn't it?' The next thing I knew she had grabbed the wheel and twisted it. I grabbed her wrists and wrestled with her. I tried to jam on the brakes. My foot slipped off the brake pedal and jammed down on the accelerator. The car leaped forward out of control and went over the embankment. I remember it turning over and I don't remember anything else."

"What did you tell the police?" I asked.

"I told them a dog suddenly shot in front of the car and I jammed on the brakes and my foot slipped off onto the accelerator and we went off the road and over the embankment."

"Thank you for telling me, Charley," I said.

"I had to tell it to somebody. I was going out of my mind, sitting here with it. I did kill her, Margaret. You see that now, don't you?"

"I don't see anything of the sort. If anything, she killed herself."

"I shouldn't have tried to take the wheel away from her. I should have let her have her small accident. At the speed we were going it wouldn't have been serious."

104

"Are you serious, Charley?"

"Of course I'm serious."

"Suppose you had. Suppose it all worked out. Suppose you had your small accident. Suppose Helen had a miscarriage? You don't really think that was any solution, do you?"

"Was there a solution?"

"I think you were on the way to it. Under whatever pretext, you had to get Helen to tell Mom and Dad. You're right, they'd have talked her into marrying you. I think she probably realized that. That's why she tried to arrange the accident."

"Maybe. Should I tell them?"

"Mom and Dad?"

"Yes."

"What will that accomplish?"

"Nothing."

"What are you going to do now, Charley?"

"Go back to the Point. What else can I do? If it hadn't been for that goddamned Point, Helen would still be alive, wouldn't she? It's like they say in the recruiting posters: 'They shall not have died in vain.' I'm sorry, Margaret, that sounds hard-boiled and callous, doesn't it? I don't mean it that way."

"I know you don't, Charley."

"I have another pressure on me now, don't I? My father's memory, my mother's sacrifice and Helen's death—all on the altar of the United States Military Academy. I have to go back now. I have to make First Captain, graduate at the top of my class and turn into a general, don't I? Why can't life leave a man alone and give him his own choice?"

"Now you do sound young."

"Yes. I guess I do. What am I going to do with the rest of my life, Margaret?"

"Live it."

"Without Helen? I adored her. Everything that was going to happen included her. I'm not being melodramatic now, Margaret. I mean it just this simply: how am I going to live wthout her?"

"Somehow, Charley, we all manage to live without the people we can't live without."

Charley got out of the hospital three days later and left the following Monday for West Point. He wrote a long letter to my mother and father and sent me a note that just said: "Thank you for listening and understanding. . . ." At the end of his second-classman year he went on maneuvers in Georgia. He sent me a penny postcard from there that said: "Everything fine. Beat Navy!"

The nursery school prospered. It got to be so successful that we hired two other girls to work with the children and I spent most of my time working on the books and mailing out brochures and promotion pieces. I kept Eddie Price dangling for a very selfish reason. I needed somebody to go out with and the supply was reasonably short. Eddie was ideal. As long as he felt we were "sort of engaged," he was no problem. Mother liked him very much. At this point, I think, Mother would have liked Mr. Hyde. Eddie was, in Mother's eyes, my last good hope of escaping old maidhood. My father took a jaundiced view of the whole situation.

"You're not really serious about Eddie Price, are you, Maggie?" he asked. Since Helen's death he'd started calling me Maggie again.

"Not really, Pop," I said.

106

"What does that mean? Are you or aren't you?"

"It means not really. It means there are very few dates around for a twenty-eight-year-old girl these days. It means Eddie pays for my movies and he's somebody to go out with."

"Are you considering marrying him?"

"Is that what you mean by serious, Pop?"

"That's what people usually mean by serious. Are you or aren't you?"

"I'm not considering marrying him, Pop, for ten consecutive seconds."

"Good. He's not for you, Maggie."

"Who is?"

"Somebody. Fallview isn't the world."

"Pop, are you suggesting I leave home?"

"Your mother would kill me if she knew it, but that's exactly what I am suggesting. You're too smart, too bright and too alive for Fallview. And, as you say, the supply of eligible young men is rather limited."

"I've thought of it. I may do it, Pop. I want to give the nursery school a whirl for a while and see if it really develops into something."

"I'm not belittling the nursery school, Maggie, but you have to have something more than that in your life. Besides there's a depression on. It hasn't really hit Fallview yet. But it will. And one of the first things to feel it will be your nursery school. When money gets tight and people get scared, the first things to lop off are the things they can really do without. A woman can always put up with a four-year-old for a couple of extra hours a day if she has to."

"Pop, you don't really think the depression is serious, do you?"

"It's damned serious. And it will get more serious."

107

Pop was right. The depression hit Fallview hard that winter of 1930. Three of the factories closed down completely, the others cut down their labor force drastically. Of course, Swede's Hill was hardest hit. I remember my mother headed up a private relief committee that supplied the unemployed families there with food baskets and wood for their stoves. Pop was right about the nursery school, too. We finally faced the inevitable and closed up for good just before Christmas. Eddie Price started pressuring me about marrying him. I no longer had any excuse for putting it off as far as he was concerned. He felt he'd been very patient, he told me— giving me a chance to have a fling at a career, but now it was time to settle down to the really important things, like marrying him and raising a tribe of young lawyers. I had half decided to follow my father's advice and move out of Fallview, but somehow I couldn't get up the energy, the ambition or the real desire to do anything about it. I should have broken the whole Eddie Price situation off, but I let that dangle and hang on, too.

I had one fast note from Charley Bronson at the beginning of his senior year at the Point. "I've lived up to my bargain," it said. "I've made First Captain." I knew enough about the Point, thanks to Helen, to know that being First Captain was the biggest of big deals. It was like being tapped for Bones at Yale or winning the sweepstakes or being football captain at Notre Dame.

I finally broke up with Eddie Price in the spring of 1932. He took it fine. Too damned fine for my pride. He acted like I was a court case he'd lost. It was too bad, but what the hell, it happens. So I started going to movies alone from then on. I just wasn't up to finding another beau and going through the hand-holding, pawing routine in return for a frosted and somebody to pay my way into the movies. I started playing a lot of bridge. I studied Culbertson and Lenz as if I was cramming for a college exam. My father kept trying to light a fire under me, but he didn't have much success.

"For God's sake, Maggie, bridge is just a game of cards, it's not a way of life."

He used to call it "The Old Maid's Sex." Not around Mother, of course. She was the best and busiest bridge player in Fallview. I think two dedicated bridge players in one family was more than father could stand. In April I got a letter from Charley, scrawled on West Point stationery.

He'd sprained his ankle playing football.

"I'm damned glad it happened," he wrote. "I only went out for the team because it's good army politics to have played a major sport at the Academy. Thanks to a bad tackle and a weak ankle that's behind me. I was a lousy football player, anyway."

His grades were very high and he was sure to be at least in the first ten in his graduating class. The last paragraph of his letter surprised me.

"I've thought of you a great deal, Margaret," he said. "And not only because you're Helen's sister. I suppose you know by now that I have very few friends. I have no really close friends here at the Academy, for instance, and outside the Academy you're the only one I can think of, offhand. Would you be my drag at June Week? I'd like it very much and I can promise you a good time because as the First Captain's OAO you'll be a very big wheel, indeed, on campus. If you refuse the invitation, you'll be responsible for breaking one of the oldest and most honored of the traditions at this most traditional of all penal institutions. I will be the first

109

First Captain who ever stagged it during June Week. Seriously, Margaret, please come. I miss seeing you very much. Give my love to your father and mother and write and say yes very soon . . . love, Charley."

Father drove me to Buffalo where I caught the afternoon train to New York. I took a train out of Grand Central and they flagged it down at Garrison, which is just across the river from West Point. We crossed on a small ferry. It was all very gay. The ferry was loaded with sweet, bright-eyed and, I assumed, bushy-tailed coeds, who were just thrilled that they'd been invited to June Week at the Point. I felt absolutely ancient and a little like the house mother at a sorority house.

Charley was right. It was fun. There were hops, dinners, movies, picnics, parades, reviews, and we swam and canoed at the lake, played golf and teamed up in doubles at tennis. Charley hadn't changed much physically. He was still almost too handsome, but I found him quieter, more mature, somehow, than his contemporaries and very obviously glad to see me. We spent every moment we could together. The only thing that disturbed me was Charley's attitude toward the army and West Point. The whole thing was still just an obligation he had to face up to and he was determined to do it as well as it could possibly be done. It was a little like talking to a priest and suddenly realizing that he really didn't believe and was in the Church because it offered a good, steady, responsible job with great opportunities for advancement.

By the night of the graduation hop in Cullum Hall, I was hopelessly in love with him. I realized it was ridiculous. I realized that I was seven years older than he was, that nobody was ever going to take Helen's place in his life and that I had no desire to spend my life as an army

110

wife. None of that mattered. I adored him. Up to then he'd really kissed me only once. After I arrived at the Point, Charley had taken me on a sight-seeing trip. He pointed out the various points of interest like a real-estate agent who knows in his heart that the subdivision is apt to be underwater during the spring thaws. The tour included, of course, Flirtation Walk. It was just after dusk and we stopped walking and Charley put his arm around me.

"Tradition," he said and took me in his arms and kissed me. It started as a light, amusing kind of kiss, but suddenly I was holding him very tight, digging my nails into his shoulder blades and feeling lightheaded and dizzy. It was a long, passionate kiss.

"There's a lot to be said for West Point tradition," I said.

"A lot."

That was all. We continued walking and the rest of June Week we behaved like brother and sister. We laughed a lot. That is, I laughed a lot. Once in a while he smiled. It was worth waiting for.

Mrs. Bronson arrived the day of graduation parade. She kept up a running commentary all the way through.

"This," she said, "is one of the great traditions at the Academy. The music for graduation parade is never used for any other parade or ceremony. . . . I remember it so well when I was here for Charley's father's graduation parade."

She cried when the battalions marched onto the plain and the band played something she called "Dashing White Sergeant." She cried when "Home Sweet Home," "The Girl I Left Behind Me" and "Auld Lang Syne" were played. She sobbed when the graduates marched on to "Army Blue." She really saved her tears

111

for the moment when the Corps passed in review while the band played "Alma Mater." I'm a sucker for tears. I cried right along with her.

When it was over, she embraced Charley and cried on his shoulder. "Your father would have been so proud of you," she said.

"Would he?" asked Charley. "Does that finally make me even, Mom?"

"What?"

"Nothing, Mom. Nothing."

Charley had been posted to Fort Ontario, New York. It was considered quite a plum assignment and carried with it a two-month furlough before reporting for duty.

We rode back to Fallview together, Charley, Mrs. Bronson and I. All I could think of was that Charley would be home for two months. We would have two whole months together.

The third night at the lake he proposed to me. I don't suppose it was a very romantic proposal, but I wasn't aware of its shortcomings at the time.

"I think you know, Margaret," he said, "that I've always loved you. I think we're genuinely fond of each other, like each other, understand each other and could be happy together. Will you marry me, Margaret?"

We told my family first. Mother cried. Father cried. I cried and finally even Charley cried. Mrs. Bronson was very pleased, too, but for a rather special reason.

"I'm very happy about this, Margaret dear," she said, "because, Lord knows, I know how important it is for a young officer to have a good, solid, level-headed wife. The fact that you're so much older than Charles is a very fortunate thing."

We wanted to get married right away, but the

family took over. The wedding was set for the middle of August. That meant that we would have time for a week's honeymoon before Charley had to report to his post.

It was a wonderful summer. I think all of Fallview breathed a sigh of relief. The pattern was now complete. Not only was Charley Bronson getting married after that terrible experience, but the older Davis girl was being saved from spinsterhood. It had a kind of neatness that Fallview admired. There were lots of parties for us that summer and I don't think Charley and I were ever apart except when we were sleeping. About a week before the wedding, I had a serious talk with him about our future. We were sitting on the porch of the house at the lake. Mother and Father had gone into town to see a movie and we were alone.

"Charley, can I say something that's been on my mind?"

"Sure."

"I keep remembering something you said at the Point to your mother. Remember what it was?"

"No."

"It was after the graduation parade. You said, 'Does this finally make me even, Mom?' Remember?"

"Yes, I remember. What is it you're saying, Margaret?"

"You are even, Charley. You did what you set out to do. You went back to the Point, you made First Captain and you graduated. You are even. I know how you feel about the army, and I just wanted you to know that it's all right with me if you want to chuck the whole thing and resign your commission."

"Why would I do that?"

"For all the reasons you've been talking about all

113

these years. You were pushed into it. You never liked it, but you went through with it. You lived up to what was expected of you. Feeling as you do about it, Charley, you're bound to be something of a misfit in the army. Your attitude is bound to come through. I don't want you to not quit, if you want to quit, because of me. Does that make sense?"

"The sentence or the suggestion?"

"Both."

"The sentence is a little confused, but I understand what you mean. I'd be out of my mind to quit now, Margaret. I went through all that hell and now I can start getting something back for it. Listen, the army is a snap. It is for me. They shoved me into it, O.K. I'm in and by the time I come out I'm going to have some stars on my shoulder. Honey, I guarantee you I'll be a general by 1950 . . . sooner if there's ever another war. Now let's forget all about it. I'm in the army and I'm gonna stay there. And you're wrong about my being a misfit. I'm the best damned fit the army ever saw."

"I didn't mean it that way, Charley. I meant that you weren't cut out for the army from the start and you were forced into it against your will and this is your chance to get out."

"Does it bother you, being an army wife?"

"No. To tell you the truth, Charley, I'm kind of excited about it."

"Fine. Now, let's talk about our honeymoon. Would it be terrible if we went to Niagara Falls?"

"It's traditional. Like Flirtation Walk."

"It's just that Fort Ontario is close by and we could work in a couple of extra days on our honeymoon that way."

Niagara Falls it was.

Eventually.

The wedding was a big splash by Fallview standards. Afterwards there was a reception on my parents' back lawn. Seven of Poppa's employees at the factory had a pick-up band that played Swedish and French-Canadian weddings and we hired them for the occasion. There was a large buffet table loaded down with hams and turkeys and all the trimmings and plenty of champagne. There were pictures of us cutting the cake, drinking champagne, toasting each other and standing with our arms around our parents. About nine o'clock I slipped upstairs to change my dress. We had reserved the bridal suite at the hotel for the night and planned to drive to Niagara Falls the next morning. When I came downstairs, my father was waiting for me.

"Maggie, I have something to tell you."

I went cold inside. It must have shown on my face.

"Relax, honey, it's not so terrible," said my father.

"What is it, Pop?"

"It's Charley. He had a little too much champagne. He passed out cold."

I started to laugh. I don't know whether it was relief that it wasn't anything more serious than that or whether I'd had a little too much champagne myself.

"That's the way to take it, honey. It happens to the best of grooms. As a matter of fact, I've had a little too much champagne myself."

"Where is he?"

"We put him up in your room. It may be that he'll sleep it off in a couple of hours and you can go on to the hotel like you planned."

"Thanks, Pop."

So I rejoined my wedding party. There were some very funny jokes about the bride being deserted on her

115

wedding night and some offers of substitutes for Charley. I went upstairs every twenty minutes or so, but there wasn't the slightest sign of life out of him. Finally at eleven o'clock I went upstairs, undressed in the dark and climbed into bed beside him. He grunted as I moved him over, but he didn't wake up.

I was awake most of the night. When I came down to breakfast the next morning, Poppa was grinning.

"There's nothing in the world like the face of a bride the morning after the wedding," he said.

"Shut up, Carl," said Mother.

"How is Charley?" she asked me.

"I think he's dead."

"That's a shame," said my mother. "And on your wedding night, too. Do you think he could have gotten some bad champagne? Carl, are you sure that champagne was all right?"

"Of course it was."

"Good morning."

We looked up. Charley was standing in the kitchen doorway wearing a bathrobe. He walked over and kissed me. "Good morning, darling," he said.

"How'd you sleep, Charley?" asked my father.

"Now, Carl, you stop that," said Mother.

"I just asked him how he slept."

"I'm very sorry," said Charley. "I owe you all an apology. I don't know what hit me. I just went out cold. Did I do anything outrageous? Was I loud drunk? Did I get into a fight with anyone?"

"You were just fine," said Mother. "You just celebrated a little too fast."

"And a little too soon," added Father.

"What a lousy thing for you, darling," he said putting his arm around me.

116

"Don't be silly, Charley. We're going to be married a long time."

"I certainly hope so."

We packed the car right after breakfast and left shortly after eleven for Niagara Falls. We had lunch on the road and got to the hotel in time for dinner. Charley was very sweet and thoughtful all day. I think he felt guilty about passing out on his wedding night and was trying to make up for it. At least it seemed that way.

There's at least one thing to be said for Niagara Falls for a honeymoon. Practically everybody else in the hotel was on a honeymoon, too, and we didn't feel self-conscious or embarrassed. By the time we finished dinner it was almost ten o'clock.

"How about a walk? We could see the falls," suggested Charley.

"Fine," I said. "It may be the only chance I'll have."

"What do you mean?"

"It's a honeymoon kind of joke, Charley."

"Oh."

The falls were wonderful. I suppose they still are. We stood and watched them awhile, holding hands.

"Margaret."

"Yes, Charley?"

"You're not . . . you know, embarrassed about tonight. I mean, you're not frightened or anything."

"No, Charley. I'm a big girl. Let's go back to the hotel now, darling."

We walked back slowly, walked through the lobby holding hands, held hands all the way up in the elevator and Charley carried me across the threshold of the room.

"That's ridiculous," I said. "We've already been up here to leave our bags when we checked in."

"That doesn't count. Besides it would have been a

pretty silly thing to do with a bellboy standing behind you."

He put me down in the middle of the room and kissed me. We had already unpacked our suitcases and laid out our nightclothes. I took my nightgown and my robe into the bathroom with me. I brushed my teeth, combed my hair, soaked in a hot tub and put perfume everywhere you're supposed to put perfume. When I came out of the bathroom, Charley was sitting on the edge of the bed reading a magazine. He looked up and smiled at me. That wonderful smile.

"All yours," I said, motioning toward the bathroom.

He went in and I heard the shower run.

I put the light out and climbed into the double bed. I was as nervous as a—well—as a bride. I could feel my heart pounding and I could hear my pulse pounding in my ears. The bathroom door opened and Charley came out and took off his robe in the dark. He turned back the covers and climbed into bed beside me. He turned and we were facing each other. He moved over and put his arms around me.

Right from the start there was nothing awkward or hesitant about it. We made love to each other as naturally as if we'd been married for twenty years. Charley was warm and gentle and yet there was a firmness about what he did and how he did it. We stopped momentarily while I put my hands over my head and took off my nightgown and he removed his pajamas. It was wonderful. It was warm and exciting and satisfying. Then he grabbed me by both arms and held me tight. I knew my fingers were digging into his shoulder, but there was nothing I could do about it. We were moaning and making noises and knowing it and enjoying knowing it.

"Oh, darling, darling," he said in a throaty whisper.

118

"Oh, darling . . . darling . . . Helen. Darling Helen . . . I love you, Helen."

I went rigid in his arms. He stopped and we stared into each other's eyes. . . .

"Oh, my God!" he said. "Oh, my God!"

I put my arms around him and held him close to me. He put his head on my breast and started to sob, deep in his throat. "Oh, my God!"

"It's all right, Charley," I said. "It's all right, darling."

He fell asleep in my arms. He woke up toward morning and made very careful, very controlled and very quiet love to me. We slept late and had breakfast sent up by room service.

Maybe I made my first and most important mistake right then.

I was terrified by what had happened. I was numbed by it. But I wouldn't face it. I acted as if it had never happened. Charley never mentioned it either. Ever. On our honeymoon or after. Never.

I thought the honeymoon would never end. Oh, we carried it off all right. We were gay and amusing. I told jokes and laughed and every night Charley made love to me. It was never like it had been that first time. He was always in control of the situation. He would finish, kiss me lightly on the cheek, go into the bathroom, come back, turn over and go to sleep. I'd be awake most of the night, just lying there, thinking, crying quietly to myself, wondering what I was going to do. He made love to me the way he went to West Point. It was something that was expected of him, so he did it.

We came back to Fallview, packed up our clothes and went to Fort Ontario to our first post. I tried, dam-

119

mit. I was the best army wife any second lieutenant ever had for the first year.

About three weeks after we got to Ontario, Charley got very drunk at a party on the post. After we got home, he made violent love to me. At the climax, again . . . he called me Helen and broke into tears and sobbed on my shoulder until morning. He stopped sleeping with me for a long time after that. He didn't even go through the motions. He stayed up working late, or he complained about a terrible headache, and I could almost see him breathe a sigh of relief when he discovered I was having my period. He was almost lighthearted for the whole week. He was relieved of finding an excuse to avoid making love to me for that short period of time. Goddammit, if I'd only had sense enough to talk to him about it. We never mentioned it. I started drinking after we'd been on the post about six months. I played bridge in the afternoons with other army wives and there was always liquor served. I started drinking heavily. And, of course, there were always parties on the post and plenty of liquor available. I drank for the same reason Charley drank right after we were married, as an excuse for avoiding the reality of the bedroom. It stopped his drinking. He didn't have to drink any more. It was horrible. One night after a party I came home with him, drunk, and tore off all my clothes in the bedroom.

"You're my husband, goddammit," I said. "Make love to me." I suppose you could say I raped him. We never mentioned that either. It only happened a couple of times. I was hurt, angry, rejected and miserable. I suppose Charley was having a rough time of it, too, but I didn't care about that. It just never occurred to me. The affairs were a natural outgrowth of that. The first one was with a bachelor officer who had just been transferred

120

to the post. It happened at a party. I got drunk very fast and on the way back from the bathroom I stopped to talk to him. We talked for about ten minutes and it was apparent what was on his mind. I was disgusted to find I was excited. He must have noticed that, too.

"Do you like new cars?" he asked.

"Love them."

"I just bought one last week. Would you like to see it? It's right outside."

"I'd love to see it."

I knew Charley wouldn't miss me. He usually found me asleep on a bed somewhere and never started looking for me until the party broke up.

I followed the lieutenant out to the car.

It started that simply and after that it happened every once in a while. Not often enough to become a public scandal, but often enough to have the word get around that Lieutenant Bronson's wife was a swinger if you played your cards right.

We never talked about that, either.

Maybe that was the whole trouble with our marriage. We never talked about anything after that night at Niagara Falls.

La Guardia ☆ 1953

Margaret sat for a minute without saying anything, staring at her hands. She lit a cigarette and took a long drag and let the smoke come slowly through her nostrils.

"You know something, Harry?"

"What?"

"That's the first time I ever told that story to anybody. It was strange, laying it out, piece by piece. Once I tried to tell it to my father, but I couldn't."

"Why not?"

"He didn't really want to hear it. It was about a year after we were married. Charley was out on a field problem and I went home to Fallview to visit my family. Pop asked me how things were working out. You know the way people ask you things like that—as a kind of ritual. The last thing in the world they want is an honest answer. I started to tell him about it. I had the feeling that, if I could just talk it out once—have somebody listen to it and tell me what to do, it might be solved. He didn't let me get far. He started turning a verbal prayer wheel. 'Marriage is a period of adjustment, Margaret,' he said. 'It's a period of compromise. You have to keep giving a little here, taking in a little of the stress there. And it's not just at the beginning that it's like that. It keeps on being like that and you never really adjust to it.' So I shut up."

"What made you tell me about it?"

"I don't know. Vanity maybe."

"Vanity?"

"Sure. Vanity. I know what you were thinking about me. For once I wanted to lay it out and say, 'Look—I didn't get this way all by myself.' For once I wanted the luxury of self-justification. Or maybe you're right, maybe I have had too much to drink and I was wallowing a little in self-pity."

"Did it ever occur to you to sit down with Charley and talk it out with him?"

"You bet it occurred to me. He wouldn't talk about it. Just as he wouldn't talk about my drinking or my tom-catting around. He wouldn't talk about it. I spoke to a doctor about it once. Not the way I just told it to you . . . a sort of abbreviated version with some of the more personal things left out. You know what he said?"

"No."

"He said the drinking and the playing around and the affairs were a result of the guilt I felt because I married my sister's lover."

"You buy that?"

"I buy some of it. I felt that way once in a while. If Helen was on Charley's mind, she was on mine, too. I think it worked the other way, too, Harry."

"What do you mean?"

"I mean Charley felt guilty about the accident. He used to have nightmares about it the first year we were married. I think being married to me made it worse. I was Helen's sister and I was a constant reminder to him of Helen. I think that's why he never said anything to

123

me about the drinking and the men. I think he felt that was a kind of penance for Helen's death."

"You really think that?"

"I really think that. I think both of us felt guilty about the marriage and I think both of us were working to make it a failure. You know it's funny, Harry, but I think I helped Charley's career more by being what I was than I could have possibly helped it by being a nice, clean-cut, decent, government-issue army wife."

"How do you figure that, Margaret?"

"The army is full of nice fresh young officers doing their jobs pretty well. But if that nice clean-cut young officer has a real bum of a wife and he goes on doing his job, he has to get all the sympathy. You have to start calling him 'Poor old Charley,' and you have to start giving him the benefit of the doubt. He has a built-in excuse if he louses something up. 'Why wouldn't he goof? How'd you like to be married to Margaret?' "

"You're justifying up a storm, aren't you, Margaret?"

"Why not? I've never done it before. You think I'm doing it to impress you? You think I really give a damn what you think of me? I'm doing it to remind myself. I may get carried away a little. I've never done it before."

"What happens now?"

"You mean between Charley and me? That depends on him. You know, Harry, every time something big or something important happens in his life I keep thinking he must have thought the whole thing out, he must be old enough now, or wise enough, or mature enough to have come to a decision about us. Or at least to have conceded that something is wrong. I keep waiting for him to sit down and talk to me about it. So far he's batting a thousand. He never says a word about it. He

124

refuses to face it or talk it out and we just drift into the same pattern. You know it might help if he got mad once and told me off or took a swing at me. Maybe I do it because I just want him to acknowledge my existence. Maybe I'm like a child who is bad because he knows his mother will notice him. A spanking is sometimes better than indifference, Harry."

"You think that would solve the other problem?"

"The love-making? Probably not. . . . I'd never be sure he wasn't thinking of Helen while he was making love to me. How could he ever make me forget that?"

"I don't know."

She started to laugh.

"What's funny?" I asked.

"I was just thinking of a joke. We were great ones for jokes, we army wives. You know the one about the couple in bed and the husband leans over and puts his arm around his wife and starts to make love to her?"

"Not so far, go ahead."

"He starts to caress her and she says, 'Not tonight, Herman, I'm too tired to think of somebody.' Pretty ironic little joke."

"Pretty ironic. . . . Don't you think Charley's a pretty good army officer?"

"He's a very good army officer. He made a bargain."

"A bargain?"

"Or I guess you could say a bargain was made for him the day his father was killed in World War One. Charley confirmed it when he accepted the appointment to West Point. And God knows, Charley's a man who lives up to a bargain. I'm probably the world's greatest authority on that."

"Of course, I know a side of him you don't know, Margaret. He's a hell of a combat soldier."

"Sure he is. You know, in order to be a good army officer—in combat, I mean—the army requires that a man be willing to die if necessary. It's that simple, isn't it? A good soldier is a man who, when the necessity arrives says, 'That's my job and, if it carries with it the risk of dying, that's just too damned bad . . . that's the way it is.' That's what it's all about, isn't it?"

"I suppose so. It's certainly one of the occupational hazards."

"It's what it boils down to. An army officer always has to face up to the necessity of dying. Charley qualified a hundred per cent on that score. He was not only willing to die as a soldier, he looked forward to it. I think he figured that was the only way he could really get even and square the account, pay off the debt his mother contracted for him when he was nine."

"You never saw him in combat. He was a hell of a soldier."

"Of course he was. Charley, I'm sure, was one of those 'I'd never ask my men to do anything I wouldn't do myself.' Wasn't he?"

"That's one way of looking at it."

"Another way of looking at it, Harry, is that any field-grade officer who does that is trying to prove something. You don't think you can really equate, on a battlefield, the value of a regimental commander and an infantry private. I know it sounds callous, but if you lose an infantry private, the replacement centers are full of nameless faceless GI's to replace him. If you lose a colonel, you lose twenty years of training and preparation. They're not the same at all and any man who willfully jeopardizes a colonel for some quixotic reason of his own is insane. Or proving something. Take that patrol you're so proud of. Was that a sensible thing for Charley to do?

126

It wasn't even useful. He just wasn't as well equipped to do the job as any man in that infantry squad. He was including himself and he doesn't have the right to do that."

"It still took a lot of guts."

"Guts my foot!"

"Don't be so damned smug, Margaret. Sometime in the next half hour a plane's going to land and Charley's going to get out of it and a hundred and seventy million people are going to cheer their heads off."

"Hooray. Hooray for Charley Bronson . . . Bronco Bronson! Remind me to tell you something about Charley's glorious football career."

"I was a kid, Margaret, when Lindbergh came back and I stood on a fire escape on Fifth Avenue and watched him ride up the avenue in an open car. I've grown a lot older since then and I've learned a lot of things about heroes since then. But I still remember how thrilled I was to look at Lindbergh and think: This is the man who did it. . . . It doesn't matter a damn why he did it or what he was really like or what he turned into. He did something brave and important, and we need that, all of us, as a race, every once in a while. That's what Charley represents. What he did in Korea was thrilling and exciting and important."

"You're really a boy scout, aren't you, Harry?"

"We're all boy scouts."

"You keep talking about guts. I don't think, in Charley's case, guts has anything to do with it. It takes guts if you have something to lose. If you're afraid. If you don't want to die. Charley never had anything to lose after that car went off the road at the lake. Charley was never afraid. Charley didn't care if he did die."

127

"You going to give me that mumbo-jumbo crap about a death wish?"

"Why not? The Japanese make a ceremony out of it. I remember once, after we were married a couple of years, Charley had a training company. He was instructing them in hand-grenade throwing. You know how they do that?"

"No."

"They spend a week showing them how a hand grenade is put together, how it works and then they have dry runs with dummy grenades, showing them how to extend the left arm to sight on, pulling the pin, throwing it in a kind of overhand loping movement and then taking cover before it explodes. Finally they march them out to the field to throw real ones. They take plenty of precautions. They have deep foxholes for the men to jump in after they throw a grenade. Anyway, one of the kids pulled the pin and the grenade dropped out of his hand. It takes about eight seconds for a grenade to go off after it's thrown. There was plenty of time. The kid jumped in the foxhole. Everybody else was in foxholes. At the very worst a couple of hunks of shrapnel would have gone whirring over the top of the holes. It might have even kicked a little dirt into the holes. But that's all. Nobody was in any danger. Charley jumped out of his hole and threw himself on top of the grenade. Do you know what happens to somebody who's lying on top of a grenade when it goes off?"

"I've seen it."

"The grenade was a dud. It never went off. Everybody talked about how brave Charley was to protect his men. Everybody lost sight of the fact that nothing would have happened if it had gone off with everybody in a foxhole. Charley was a big hero around the camp."

128

"And you think he was trying to kill himself?"

"It's not that simple, Harry. He moved instinctively. I don't think he realized it himself, but he just saw an opportunity and he took it. He said later that he was afraid the kid would get panicky and climb out of his hole. Maybe he would have. He didn't. I just say that, whether Charley recognized it or not, he was looking for an excuse to get himself killed. So far, he hasn't been able to do it."

The door opened and Buddy came in.

"Excuse me. The newsreel men wondered if they could have Mrs. Bronson for a couple of minutes. They want to take some stock shots of her, looking up in the sky for the plane, walking across the field—things like that. They won't have time later, after the plane lands, and they'd like to get them now."

"How about it, Margaret?" I asked.

"Sure. Why not?"

She left with Buddy. I called the army's PRO office and found out that they were in radio contact with the plane. They were estimating its arrival in twenty-five minutes.

Europe ☆ 1944-45

After that patrol, I lost track of Charley Bronson and his division for a while. The front started moving and I don't think you'd have been able to find any particular division on any given day. The war got mobile again and I'd had a cable from the home office telling me to get around more, cover more units and stop filing stories exclusively about the infantry.

Like a lot of other correspondents, from Ernie Pyle on down, I'd become an infantry buff. I never quite lost my awe of the honest to God guts of the GI's with the crossed rifles on their collars. I kept wondering if I could have taken it the way they did if the fickle finger of a draft board had landed me with a line company. Getting shot at was only one part of what it was like to be an infantryman. It meant living in the same clothes for a month at a time, not shaving or washing because you couldn't spare the water. It meant lice and living on a cold slice of canned cheese, a fruit bar and hard, tasteless crackers. It meant watching your buddies disappear and wondering when the law of averages was going to work against you. I put in a lot of line time, sweated out mortar barrages, shellings, flushed snipers off rooftops and even had trench foot and the GIs. But there was a big difference between us. I could only

130

approximate what it was like to be a combat soldier. I always had an out. I could always leave if things got too rough. The GI couldn't leave until they carried him out on a litter, stuck a dog tag between his teeth and buried him. Or, unless he survived and the war ended. No GI ever really believed the war would end. Even after a month of it, I found myself falling into the GI frame of mind when I got back to a city. I found myself drinking every drink like it was the last drink I was ever going to have, looking at every woman like she was the last woman I'd ever see. I began to notice sunrises and sunsets with a new perspective. If there isn't much life that's beautiful or attractive, a sunrise can be quite an experience. I did a piece on a GI who had been through the war with one of the top combat divisions. I just documented one day in his life. Not a particularly rough one, just an ordinary day. It went like this:

The day started an hour before dawn when his company got in position for an attack. The objective was a line of trees over a small rise. It was slightly more than five hundred yards away. At dawn they jumped off in the attack. They got three hundred yards when the Germans pinned them down with rifle and automatic fire. They hit the ground. As the bullets flew around, they tried to force the ground to give and afford them some cover. A small clump of dirt was like a Christmas present. They remained pinned down for a couple of hours, and being pinned down meant that you couldn't move your head up or aim your rifle or fire back.

You were immobilized. Your weapons platoon in the rear opened up with the heavies and their mortars to keep the Germans from just walking over you and bayoneting you where you lay. You depended on the company on your left or right that wasn't pinned down to

131

divert the Germans, put pressure on them and give you a chance to get up and move forward a couple of hundred yards toward your objective. That went on all day. Every once in a while you'd hear the cry that you dreaded, "Medic," and another of your buddies had caught one. By nightfall, on a good day, you'd have reached your objective, you'd have captured five hundred yards of real estate. You'd have been five hundred yards closer to the end of the war. You weren't through when you captured your objective. A squad would have to go out and secure the ground ahead of you to set up a defense perimeter. While they were doing that, you started digging in. Digging in meant digging a hole in the hard, rocky, frozen ground with a folding shovel you carried on your belt. It meant doing with a makeshift tool, a job that would have proved difficult for a pneumatic drill. But you dug because every inch farther below the ground you got was that much more protection for you when the inevitable counterattack and artillery barrage came.

By eleven o'clock at night, the company would have secured the position, been dug in and ready to get some sleep. The water would have been brought up in five-gallon jerricans and the cold, tasteless rations eaten. But you pulled guard duty. There were two men in a foxhole and you slept two hours while your buddy watched, and then he watched for two hours while you slept. At four in the morning you were roused out, saddled up and got ready to jump off again and go through the same thing all over again. Only it was a little tougher this time because you had to fight through woods where you had very little visibility and had the added problem of snipers in trees above you. That's what it meant being a combat soldier. That was a normal,

132

ordinary day and, if you survived, it became the pattern of your life. It became after a while the only life you remembered. The GI I wrote the story about had gone through 511 of those days.

I don't know about the rest of the correspondents but the GIs treated me fine. All of them I think were hoping I'd do a story about them. It wasn't pride that made them want the story. I think it represented to them a proof of their existence to the people back home. It's funny, but none of them resented me. They'd long since gotten over the initial human reaction of feeling sorry for themselves because, out of an army of ten million, they, personally had been chosen for the dirty work of killing and being killed. That was the way it was. Most of them had a kind of grudging respect for the correspondent. They had to be there. We didn't. Every time I left an infantry outfit they were almost glad to see me go.

"About time," one sergeant told me. "If it was me and I coulda, I'da hauled ass outa here long ago. What're you, a hero or something?"

I think they were glad I hadn't been killed. If I'd been killed, I couldn't have written that story about them. In a way, I suppose, I was their only hope of immortality.

After a while I found myself insulating my feelings. I stopped looking at the pictures of their fat wives in Cleveland—or their three kids in front of the family car—or the picture of the self-conscious teen-age girl, wearing the short bathing suit, staring into the camera and smiling. I refused to give them an identity in my own mind. I refused to get involved emotionally with them because these were doomed men. These were the expendables of war. All of them were going to die and

133

if they were just nameless, faceless, pictureless statistics in a morning report, I could survive their deaths. If I knew them, listened to them talk of home and family, girl friends, wives and kids, I found part of myself dying with each death. And so I stopped making friends with the GI's—to save my sanity—so that their inevitable deaths wouldn't touch me or move me.

And yet they had an irresistible pull. I found myself drawn back to an individual company or an individual battalion, regiment or division, noticing who was missing and not mentioning it because the men, too, had written that death off in their own minds.

Anyway, all through the break-through in the Siegfried Line and the rout in the Rhineland, I kept thinking of Charley Bronson and his regiment. I wondered if Father Barry was still censoring mail in a foxhole, if the company commander was still alive and who Charley was playing chess with these nights.

I was on my way back to army press headquarters after spending two weeks with an ack-ack outfit when I saw the division insignia outside one of those towns with Baden on the end of its name. I hitched a ride into town and discovered that the whole place had been turned over to the division as a rest camp. That meant they were off the lines. It meant Red Cross girls, doughnuts, hot food, daily showers, clean clothes, nightly movies and cognac. It meant a chance to write letters home and a chance to sleep in a bed again and a two-week respite from shooting and being shot at. I found the division press headquarters and looked up Bill Ames. I figured he could tell me where Bronson's regiment was put up. He looked about the same. He was still the best-groomed officer in the ETO. He was also still a captain. He greeted me like a long-lost brother.

134

"Harry. Great to see you."

"Good to see you, Bill."

"I never thanked you for that story you did about me. Did you know CBS picked it up and reprinted it in their house organ?"

"No."

"A fact. I'm very big on Madison Avenue these days. I like to feel I'm out here making the world safe for Arthur Godfrey and Margaret Arlen."

"That's the best war aim I've heard all week."

"Sure. It'll be in all the history books. Been back to Paris lately?"

"Nope."

"I'm trying to promote a trip for myself. Old Corn Cob has the feeling the war is coming to an end and he's beginning to worry about his place in history."

"What does that mean?"

"It means you're looking at a man who has been assigned to write the official history of this here now famous division. It means you're looking at Corn Cob Corridon's official biographer. He figures when this war is over every general in the ETO will be breaking into print with his story, and he wants to beat them all to the punch. So I have been assigned to get to work on that future Book-of-the-Month-Club selection."

"What's that got to do with Paris?"

"I was hoping you'd ask that. Old Corn Cob was all for letting some Kraut publisher put the book out. I told him that a man of his importance in the history of our times shouldn't settle for second best. I told him that——"

"The only place in the world with publishing facilities worthy of his book was Paris," I finished for him.

"I'm glad you agree with me, Harry. Listen, you

135

can do something for me while you're here. Would you go and interview him?"

"For what?"

"For me. For my trip to Paris."

"I thought he ate correspondents for breakfast?"

"He used to. He has a slightly different attitude now that he's about to be the subject of the year's most important biography."

"O.K."

"You're a sweetheart, Harry. I always said that."

"I know. It'll be in all the schoolbooks."

"You got any ideas what's coming up, Harry?"

"What do you mean, coming up?"

"I mean, the last time we had a division rest camp we made an invasion. What have they got up their lousy little olive drab sleeves for us now?"

"You promise you won't tell anyone, Bill?"

"Sure, Harry. Honest to God, you know something?"

"Look, Bill. I'm the confidant of generals; they don't make a move without clearing it with me from a public-relations angle."

"Come on, come off it. Do you know anything?"

"You promise you can keep it to yourself? You won't get loaded and blurt it out?"

"Loose lips sink ships, Harry. I know that. Come on—give."

"I understand there's a move afoot, originating at SHAEF . . ."

"Yeah?"

I lowered my voice to a whisper:

". . . a move afoot to—put Paris off limits to division press officers who haven't made major."

"I asked for that, didn't I?"

"Sure," I said. "Seriously, Bill, I don't know a

damned thing. I've been traveling with the lower ranks lately. I suppose sooner or later somebody is going to have to cross the Rhine."

"Did you get a look at the local talent?"

"No, I must admit I didn't."

"Nothing! Clean but nothing!"

"I'm sorry, Bill. It'll be different in Paris."

"Listen, I do all right."

"I thought you said it was nothing."

"It is but what the hell, it's better than nothing."

"I'll tell you what I really came to see you about. Where is Charley Bronson's regiment holed up?"

"Didn't you hear about him?"

"Hear what? Is he dead?"

"You were a pretty good friend of his, weren't you, Harry? He talked about you a lot. He said you were one of the best chess players he ever met."

"Come on for Chrissakes. What happened to him? Is he dead?"

"No. He isn't dead. He went off his rocker."

"What do you mean?"

"I mean he went psycho. They evacuated him to a general hospital."

"What happened?"

"They were making up a task force under the command of the French and they took one of his battalions on detached service. He requested permission to go along on the mission. I don't know how he did it, but he talked Corn Cob into letting him go. You know how the war's been going lately. The Krauts stand and fight for every inch of ground and then you wake up the next morning and they've hauled ass out of the country. You move for five days without any contact and bang—there they are again—fighting like hell."

"Yeah, I know, Bill. They hold you long enough to build a line behind them and pull back to it. What happened to Charley?"

"All I know is they formed this task force—a mobile unit to chase the Krauts . . . fast as hell . . . mounted infantry on tanks, half tracks and weapons carriers. . . . They take off, find the Krauts, engage them and start a fight for the rest of the unit to push through. It keeps the pressure on that way. They did fine. He got a silver star out of one action. He was a demon. He was the commanding officer, but from what I hear he was acting like a platoon sergeant."

"What happened to him, Bill?"

"I don't know all the details, Harry. He got trapped in one of those big goddamned villas with two of his companies. The Krauts sucked them into an attack, cut off their retreat with tanks . . . pulverized them with eighty-eights and mortars and then moved in and mopped up on them. The two companies had ninety eight per cent casualties. Charley got a couple of flesh wounds from shrapnel, but he was alive. The rest of the task force pushed into the town and drove the Krauts off. Like I said, there wasn't much left of the two companies, but they found Charley alive."

"But what?"

"He'd had it. He didn't recognize anybody. He kept staring straight ahead, mumbling to himself. They took him back to regimental aid, but they sent him back here to division. Doc Watson, the Division Psychiatrist, had him shipped back to a general hospital. He may even be on his way back to the States right now. He'd really had it. They were cut off for three days and the Krauts really pounded hell out of the place."

"How'd he get sucked into the trap?"

138

"Who knows? I do know this. They say he coulda got out. As a matter of fact, the commander of the task force ordered him to pull back. He acknowledged the order, but said he was having trouble hearing and then the phone went dead. They found the wires pulled out of the field-phone set. It coulda been done by a shell, but they say it looked like he'd yanked it out himself so he wouldn't have to pull out of there. He had guts. You oughta know that. You went on that patrol with him, didn't you?"

"Yeah."

"I read the piece. Great story. Corn Cob reamed him out good when he saw the clipping. That didn't stop Charley. He kept going on patrols. For a while he used to go out ahead of the division front when his regiment was on the point of the attack . . . out there with the first goddamned scout, drawing fire from the Krauts. He had guts all right. He was the kind of a guy winds up a general or dead."

"Or psycho."

"Yeah. Listen, why don't you go over and talk to Doc Watson. He can fill you in on what actually happened after they found him."

"You have no idea where he is now?"

"None. You could find out from Doc which general hospital they sent him to and check him from there. I saw him when they sent him outa here. It's my guess he's been Z-I'd by now and is back in the States."

"I think I will look in on Doc Watson."

Doc Watson looked like nobody's idea of a psychiatrist. He looked as a matter of fact a little like Guy Kibbee and just about as warlike. He was one of those men who just resist looking like a soldier. You could

139

have put him in a suit of armor and he'd still look like the corner druggist dressed up for a masquerade ball on Halloween. I introduced myself, told him I was a friend of Charley Bronson's and hoped he'd tell me what he knew about him.

"Your friend, Lieutenant Colonel Charles Bronson is a damned fool and a dangerous one."

"That's a nice, unemotional scientific judgment, Doctor."

"It wasn't meant to be either unemotional or scientific. I'm talking as an individual now. I think your friend Bronson is high on the list of the most dangerous men I've ever known."

"Would you like to run down your list of reasons, Doc?"

"I'd be glad to. First, I'd like to know whether I'm talking to a newspaperman or a friend of Charley Bronson's."

"I couldn't write about this if I wanted to. It would never clear the censor. You know that."

"I just wanted to make sure you did. O.K. First of all, Bronson had no right being in command of that battalion. He's a regimental commander and when a battalion is detached from a division to join a task force it is still commanded by its normal battalion commander."

"Isn't that something between Corridon and Bronson? Corridon had to approve Bronson's suggestion."

"You don't think Corn Cob is sane, do you?"

"Let's stick to Charley."

"All right, Williams. You know something of Charley's record around this division, I assume? His eager-beaver tendencies, his fondness for getting shot at, his eagerness to issue an order and turn around and

140

act like the Pfc that has to carry it out. Did you know, by the way, what his nickname is?"

"No."

"Rover Boy. You'd think he'd have the respect of his men, wouldn't you? Command officers willing to get up close enough to make a target are reasonably rare. You'd think they'd respect his guts, wouldn't you?"

"I would think so, yes."

"Well, you'd be dead wrong. He frightens them. If he sticks his neck out, that's his own business, but most of the time he's sticking their necks out, too. He's taking unnecessary risks, refusing to face facts and withdraw when it's prudent to do so. He's putting them in a position where he's cutting down on even the low odds they have left with the law of averages. They hate his guts. Take a look at the regiment casualty record sometime. It will amaze you, Mr. Williams. The other regiments in this division aren't exactly goofing off, you know. His casualties are almost twice as high as theirs. The fact that he exposes himself to the danger too doesn't excuse it."

"You don't give him credit for being a good officer?"

"You're damned right, I don't. He's maybe the worst officer in the United States Army. If the value of an officer is taking calculated risks, avoiding unnecessary sacrifices and using a little God-given prudence and caution, he's way down at the bottom of the list. Let me make myself clear, Williams. What's your first name?"

"Harry."

"Let me make myself clear, Harry. I'm not a warrior. I practice a profession that most of my fellow countrymen view with suspicion, alarm and derision. I'm the division psychiatrist. When a man is in shock or is crying or is terrified and the battalion aid station

141

and the regimental station need the space to fix up somebody with a shattered leg or a shrapnel wound— they send the patient back to me because he has 'battle fatigue.' " I'm supposed to somehow make them well and send them back to fight again. In most cases it is a simple matter of exhaustion—physical and emotional, a case of living with fear twenty-four hours a day, not enough sleep, not enough to eat."

"And what do you do, Doc?"

"You know what I do? I talk to them as though they're human beings. That hasn't happened to them for a long time. I get them clean clothes. I send them over to the division chow lines to get a hot meal. I send them over to take a shower. I send them to see a movie. I give them something to make them sleep and three days later I send them back to the lines. See what a medical wizard I am?"

"Is it always that simple?"

"Of course it isn't. I'm telling you what the run-of-the-mill job is like. It bears as much resemblance to psychiatry as war does to a football field. Once in a while there is a true case of shock. A man who has seen his best friend blown to pieces next to him—a boy who cracks under the terrible strain of living, feeling and acting like a brute. Charley Bronson doesn't fit into any of those categories. The army in wartime is full of misfits. Nobody can predict how any given man is going to react under the stimulus of the kind of life he's forced to lead in combat. You know what the induction center psychiatrist asks the draftees? 'Do you like girls?' If he answers no, he likes boys, he's considered a poor risk. If he likes girls, he's going to be fine and brave and upstanding and make the world safe for democracy. To get back to Bronson. You know his background in combat.

He's a damn fool, but even a damn fool wouldn't have walked two companies into the kind of trap he walked them into. The Krauts sucked him in. Suppose he didn't know it at first. He should have tumbled to it and gotten out after it happened. There was one escape route opened. He ignored it. He was ordered by his commanding officer to pull out. You know what his reaction was? He said he never received the order—the connection was bad. And to prevent getting another order that might compromise his image of himself as the brave crusader, he yanked the field phone out by the roots."

"The phone might have been hit by shrapnel. Isn't that possible?"

"Sure, it's possible. Do you believe it was?"

"I don't know."

"*I* do. He yanked it out by hand. He told me so."

"Why? He's enough of a soldier to accept an order whether he agrees with it or not."

"*Is* he? And what do you think he accomplished after he was cut off. He couldn't make an aggressive move. He took two companies in with him as targets. About all he succeeded in doing—except, of course, killing off most of his men—was to give the Krauts target practice and use up their ammunition. They also had to pull a battalion off the flank to attack a target they should have by-passed.

"This must sound like strange talk coming from a psychiatrist, Harry, but there are enough hazards against staying alive in combat without adding an officer who plays with your life like it's Confederate money. It doesn't excuse it that he treats his own life the same way. Not by a good goddamn, it doesn't."

"Give me the details, will you, Doc?"

"Sure. I told you, they pulled a battalion off the

flank to rescue him. They found him in the cellar surrounded by dead men and debris. He'd gone into shock. They evacuated him. He passed through the battalion and the regimental aid stations and wound up here with me. When he came out of it, he kept repeating, 'Why wasn't I killed, too?''

"That's normal, isn't it, Doc?"

"Sure. It's normal. He felt guilty about the men who had been killed. I've seen it before in commanders who have sustained heavy losses. They feel the only thing that would have expiated the guilt was to be killed along with their men. Commanders who go through that kind of thing are usually worthless as leaders. They get buckshy about making decisions or issuing orders because the orders they have issued have led to large casualties."

"Where is he now?"

"I haven't the faintest idea. I can tell you one thing though. He isn't commanding any combat soldiers. I made sure of that."

"How?"

"I wrote a long report of my feelings and my medical opinion of Charley Bronson and sent it to the head of the general hospital. I doubt that they would send him back to combat in the face of that report."

"I want to find him."

"Why?"

"I like him."

"I'll tell you something, Harry. I do, too. I hate everything he's done and can do if he ever gets back in command, but in spite of all that, I like him very much, the poor, miserable bastard."

"Why do you say that?"

"Do you know anything about his personal life?"

"Nothing, except that he's married."

"Gets along with his wife?"

"I suppose so. I don't know."

"He kept calling her name over and over again when they brought him in here. The injection we give these cases is designed to get them talking—to get things out of their systems. He kept saying, 'You see, Helen. I did it. I did it, Helen.'"

"I think his wife's name is Margaret."

"Maybe he's got a girl friend. Maybe like a lot of his fellow crusaders his hatred of the Germans doesn't include shacking up with their women. Helen was the name all right. I'm sure of that."

"What will happen to him? He's a career officer."

"He'll sit the rest of the war out in Texas or North Carolina or maybe even the Pentagon. He'll be all right. If he has the West Point ring, they'll take care of him. He belongs to the most exclusive and most protective club in the world. He'll be fine. I'd just hate to have him commanding my son in combat, or anyone else's son, for that matter."

"That's a pretty harsh judgment, Doc."

"What's harsh about it? You and I are lucky."

"How?"

"By the pure accident of the timing of our birth. This is evidently a world that has to have a war every generation. It just happens that when our war came along we were far enough along in our lives to be lucky. You had the background, experience and skill that permitted you to at least work at your trade during the war. As a matter of fact, looking at it from a purely selfish mercenary point of view, you'll have gained a lot from it. You'll come out of the war a better, more experienced writer. It's a kind of laboratory for you—a chance to see major emotions close up. Suppose, Harry, the war came

145

when you were fresh out of high school or college. You'd have been drafted right into the infantry and you might have ended up being commanded by somebody like your friend Bronson. You'd have been as expendable as a tent peg with the life expectancy of a lit match. Knowing what you know about Charley Bronson, how would you like to be an infantry private under his command?"

"How about you, Doc? What are you learning from the whole thing?"

"My contribution to the war effort is to give up God knows how many of my most productive years as a psychiatrist. Your friend Bronson intrigues me, professionally. I wish I had the time to really treat him. What's the root of this sickness he has? Where did it start? You know the system stinks, don't you?"

"What system?"

"They start with a bright kid. He has to be bright or he wouldn't get the appointment to the Point. They give him a pretty good, pretty sound education . . . pretty sound if you measure it by knowledge and not by the intangibles that are the special kick of the Ivy League schools. They fill him full of mumbo jumbo, tradition, the feeling of being unique, important and special. They graduate him, turn him into a second lieutenant in the United States Army and in wartime they turn over to his care the cream of our youth. It is automatically assumed that he is capable of making decisions that affect the life or death of the men under his command. They suddenly put him in a position that allows him to play God and decide who shall live and who shall die. I know, you're going to tell me that it's one of the penalties of war. Sure. But we can have some safeguards built in. We can protect ourselves from the arrogance, the ambition and the unbalanced glory-seeking of the

146

men we put in control of the destiny of our sons. Every army officer ought to have to go through an examination every two years to find out when he's crossed the line between being a leader of men and a paranoiac."

"And who's to decide?"

"People like me, for one. People who are trained to diagnose the illness before it kills a whole company or a whole battalion. The enemy, Harry, isn't always in front of you in another uniform."

"You sound to me, Doc, like a man with his own little store of arrogance, ambition and godlike tendencies."

"Sure. That's where the whole fallacy comes in. Suppose you figure, for the moment, that the infantry is like firewood. You throw so many logs into a fire. The logs are consumed, but they keep you warm, heat your food, and keep you alive. And if in the process, they're consumed, that's too bad, and after all the woods are full of trees to make logs to replace the ones that are burned up. Isn't the infantry—and to a lesser degree the other combat units—in that position? We trade so many bodies for so much real estate and sooner or later, if the supply of bodies doesn't give out, we buy enough real estate to win a war."

"Funny, Doc. I haven't seen that particular analysis on any of the recruiting posters."

"And what does it take to make a log? Damned little. The amount of skill involved in firing a gun, living like an animal and dying can be taught in a ten-week basic-training camp. And have you ever been through a basic-training camp? The routine is so backbreaking, the humiliation of the individual is so complete that going off to war and fighting an enemy is the lesser of two evils."

"You're a pretty subversive old man, Doc."

147

"Let me finish the Watson Theory. Suppose, somehow you find a way of putting in the infantry only the ones you can spare—the inferior products of our civilization—the waste products we can spare—the expendables of peacetime? But we can't do that, can we? Who is to say which is inferior, which is expendable? So we practice the ultimate in democracy—the democracy of death. We throw them all in the fishbowl and say, 'You're it.' You see how lucky we are, Harry? You'll come out of the war a better writer. If you have any compassion in you, you'll come out of it understanding yourself, your world and the poor goddamned expendables better. Either that or you'll be shocked into a permanent silence."

"And what about you, Doc?"

"Me? So a few heads that should have been shrunk won't have been shrunk for a couple of years. It may even cause me to doubt the certainty of my godlike pronouncements a little."

Doc Watson broke out the bottle of cognac and we sat drinking and talking for about an hour. I found out which general hospital Bronson had been sent to. I knew it very well. It was on the outskirts of Paris.

I stayed around the division long enough to interview Corn Cob Corridon, as a favor for Bill Ames. I disliked him on sight. I don't think he was aware enough of my existence to like or dislike me. I was an instrument to him and he made only the minimum attempt to be ingratiating and pleasant. I filed a rather nondescript story on him, certain that my editor would recognize it for what it was, a bread-and-butter piece.

I'd been away from Paris almost three months, but it hadn't changed much. I spent a week catching up on black-market steaks, French girls, the gossip around the Scribe and my sleep and then went out to the general hospital outside Paris. I was shown into the office of the chief psychiatrist, Colonel Richard Armstrong. I told him I was interested in finding Charley Bronson.

"That's easy," he said. "He's about thirty miles south of here. He's commanding officer of a replacement depot."

"Good God," I said.

"I know," said the colonel. "But it was that or back to the States. The division psychiatrist who sent him here made some rather strong recommendations. I didn't quite agree with all of them, but in the face of it, once we discharged him from the hospital, we could not send him back to a combat command. He had to appear before a fitness board for an examination and they gave him the choice—back to the States or take over the command of the repple depple."

"And he took that?"

"Reluctantly he took it. He was very firm about going back to the States. We could never find out from him why he was opposed to going home. Most of the officers we get through here would give their right arms to be Z-I'd, but not Colonel Bronson. He would only say that he had personal reasons for not wanting to go back to the States. I assume it had something to do with his wife."

"Why would you assume that, Colonel?"

"Just a guess based on past experience. Maybe you know more about that than I do. Has he had any family trouble?"

"Not that I know of. Of course, Bronson and I aren't old—or, I suppose, even close—friends. I covered his regiment for a while, we talked a lot, played some chess and got to be good casual friends. How is he?"

"He's fine now. He made colonel."

149

"He did? When did that happen?"

"A couple of weeks ago. He's evidently doing a pretty good job at the repple depple. I had a note from him last week. I've been meaning to run down there and see him."

"A purely professional call?"

"Half and half. I'm curious about him and I liked him a lot."

"Most people do."

"When he got here he was going through a profound depression. He saw a copy of Watson's report and he was certain that it would spell the end of his army career. He knew, at the very least, he'd be shipped back to the States. Somehow, to him that represented the end of the world."

"How did you treat him?"

"I gave him a prescription that I have a great deal of confidence in."

"Which is . . . ?"

"I told him to go into Paris and get loaded and laid. I told him to forget about the war for a while. I told him to go to the opera, take a walk in the Bois, hire a carriage and go out to Versailles, take a boat up the Seine, go through the Louvre. He didn't want to do any of those things. He moped around the hospital. He found a patient who'd play chess with him. Finally, one night I insisted he go into Paris with me. Do you have the time, Mr. Williams? It's a rather amusing story."

"Sure. I have all the time in the world. I have between now and unconditional surrender to kill."

"I kept telling him what a wonderful opportunity he was missing—the opportunity to get to know Paris. That didn't interest him at all, but, as I say, one night I finally talked him into going into Paris with me. I know

Paris rather well, Mr. Williams. I'd been here studying before the war and since I've been attached to this hospital, I've gotten to know the city better than I know my own home town."

"Which is . . . ?"

"Philadelphia. Anyway, we went into Paris. We had a wonderful evening. I took him to a restaurant I knew from the peacetime years. They remembered me very well and we were served a magnificent meal. After dinner we strolled around and finally sat at a sidewalk café on the Grand Boulevard. We sat drinking a watery cognac, watching the parade of the whores. I'm not sure you could get it through the censors, but it would make a wonderful story for you. Do you know about the parade of the whores?"

"I guess not the way you say it with capital letters."

"There's one section of the Grand Boulevard, down near the Rue Blondel where the parade takes place every night."

"I know the Rue Blondel——"

"The spiritual home of every whore, pimp and black marketeer in Paris. Anyway, every night from eight until eleven the whores parade down that two-block stretch of the Grand Boulevard. The audience are the GI's who are looking for a woman to shack up with for the night. They sit at the tables at the sidewalk café and look over the crop. It's very much like an old slave market. If a GI sees something he likes, he crooks his finger; the girl comes over to the table, has a drink with him, talks price; they negotiate and disappear into one of the tenth-rate hotels in the side streets. It's always fascinated me. As you know, there's an eleven-o'clock curfew for military personnel in Paris, so around ten thirty the whole business gets rather frantic. The GI who

151

has held off making his purchase until late because he knows the price will come down is beginning to wonder how wise he's been. The poor whore, facing a profitless night is equally frantic and much bolder. The pimps, going from table to table, make wilder and wilder claims for the women who support them. I should think it would make a rather poignant story for you."

"Yeah. You bet, Colonel."

"Wouldn't it?"

"You don't think any clean-cut American boy has anything to do with prostitutes, do you? He's too busy thinking about Mom's apple pie and the girl next door to have any carnal instincts that aren't satisfied by a soggy doughnut and a jukebox in a Red Cross canteen."

"Anyway. Bronson and I sat at the sidewalk café, drinking that bad cognac, watching the parade. Suddenly he pointed to a girl walking past. 'Is she a whore?' he asked. I nodded. 'She can't be,' he said. 'Why not?' I asked him. 'She looks like somebody I used to know. She can't be a whore.' 'No?' I asked. And I crooked my finger and she came over and sat with us. Have you ever taken a good look at the whores of Paris, Mr. Williams?"

"Not a really good look, Colonel."

"They're fantastic. They're all playing a part. One is made up to look like a countess, another looks like a tweedy horsewoman. Each of them has a type she plays. This particular one looked like an American college girl. She wore a skirt and blouse and the dirty white kind of saddle shoes that would look at home on any college campus in the United States. Bronson was fascinated by her. She spoke English with a rather charming accent and every once in a while she'd throw in a word or two of American slang. Bronson asked her how much she got for spending the night with a soldier. She told

152

him twenty dollars plus the rent for the hotel room. He asked her where she was from, how old she was, how she got into the business of being for hire. That was the way he phrased it—'got into the business of being for hire.' He couldn't quite bring himself to use the word 'whore' with her. Then he asked her what her name was. 'Helene,' she said. He grabbed her by the wrist . . . 'You're lying,' he said. 'You're lying. . . .' He was hurting her and when he realized it, he let go and apologized."

"Was that the end of it?"

"No. That was the beginning of it. He told me I was right, that he should take this opportunity of getting to know Paris. Then he asked the whore if she'd be his guide. He wanted her to show him Paris—all of it, not just the tourist's Paris but—even if he wouldn't use the word—a whore's Paris. He gave her twenty dollars and told her to meet him at the café at ten o'clock the next morning. He told her he would pay her twenty dollars a day if she would show him Paris. For the twenty dollars she was to be with him every day, from ten in the morning until curfew at night. He made it plain to her that he had no intention of sleeping with her and part of the bargain was that after she left him at curfew she was to go home and not sleep with any soldier. There was no danger of that if he was with her from the morning until curfew. She smiled at him and agreed to the bargain. 'O.K.,' she said. 'O.K.' "

"Did he do it?"

"He did it. For two weeks. They covered every inch of Paris. As I said, I've lived in Paris before the war. I know it intimately, but Bronson knew it better. At the end of the two weeks, he went before the Fitness Board, convinced them that it was unnecessary to send him back to the States and was given his new assignment. I helped there. I thought he was in good shape. I wasn't sure he was fit for a combat command, but he was so very anxious to remain in Europe that I recommended he be given a noncombat command here. Before he left he told me about the two weeks with the whore. At first she didn't quite believe that he meant what he said. Then, when she did believe it, she resented it. Somehow it was an insult to her as a woman. So she started trying to make Charley. It became very important to her that he want to make love to her. She had, like most whores a great contempt for sex, but this was something else again. By not being interested at all, he was paying her the most horrible of insults. She knew he wasn't a fairy. She took it as a very personal insult. Their last night together they held hands, had a drink in the café where they'd first met, he kissed her on the forehead and said good-bye and walked away."

"Did you ever ask him about it?"

"Of course I did."

"And?"

"I couldn't understand why he wouldn't sleep with her. Between the two of us it would have done him the world of good. And she was an appealing little piece. He said he couldn't for two reasons. Reason number one was that she reminded him of someone he loved very much. Reason number two was a very romantic sort of reason. He said that he was very attracted to her, but, if he gave in and slept with her, he'd be just another soldier who paid her for her body and she'd be just a Paris whore. This way, they were each something very special to the other."

"As a psychiatrist would you consider that a normal reaction?"

154

"As a friend of Charley Bronson's I would consider it something he would do."

"What happened to the girl?"

"Oh she's still around. You can see her any night in the parade on the Grand Boulevard. I saw her myself only two nights ago. He was right, you know, she talks about him in the proper shopgirl, romantic terms you find in bad movies."

"And how does he talk about her?"

"He's been up to Paris once or twice since he took over at the repple depple. He carefully avoids the Grand Boulevard. Twice he left money with me for her. 'To buy her something,' he said."

"What'd you do with the money?"

"Spent it on books for the day room."

"You think he'd resent it if I went to see him?"

"Why would he resent it? You're friends, aren't you?"

"I suppose we are. Quite honestly, Colonel, I don't know why I'm so interested in Charley Bronson. I've spent a lot of time with a lot of other officers in combat. There are a lot of them that I know a lot better than I know Charley, and yet I keep wondering about him, thinking about him, worrying about how he's making it."

"Why do you suppose that is, Mr. Williams?"

"I went on a patrol with him once. He's a damned fool in combat, Colonel. He takes a lot of unnecessary risks. He's always sticking his neck out. I keep expecting to hear that he's killed himself."

"Killed himself?"

"I don't mean that literally. I mean I keep worrying that he's gotten himself into a position he can't get

155

out of. I guess I don't have much confidence that Charley Bronson is going to survive the war."

"I think you can bet on that now, Mr. Williams. The chances of Charley Bronson getting back into combat are very slim, indeed."

"That saddens me, too."

"Does it? Why?"

"Because combat, it seemed to me, was his natural habitat. Even his fascination with chess is a sort of sublimation of that. He plays chess the way he fought the war, daringly, impulsively, with a kind of calculated abandon."

"But all you lose in chess are some wooden pieces and, when the game is over, you set them back on the board and they're ready to fight again."

"It sounds like you go along with Watson's theory that he's a dangerous man."

"He's a very dangerous man. He's a button pusher."

"What does that mean?"

"You know the old chestnut about 'if you could press this button and destroy the whole world, would you push it?' Charley Bronson would push it."

"Provided he didn't survive."

"Provided he didn't survive. I'm being very glib, Mr. Williams. My relationship with Charley Bronson, professional and personal has been very casual. I can't diagnose or even attempt to cure. That would be a long, painstaking process. I can, however, venture the opinion that he is a very sick man. And in a very special sense, a very dangerous one. I think that's what Watson was talking about and guarding against."

"I'm sorry, Colonel, but I think both you and Watson are blowing something up out of all proportion. What did he do that was so terrible? He's a soldier. He's

156

fighting a war. He fights that war with some distinction, some style, some daring. People are killed. People are always killed in a war, Colonel. I'm not speaking theoretically now. I'm speaking from experience and knowledge. I went on a patrol with Bronson. I know that his courage, his leadership and his experience saved us all from being ambushed and killed. What the hell is so abnormal about a soldier that wants to fight?"

"Laymen, Mr. Williams, throw the words 'normal' and 'abnormal' around very carelessly. I'm sure Bronson is, in theory, a fine soldier."

"In practice, too."

"You say that, based on your one experience with him on a patrol. Being a good soldier requires a little more than being brave or daring. It requires some sense of prudence, some weighing of the odds before a decision is made. Bravery may be fine if you mean marching two companies into a trap and losing them, man by man. That, on the surface is a brave thing. It is also a foolhardy, criminal act for a thinking man. And I think you have to go one step further in the case of Charley Bronson. What motivates that kind of action on his part? Is it glory he's after? Is he bucking to make colonel and then to make general?"

"I don't know him well enough to answer that."

"Seeking after glory, regardless of the consequences, is fairly common among career army officers. It is even, in a distorted way, understandable. After all, war is their trade. They have a certain limited time to practice it. They have to make the most of it. And you know, as well as I do, that promotions and honors come slowly in peacetime. You know how long a major in the peacetime army can expect to remain in grade. Give them a good war, a little impudence, a little daring, some guts and a lot

157

of ambition and they can run from captain right up to general in one war."

"Is it that simple with Bronson?"

"I think that's part of it. Don't you?"

"I don't know. It's not so different for a correspondent, Colonel. I might still be covering City Hall or chasing fire engines. Because I'm willing to get myself shot at once in a while and was able to talk my editor into sending me I can get a cheap by-line and a quick reputation that pays off after the war is over. Who ever heard of a guy named Ernie Pyle who was doing a travel and nature column five years ago?"

"There's more than just that, however, in the case of Charley Bronson. I said that, when he came back here, he was suffering from a profound depression. He was also suffering from a severe sense of guilt."

"He lost almost three hundred men, Colonel. Three hundred men died because they followed him into that building."

"Yes. You would think that would bother him, wouldn't you? That would be what you like to call, so glibly, 'normal.' I'm not sniping at you, Mr. Williams. Not you personally. When I say 'you,' I mean, the lay public who've added the language of psychiatry to their vocabulary the way they add the latest in teen-age slang. They have the words right, but they use them wrong. It would be 'normal' to feel that you, personally, were responsible for the death of three hundred men, wouldn't it?"

"I said that." I answered him rather sharply. I was getting a little annoyed with the colonel's superior attitude and his classroom manner.

"Yes, you said it. But you were wrong. Because I told you Bronson was feeling depressed and guilty, you

158

jumped to what seemed to you to be a logical conclusion."

"Which is what?"

"Which is that he was depressed and guilty about the men with him who died. He never even thought of them—not before it happened, while it was happening or after it happened. He was depressed and guilty because he was still alive. I told you I don't know enough about your friend Charley Bronson to even attempt a diagnosis, but I do know this—Charley Bronson, I would be willing to bet, is a man who has sat with a loaded revolver in his hand—perhaps even at his forehead—and not been able to pull the trigger."

"Come on now, Colonel——"

"You asked my opinion. Charley Bronson is a man who has lived with the thought of his own death for a good long time. For whatever reason, responsibility, moral scruples, a fear of being thought a coward—whatever the reason may have been, he's been unable to pull that trigger. And he's spent a good part of his life since that decision was made trying to find somebody else to pull the trigger for him. In this case, he has attempted to have the German army do it for him. I would venture the guess that Colonel Bronson drives a car at fantastically high speed, dives off the highest diving board, skis on only the most suicidal slopes. Charley Bronson is a man trying to find somebody to countersign his death warrant. And that's why Doctor Watson considers him a dangerous man. He *is* dangerous."

"Well if he is, Colonel, you've removed his fangs—you and the Fitness Board."

"Have we? All we've done is put him in a spot where it will be a little more difficult for him to carry out his intentions."

"The last I heard, Colonel, nobody was leading any patrols thirty miles south of Paris. I haven't heard anything about eighty-eights zeroed in on repple depples or snipers shooting at the brass."

"You wanted to go down and see him. Fine. I suggest you do that, Mr. Williams."

"You sound as if that is going to take care of some point you're trying to make."

"Maybe it will. Just be prepared for a rather different Charley Bronson than the one you've known. It's funny. We get a lot of correspondents through here. Almost all of them adopt some GI. They bring him books, smuggle in booze, come to visit him and show him a big time when he gets into Paris on pass. That's reasonably common. You, however, Mr. Williams, are the first correspondent I've ever seen who has adopted a colonel."

"I haven't adopted him."

"You may not want to when you get a good look at him this time."

"Thanks for the warning."

Colonel Armstrong had annoyed me by his manner and his attitude and yet I left feeling slightly apprehensive about the trip down to the repple depple. I began to wonder about my fixation on Charley Bronson. Why *had* I adopted him? What the hell did I care what happened to one officer? Just because I'd played chess with him and gone out on that patrol with him didn't mean we were suddenly bosom buddies or relatives. I almost decided against going. I got back into the Paris swing and started pulling my stories off the big board at the Scribe like the rest of them. I got into the all-night poker sessions with the network radio correspondents, who had better billets and bigger expense accounts than the rest of us. I started seeing a lot of one of the dancers in that

160

crazy night club out near the city line where they had the parrot that sang close harmony on "Sweet Adeline" with a nude girl. I was prepared to sit out the rest of the war without getting shot at, without going hungry and without getting trench foot. I put Charley Bronson out of my mind until one night I found myself over near the Opera after dinner. I remembered about Colonel Armstrong's parade of the whores and headed toward the Rue Blondel. I sat at the sidewalk café, ordered a cognac and watched the girls parade by. It was as advertised even down to the watery cognac. I was the only non-GI in the place, but my olive drab correspondent's uniform gave me a kind of protective coloration. It looked exactly like a class-A uniform except for the patch on the left shoulder that said "Official U.S. War Correspondent." It *was* a little like a slave market and I was amused, watching the two soldiers at the next table as they looked over the wares on display. I even played a mental game with myself. I found at least three of them that I'd have been perfectly willing to spend the night with, all other things being equal. Then, as my eye wandered along the pavement I saw the girl Colonel Armstrong had told me about. It couldn't have been anyone else. You really would have cast her as the All-American college girl. Even here on a boulevard in Paris she looked as if she was ready to take her place in a Middle Western football stadium in front of the cheering section with a paper pompom in her hand. She was wearing a white blouse, a dark blue cardigan sweater left open, a dark skirt, a pair of white anklets and the dirty white saddle shoes. She caught the eyes of my GI neighbors and they beckoned her over. I eavesdropped shamelessly and heard her sprinkle her conversation with references to how tough things were in the ETO. She talked about her "aching

161

GI back," admitted she "never had it so good" and showed enthusiasm by saying "Oh, boy" and "Roger." The younger of the two GI's was obviously enchanted with her and they left together within fifteen minutes. The other GI stopped being a connoisseur, picked a girl more or less at random and followed his buddy and Helene up the street. I paid for my drinks and went back over to the bar the correspondents were hanging out in that winter, a clip joint on Rue Lincoln. The incident, of course, started me thinking about Bronson again. The next day I was passing an antique shop on the Avenue Wagram and my eye was caught by something in the window. It was a chess set, but the most unusual one I'd ever seen. The base was made out of the polished brass of an artillery shell. The tops were the carved heads of American generals with Roosevelt as the king. The pawns were simply Garand rifles mounted on the brass shell casing. They were covered with what looked like felt on the bottom, but on examination the felt turned out to be a GI blanket dyed green. On one or two you could clearly make out the U.S. burned into the material. I thought it would make a wonderful present for me to take to Charley Bronson and then reminded myself that I had no intention of visiting him.

The hell I didn't!

I went into the shop and priced the chess set. The owner of the shop wanted a hundred and fifty dollars for it and went on at great length about the careful carving and the importance it had as a souvenir of the war. I promised to write something about his shop for the *Stars and Stripes* and got him down to a hundred and ten bucks. I closed out the deal at a hundred and five and four cartons of Chesterfields.

It was quite a set. The bishops were very good likenesses of Mark Clark. The knights were General Patton; the rooks, Omar Bradley. The queen looked like a cross between Eleanor Roosevelt and Mae West—the two most typical American women the carver could think of, obviously. I was enchanted with it and I dropped by the shop the next morning and commissioned the shopkeeper to have another one made for me.

I packed a musette bag and caught a train heading south. I felt like a suitor bringing his best girl a hell of a Christmas present. I kept feeling the package to make sure the set hadn't fallen out or wasn't being crushed.

I don't know whether you know what a replacement depot is. In army talk, it's called a "repple depple" and I suppose the best way to describe it is to say that it's a sort of army used-car lot. Instead of cars, its product is men. The majority of its personnel consists of replacements fresh from the States, awaiting shipment to combat divisions. The troops are sorted out according to branch, army specialization number and special skills and, as the divisions request replacements for their casualties, shipments are made up and sent off in the cattle cars that pass for transportation in wartime. Soldiers back from hospitals and on their way to rejoin their outfits at the front are sent there and held until there is a shipment of replacements going to a particular area. For the most part, soldiers never spend more than four or five days in a repple depple. They are loosely run camps. I was in one camp in Italy that was set up on the side of a mountain on top of eight feet of lava dust. The replacements that came out of there must have spent the major part of their time in combat scraping the dirt and grime off their bodies. Accommodations are crude and makeshift. The soldiers sleep in pup tents, and spend most of their time loafing around reading

163

comic books, writing letters home and waiting to get shipped out of the disorganized boredom. Nobody gets a pass out of a repple depple, but most of the combat veterans slip out at night and get loaded on whatever passes for liquor in the area. Once a day the soldiers stand roll call and once a day the shipping orders are read off and the ones who find their names on the list gather together their worldly possessions and move out, headed back for the fighting war. For the most part, the cadre and officers at a repple depple are the bottom of the army barrel. They are misfits, rejects and limited service troops. I somehow couldn't picture Charley Bronson involved in a setup like that.

I walked through the train and came into a car filled with GI's. Their gear was spread all over the floor and they were passing a bottle of Eau de Vie around. A captain who was obviously in charge of the group was sitting with his feet up on the seat in front of him.

"Wanna sit down?" he asked me.

"May I?"

"Sure."

He removed his feet and I sat down facing him.

I motioned toward the soldiers.

"The natives are restless," I said.

"What the hell. They'll need it. Thank God I'm just shepherding them down there."

"Where?"

"The repple depple. They're just out of the hospital, bound for their own outfits . . . by way of the goddamned repple depple."

"Hell," I said. "Repple depples are all right. I should think they'd be a good kind of lazy bridge between the hospital and combat."

164

"Yeah? You ever been to this particular repple depple, Mac?"

"No."

"You never heard of Bronson's Bastille?"

"Bronson's Bastille?"

"That's what they call it. I make two trips down here a week, herding these characters. It gives me the creeps just to poke my nose inside, deliver the bodies and take off again. I suppose you think it's funny my letting them drink this way. What the hell, they're gonna need it."

"Why do they call it Bronson's Bastille?"

"Where are you bound for, Mac?"

"The repple depple."

"That's what I figured. I wouldn't want to spoil it for you."

"If it's so rough, aren't you doing these guys a disservice having them show up half loaded?"

"There are thirty of them, Mac. Before we left the hospital I gave them a shakedown. They're allowed one bottle of Eau de Vie between them. How loaded can thirty guys get on one bottle? They won't be loaded, but they won't be walking into that place cold sober either. I figure, like the poet says, if you can do a little kindness on the way, what the hell!"

When the train arrived, I stuck close to the captain and the GI's. I figured there'd be transportation for them and I'd grab a ride. The captain spelled it out for me.

"I got orders for thirty GI's and myself, Mac. I'll take you as far as the gate. From there on, you're on your own. I'm sorry, I can't get you in, but what the hell, you probably got enough connections or enough gall to get yourself in. O.K.?"

"O.K."

As soon as we got to the gate, I realized I'd have to

forget equating this place with any other repple depple I'd ever seen. There was a large, heavy iron gate with a sentry box on one side. Two armed guards with white, polished helmet liners stopped the truck I was riding in and examined the captain's orders. I got off the truck.

"Your orders, Sir," the guard said.

"I don't have any orders. I'm a correspondent."

"I'm sorry, Sir. You can't be admitted without orders. Written orders."

"From whom?"

"Colonel Bronson, Sir. I'm sorry. Those are my instructions."

He waved the truck on through the gates, which had been opened by the other guard. The captain and the GIs waved to me and after the truck passed through, the gates were swung closed behind them. This was a real switch. Every other repple depple I'd ever been in was as hard to get into as Grand Central Station. I'm sure you could have marched the whole German army into any one of them and never been challenged.

"I'm sorry, Sir," said the guard.

"Would you call Colonel Bronson and tell him Harry Williams is out here and would like to be admitted to the castle. Ask him to put the drawbridge down or at least give somebody permission to row me across the moat."

"Yes, Sir," said the guard. He walked to the sentry box.

"Harry Williams, Sir?"

"Better make it Cappy Williams."

"Yes, Sir."

He disappeared into the sentry box. The other guard moved closer and stared at me. He was holding his rifle in a ready position. I didn't know what he

166

suspected me of, but damned if I didn't begin to feel guilty.

The first guard came back.

"The colonel is sending his car for you, Sir."

"Thank you."

"You're welcome, Sir."

"How long have you been here, Sergeant?"

"I'm sorry, Sir. We are not permitted to talk on duty except in the line of duty."

"That's all right, Sergeant. That's a mighty pretty helmet. I haven't seen a white, shellacked helmet liner since the last time I was in Patton's area. Tell me, Charley Bronson hasn't taken to wearing pearl-handled pistols, too, has he?"

The guard just stared at me. There was only the slightest hint of a smile on his face.

"You're very lucky, Sergeant," I said. "You are getting some invaluable on-the-job training out of this war. When it's all over, you can cross the channel and pick up a job as a guard at Buckingham Palace without any trouble at all."

"Yes, Sir."

"You consider that remark in the line of duty, Sergeant?"

"Sir?"

"You answered me. Do you consider that a proper question to answer?"

"No, Sir."

"Your secret is safe with me, Sergeant."

A staff car arrived and stopped at the closed gates, on the inside. The guards swung the gates open. I walked through and climbed into the car.

The ride was fascinating. The grounds were carefully landscaped. The grass was cut close and not a

167

piece of the gravel from the driveway had fallen on the lawn. As we drove up the large, tree-bordered driveway, a platoon of men, herded by a sergeant came marching toward us. They were in step and, so help me, they were shouting cadence at the top of their voices as they passed. The staff car pulled up in front of a two-story building. It had evidently been the main house. It looked vaguely like a chateau and I was trying to figure out whether this estate had originally been a hospital, a school or perhaps even a convent. I got out of the staff car and two guards armed with M-1 rifles sprang to attention. One of them moved toward me.

"Mr. Williams?"

"Yes?"

"Colonel Bronson is expecting you, Sir. Would you follow me, please?"

Since I had no choice, I followed him into the building, down a long hall, through a large office with four Wacs pounding away at typewriters and up to a door marked "Colonel Charles Bronson—Commanding Officer." The guard knocked, opened the door and stepped aside to let me through.

Bronson was sitting at a desk under the window with a name plate on the desk in front of him. There was a large American flag behind him in a stand, two leather chairs facing the desk and a long leather couch against one of the walls. Charley looked up at me. He got to his feet and came toward me with his hand out. I took it.

"How are you, Charley?"

"Fine, Cappy. Just fine. And you?"

"Couldn't be better."

He smiled. And the smile did something wonderful to his face.

"God. it's good to see you!" he said. He meant it, too, and I sat down in the chair.

"This is the most GI outfit I've seen since Camp Hood, Texas."

"Were you at Hood, Cappy? I didn't know that. I was at Hood, too."

"I did a story on a draftee, followed him through from induction to his basic-training camp. It was a rough go. This place reminds me of it. What're you bucking for, Charley?"

"General."

That laid it right on the line. I didn't quite know what to say for a couple of minutes. You know how it is when you see somebody you haven't seen in a long time. You wonder how they've changed and if your relationship is quite the same. You feel your way along tentatively until something comes up that gives you a clue. I lit a cigarette to stall for time.

"I suppose you know what happened to me?" he asked.

"Yes. I know, Charley."

"How did you find me?"

"I started with Doc Watson at the division."

"That son of a bitch."

"Then I looked up Colonel Armstrong in Paris. He told me you were here."

"I certainly am. How do you like it?"

"Bronson's Bastille?"

He looked at me sharply.

"What?"

"That's what they call it, 'Bronson's Bastille.' I thought you knew."

"No, I didn't know. I've been collecting nicknames since I saw you last, Cappy. That's a new one."

169

"I even know the nicknames, Charley. 'Rover Boy' . . . 'Eager Beaver.' "

"You know what my officers call me here?"

"Good old Charley?"

"Bully Boy Bronson. I've earned it."

"What the hell are you up to, Charley? What are you trying to prove?"

"I'm not up to anything, Cappy. I'm doing my job. They assigned me here as commanding officer. So I'm commanding. I suppose Watson told you I'm crazy. He did his best to get me railroaded out of Europe and possibly the army. You heard the details on the ambush, I suppose."

"Most of them."

"Watson thinks I'm a dangerous man whose problems can only be solved by having me cashiered out of the service. Armstrong on the other hand, from what I can figure out, thinks that everything will be fine if I just go into Paris and get laid. There you have the sharp gulf between two of our most brilliant psychiatric minds. Do you want to offer an opinion, Cappy?"

"Not particularly. I saw your girl in Paris."

"My girl?"

"Helene."

"Where? Where did you see her?"

"The same place you saw her. Armstrong told me about your unorthodox tour of Paris. I was curious so I sat at the sidewalk café and saw her. I couldn't miss her."

"Is she back to ———"

"Whoring? Yes."

"That's too bad."

"What did you think she'd be doing, Charley?

Teaching Sunday school? Conducting tours for GI's through Paris?"

"You saw her. You talked to her?"

"No, Charley. I saw her. I didn't talk to her. I didn't sleep with her either, if you're wondering about that. It's none of my business, is it?"

"What's none of your business?"

"Why you didn't sleep with her."

"I'm a married man, Cappy."

"So are one out of every three GI's in Europe. Does that make you immune?"

"I couldn't. I thought at first I could. You saw how she looked. And then, her name being Helene was almost like a sign. But I couldn't, Cappy. It's too complicated to go into. Just take my word for it, I couldn't."

"You mean you haven't—since you've been over here? That's a hell of a thing to ask you, isn't it? What business is it of mine and what the hell do I care about your sex life?"

"I haven't, Cappy. There's nothing particularly strange about it. I suppose I just don't have a very well-developed sex drive."

"I'll stop talking like Watson and Armstrong."

"The Boobsey Twins."

"I brought you a present."

I took the chess set out and set the pieces up on the table. He was fascinated by them. He kept picking them up one after another and examining them.

"Goddamn! Isn't that something!" he said.

"I thought you'd like it."

"Like it! It's the most wonderful thing I've ever seen. Thank you very much, Cappy."

"My pleasure."

"Can you stay awhile? I need somebody to talk to.

171

I haven't played chess in weeks. Please stay awhile, Cappy."

"Awhile. I was worried about you, Charley."

"Worried about me? I'm getting a little big for that."

"I'd heard so many strange things about you. I— it's funny, I was very nervous coming into the office just now."

"Most people are. You'd better prepare yourself, Cappy. Within the walls of this installation, I could give Hitler, Goering, Mussolini and Tojo cards and spades and still walk off with the honors as the most hated man in the world."

"You sound proud of that."

"I am. You've been in repple depples before, haven't you?"

"A couple."

"You know what they're like. This one is different."

"I've noticed that already."

"They wouldn't let me do the job I was trained to do. They sloughed me off with this job. O.K. I surprised them. I run a repple depple as if it's an army establishment and not a cub scout troop. I make them so god-damned glad to get out of here that combat seems like a vacation with pay."

"Why, Charley?"

"It's my job. They made me an administrator. Fine. I'm going to be the best administrator they've ever seen. I've reorganized this place and put it on a workable basis. Nobody goes AWOL from here. Nobody leaves here with half his equipment. Nobody goofs off. If, in the process, they all hate my guts, that's too bad. Let them hate me. I'm doing a difficult job damn well and, when they get around to making a fitness report, I may not win

172

any popularity contests, but I'll get a hell of a high rating. Let the combat boys grab the gravy and the medals. When this war is over, they're going to need administrators."

"So it's all ambition after all, isn't it?"

"It isn't all anything, Cappy. It never is. Come on, I'll show you around."

"Charley," I said, "it seems to me, for a chess opponent, I've stuck my nose pretty far into your business already. Do you mind if I stick it a little further in?"

"Go ahead."

"Who is Helen?"

He stood stock still. He stared at me and the blood seemed to drain out of his face for a minute. When he spoke, it was in a voice that I'd never heard him use before. It was a little like a voice I remembered from my childhood when I'd done something terribly wrong.

"Where did you hear that name?"

"Watson said you kept repeating the name while you were in shock after the ambush."

"He never told me that. What right did he have telling it to you if he didn't tell it to me?"

"None at all, except that he thought I was a close friend of yours and he thought perhaps I should know it. Should I, Charley?"

He lit a cigarette.

"I don't know why I should have said the name, Cappy. Helen was somebody I knew a long time ago. She died. That's all there is to it."

"A relative, Charley? A friend? What?"

"Drop it!"

There was no mistaking the note of command.

"I'm sorry, Charley. I said it was none of my business."

173

"Come on. I'll show you around."

I followed him out of the office. We got into the command car. The guards presented arms. The driver saluted. We drove all over the camp. The troops slept in pup tents. That much at least, was the same as other repple depples. But the pup tents were arranged in orderly rows. The area around them was spotlessly clean. We rode out of the camp area into the woods. We passed one group of GIs going through a bayonet drill. Another group was doing calisthenics. In one area a group of men were sitting in tiers of bleachers listening to a lecture on military courtesy. There were classes in assembling the M-1 rifle. Charley took me to an infiltration course where we watched a company of men crawl under barbed wire on their bellies while two machine guns fired a foot over their heads. It was quite a tour. When we got back to his office, he opened a bottle of Scotch and poured each of us a drink.

"What the hell are you doing, Charley, running a basic-training camp?"

"That's exactly what I'm doing. Why should they sit around on their duffs reading comic books and loafing? These men are bound for combat. The new replacements can use the extra training. The next stop from here is the place where they're being shot at for real."

"And what about the returnees, coming out of hospitals? How can you take a man who's been in combat and put him through instruction in the M-1 rifle? I suppose you send them out on hikes, too?"

"Ten- and fifteen-mile hikes with full field packs. It does them good."

"No wonder they call it 'Bronson's Bastille.'"

"You haven't seen anything yet, Cappy. They

stand reveille at seven thirty in the morning. Most of the repple depples use civilian natives for KP and the dirty details. We draw our KP's from the company roster. There's an inspection every morning."

"No passes?"

"No passes."

"What kind of an inspection?"

"A complete inspection. Equipment, clothes, person, area."

"Charley, even in basic training there's only one inspection a week."

"In basic training they're three thousand miles away from the war. Did Watson fill you full of that crap about my not caring how many men were killed, or how?"

"He said something like that."

"I care. I care a lot. Nobody that leaves here is going to be killed because I haven't done everything I can to prepare him for what's ahead of him. If he hates me in the process, that's just too goddamned bad. Maybe if one of these guys passing through here winds up in an ambush, he'll come out alive because he hasn't been coddled and allowed to goof off. They really hate me, Cappy. Don't underestimate that."

"You do sound proud of it."

"Why not? Don't you think discipline is a big part of a soldier's equipment? . . . O.K. This is where the army put me. Well, goddammit, I'm going to do the job the way I think it should be done. I don't care if the whole United States Army hates my guts. Why didn't they leave me alone—leave me where I was, leave me to do what I can do?"

"What happens if a man doesn't pass your daily inspection, Charley? Do you put him on KP?"

175

"KP isn't a punishment here, Cappy. The men get one hot meal a day. Breakfast and lunch are K rations. We give them hot water in the morning to make their soluble coffee. They eat the K's in the field. KP is a privilege. The men get more food that way. They also get out of the training for the day while they're on KP. No, I have a much better punishment than that. Can you guess what it is?"

"I wouldn't even try, Charley."

"The only thing they dream about is getting out of here, winding up on a shipment. The stupid bastards. At least nobody is shooting at them in anger here. But they can't wait to get out. So, if they don't pass inspection, I take their name off the roster that day so they can't get shipped out. I keep them off the roster until they pass an inspection. You'd be surprised how effective that is. The Inspector General himself could walk into this camp any time he wants to and the whole camp would pass even his inspection."

"You have changed, Charley."

"Have I? I don't think so. I'm still trying to do my job as well as I can. On the lines that job was fighting the Germans. Back here, my job is running this camp. They have to pay attention to it. They have to realize what a job I'm doing and lift the goddamned no combat ban on me."

"I never saw a man so anxious to get shot at in my life. Why, Charley?"

"Why not?"

"I forgot to congratulate you. A full chicken colonel."

"I'm chicken, all right. I promised Margaret I'd be a general. If they left me alone, I'd have made it,

176

too. You don't make general in the rear echelon. Watson and his meddling took care of that."

"He thought you were trying to get yourself killed."

"I know."

"Are you?"

"No more than you are, going up to the lines instead of sitting on your tail in Paris and covering the war from there."

"It's not quite the same, Charley."

"You could help me, you know, Cappy."

"How?"

"If you did a story about this place—you know, the West Point of the ETO—that kind of thing. It would carry a lot of weight."

"And it might even get you sprung, give you a chance to go back up and get your ass shot off. No thanks."

"Even if I want that chance?"

"Don't push me, Charley. I never give more than one present a week. The chess set is yours for this week."

"In that case you have to stay at least two weeks. Come on, how about trying out the new set?"

"Bully Boy Bronson."

"Don't worry, Cappy. You're safe. You're a civilian."

"I was a civilian when you talked me into that patrol."

"You came out of it alive, didn't you?"

"Come on, Charley, let's play chess."

"You and Armstrong and Watson are all alike. You put on your soldier suits and march off to a war without any idea of what it is and how it has to be fought. War is my business, Cappy. I've been training for it since I was nine years old. And now, because I fight it the way I was taught to fight it, I wind up being kicked out of the

177

game by a referee who doesn't know the first goddamned thing about the rules."

"And what are the rules?"

"Kill the enemy. Don't be afraid to stick your neck out or afraid of being shot at. I'm not minimizing the men that were killed, Cappy. Watson says I walked into a trap. What the hell does he know about a trap or a military operaton? My orders were to attack. I saw what the German commander was trying to do. I let him suck me in. It seemed to me that there was a chance I could fight my way through. I weighed the odds. I'll admit they weren't in my favor. But a lot of the battles that wound up in the history books were fought with much worse odds against the men who eventually won. I thought there was enough of a chance to push through his trap to make it worth while taking the risk. If I'd succeeded, I'd have opened up the whole flank of the German defense. All you civilians want to play it so goddamned safe. You're so smug about your B-29's and Willow Run. If you had your way, you'd load your guns with leaflets and overwhelm the enemy with your righteousness and your smug certainty that you can't be defeated. I know different. There is nothing that says we have to win and they have to lose. You still have to slug it out on a battlefield and on a battlefield men die. Our men as well as theirs."

"Come on, Charley, let's play chess."

"There's an unbridgeable gulf between us, Cappy. . . . There are two worlds, the civilian world and the army world. Most of the time you're ashamed of us. During peacetime, you look down at us from your Olympian heights. You underpay us, underestimate us and consider us the social misfits of the world. The peacetime army is filled with bums, in your eyes. Anybody who

178

couldn't make it in the big, wide, important world is shoveled into the army. You figure we drink, fornicate and live off a kind of dole that you graciously pay in the unlikely event that you're ever going to need all the brutal qualities that you're too refined, too intellectual and too fastidious to learn and use. Then when you bollix up the peace and start a war, you come running to us. You put us on the movie screens played by your biggest movie stars. You open canteens for us and let your daughters serve us doughnuts and even dance with us. You put us on your billboards and you let your sons join us. You hate our guts, but, because you somehow manage to start a war every generation, you can't do without us. What the hell do Watson or Armstrong or a bunch of reconverted civilians on a review board know about fighting a war and what the hell right do they have to say what is a justifiable risk and what isn't."

"How does this repple depple and the way you're running it fit into all that, Charley?"

"You say you've been around a basic-training camp. You've certainly been up with the line companies. Let's cut the crap for a minute and talk straight about the American soldier . . . the tools they hand the pros to fight a war with. Your average draftee comes into the army with a chip on his shoulder and a big supply of self-pity. 'What the hell am I doing here?' he asks. 'Why should I have to be the one to fight the war?' He goofs off during basic training if he can. He's too stupid to know that it's a tough grind because where he's going it will be even tougher. He's flabby and soft, he's full of self-importance. He has to be toughened up, physically and mentally. He has to stop thinking he's so goddamned important. The army is important. The division is important. The company is important. The battle is important. The objective is important. He's the most unimportant thing in the world. He's expendable. That's a hard thing to accept, Cappy. A man can't accept it unless something is more important to him than himself. He has to either believe enough or hate enough. As a nation, we're raised to listen to all the slogans and all the malarky that passes for truth. 'Don't give up the ship,' 'We have just begun to fight.' 'I regret that I have but one life to give for my country.' You've seen green troops in action. Once they are faced with the reality of trading their lives for a principle, for their country, for freedom or any of the other intangibles, they turn ass and run. It takes a lot of training to make a man accept the vulnerability of a combat soldier. They're perfectly willing to accept casualties, as long as they aren't part of the statistic, themselves. That's where we come in. We know the score. We know the odds. We know what has to be done and how to do it. And we have to do it with the material you give us. So we try to make the material workable. We beat hell out of you civilians in basic training. We frighten you, we try to knock some of the individuality of the peacetime world out of you. We try to give you some feeling of pride of belonging to something that's bigger and more important than any of you, personally. Call it a platoon, a company, a division or an army. We say, 'tough luck that you're here. Too bad you've been chosen to do the actual fighting, but since you are here and since you have been chosen, you'd damned well better learn how to do it.' And if, in the process, the soldier learns to hate us almost as much as he theoretically hates the enemy, that's fine. Hate is an emotion you have to carry into a war with you. Self-pity will get you killed. You'll operate on the principle that if you don't shoot at the Krauts, they won't shoot

180

at you. You get killed that way. But with hate, you have a chance of surviving. That's all I'm doing here. I'm giving the men who pass through here—the replacements and the returnees—one last chance to toughen up, one last chance to be a little better equipped to stay alive on the lines. Does that make me so goddamned dangerous? Or do you agree with Watson and Armstrong that I have some sort of mystical death wish, that I'm pulling the temple down around my ears?"

"You know what I believe, Charley?"

"What?"

"I believe we ought to play some chess."

"Cappy, at the risk of boring you, let me finish. I don't know why I'm trying to justify myself in your eyes. It seems to me that we're fond of each other. I don't know why. I don't think we've spent more than a total of two weeks together. We've played some chess, done some talking, even a little fighting, but it's important to me that you go away, if not understanding me, at least conceding that I have a point of view and something to say in my own defense. I never wanted to be in the army. I never wanted to go to West Point. I never wanted to go to war. But the deal was made for me when I was nine years old and by God, I lived up to it. I'm a hell of a good army officer. I've loused up the rest of my life, but not this part of it. That's why it's so important to me. I have nothing else, Cappy."

"What about your wife?"

"Margaret?"

"Yes."

"Whatever is wrong with Margaret, I made wrong. She did the best she could under a set of lousy circumstances. I never gave her a chance to be a wife. She tried hard for a while. I've been doing a lot of thinking about

181

the two of us. I'm not sure that after the war is over it makes any sense at all for us to stay married to each other. I don't know, Cappy. Maybe I'll try one more time. Maybe what I need is the same kind of basic training for normal living I was talking about before. If the draftees aren't equipped to be soldiers, I'm sure as hell not equipped to be a husband or a normal, functioning human being."

"You're a strange contradiction, Charley. Your opinion of yourself as Charley Bronson, colonel, and Charley Bronson, human being, has no meeting ground. Maybe you're overestimating one and underestimating the other."

"Maybe professional soldiers shouldn't have any private lives at all. Maybe they shouldn't get married or have children or lead lives outside the soldier's handbook. Maybe the army should have a special division of women to take care of their basic needs and let it go at that."

"In your case they'd better be sure and have somebody with a cardigan sweater and white saddle shoes."

"That's peculiar, too, Cappy. It was a little like smelling a familiar perfume in a room and going off into a reverie about something that happened once. It was the nostalgia of a familiar smell, a familiar sight or sound. In this case, those dirty white saddle shoes opened up an old wound. You know what I think?"

"What?"

"I think we ought to play chess," he said.

We did. We played chess all afternoon.

His phone rang a couple of times. The Wac secretary came in with papers for him to sign and once or twice we were distracted by cadence shouted by a group of marching men going by the window. As usual, I

182

enjoyed playing chess with Charley. Without realizing it, I found myself watching him carefully to see if he'd developed a nervous tic or a stutter. He was self-assured, calm and completely at ease.

We quit late in the afternoon, had a drink and then went out into the courtyard for retreat. I'm a sucker for retreat. The naked bugles and lowering of the flag works every time. The entire camp was in ranks in the courtyard in Class-A uniforms and it looked very impressive. They marched well and looked like soldiers. When they were dismissed, they ran off, presumably to get back into fatigues for chow. With the kind of a regime Charley had set up for them, a hot meal was the high point of the day.

The dining hall was a huge room on the second floor of the main building. The GI's went through a cafeteria line with a tin tray. The officers sat at a long table in the corner and were served by KP's who doubled as waiters. The food was good and plentiful. The Wacs ate by themselves in a smaller dining room down the hall. Charley thought it was a good idea. He didn't want them to sit with the officers and thought it might be awkward for them to sit at a table by themselves, exposed to the no-doubt-carnal glances of the GIs.

The atmosphere at the table was very formal. Everybody sat more or less at attention and Charley was called "Sir" or "Colonel Bronson." I had the cockeyed feeling that the other officers and I were the plebes and Charley was the upper classman put at our table to keep us up to snuff. I wouldn't have been surprised if he had made us all eat "a square meal." I didn't enjoy the meal at all. I felt uncomfortable and out of place. I sympathized with the officers, who were obviously terrified of Charley and his disapproval. I didn't dare show my sympathy.

183

That would have been an act of treason. So I sat and ate and found myself talking too much to the men around me. Charley asked an occasional question about the training program, but for the most part remained silent and ate. I noticed that the mess hall itself was curiously quiet. There was very little talking. The men sat with their trays, ate in silence, went back for seconds and filed quietly out of the room. There wasn't even the usual clatter as they deposited their dirty trays in the pile at the door. It was the most unnatural mess hall I'd ever been in.

Over coffee, Charley turned to the officer next to him, a captain, and asked a question.

"Grayson, why is it so many of the men in your company turn up on sick call every morning?"

"Probably because they're sick, Colonel."

"I've told all of you, I don't stand for wholesale goofing off. I'm not saying that we can deny a soldier the opportunity of going to the dispensary if he's sick. I will not have a man falling out of formation in the morning, loafing around sick call, getting two aspirins and missing the morning training schedule. I depend on all of my company commanders to make sure that a man is really sick before you allow him to go on sick call."

"We're not doctors, Colonel Bronson. If a man says he's sick, I'm in no position to tell him he's well and he can't go on sick call."

"Come off it, Grayson. You've been an officer long enough to spot the malingerers. There's one man in your company who has been here twenty-three days. He's been on sick call twenty-one of those days. In each case he's complained of an upset stomach. Upset stomach my foot! He's goofing off. He knows it. You know it and I damn well know it."

184

Grayson hesitated for a minute. The colonel tried staring him down. He didn't succeed.

"Colonel, I know the man you're talking about. He's been in combat since Sicily. He has a purple heart and three clusters. He's just out of the hospital after being shot up. I somehow don't consider it a crime that he wants to duck a lecture on the nomenclature of the M-1 rifle or listen to a T/5 tell him that in order to salute the fingers of the right hand are extended and joined. You're right, Colonel. He is goofing off. He's goofing off with my knowledge and support."

"Let me make myself clear, Captain Grayson, and this goes for the rest of you who haven't understood my orders. This is a military establishment. I am the commanding officer. All soldiers of this command take part in all the training activities. All soldiers. All. If any of you think because you're casuals here like the men you can goof off, you're mistaken. You may only be here a week or at the most a month, but while you're here and while you're under my command, you will behave like officers and obey my orders. Is that sufficiently clear? If it's not I'll be happy to explain it to you in private. Grayson, I want to see a sharp drop in the number of men from your company on sick call."

"Would you spell it out for me, Sir? Which particular diseases are allowed to be treated?"

"Don't be impertinent."

"You misunderstand me, Colonel. I'm not being impertinent at all. I'm trying to clarify the military situation. I'm asking for a clarification of my orders. Which diseases are allowed to be treated?"

"You've had a chip on your shoulder since you arrived, haven't you, Grayson?"

"No, Sir. Not quite since I arrived. I'm no ninety-

185

day wonder, Colonel. I've been in this army three and a half years. I've spent almost half of that time in combat. I learned early on that carrying a chip on your shoulder is just so much excess weight. I've been in repple depples before but never one like this."

"You don't like the way this repple depple is run, Captain?"

"Is that a rhetorical question, Colonel, or do I have your permission to really answer it."

"I asked it for an answer."

"In short, in brief, to the point . . . I do not like the way it is being run."

"Perhaps you'd care to offer some constructive criticism, Captain."

"There's nothing wrong, Colonel, in running the replacements through a sort of refresher of their basic training. It may even do some good. If nothing else, it takes their mind off their next destination and tires them out so they don't have the energy to feel sorry for themselves. I approve of that."

"Thank you, Captain."

"But I don't approve of treating the combat veterans the same way. You'll forgive me, Sir, but it is pretty ridiculous to send a man on his way back from a hospital to rejoin his outfit on the line out on a fifteen-mile hike with full field pack. Or to send him through a gas chamber or teach him how to salute Wac officers, or how to read a compass or a map. It's insulting, degrading and needlessly cruel."

"I'll take your opinion into consideration, Captain. And what would you have me do with your combat veteran?"

"Do what every other commander of every other repple depple does. Let him slip through the fence at

186

night and find booze and a broad. Let him sleep in the morning and write letters home. Show a movie in the open field every night and let him get a ring around his can from sitting on his helmet watching it. Give him a bridge back to the lines. Colonel, damn few of them goof off, take off or miss shipment. They deserve a little humanity and a little sympathy."

"I hope you're getting all this down, Cappy. Captain Grayson is the best friend the GIs ever had. When the war is over, he may run for Congress. Vote for Pete Grayson, the GI's friend!"

"It's an unfair fight, Colonel. You have a weapon I'm forbidden to use, sarcasm."

They stared at each other hard for a full minute. I don't know about the other officers, but I know I was embarrassed by the whole exchange.

"One other thing, Colonel," said Captain Grayson.

"Yes, Captain?"

"When am I getting the hell out of here? You said yourself that casual officers stay around a couple of weeks—a month at the most. I've been here almost three months. My MOS isn't that unusual, is it? I'm sure there's been a request for the services of a line company commander in those three months?"

"Oh, yes, Captain. There have been many requests."

"But?"

"But what, Captain?"

"Why haven't I shipped out?"

"You can't ship out, Captain. You see, I've taken your name off the shipping list. You've done such a sterling job here that I've requested you as a member of the permanent party."

"You've what?"

187

"A captain, Captain, normally addresses his superior officer by title or by the all inclusive 'Sir.' "

"Colonel Bronson, Sir, do I understand you to say that you've removed my name from the shipping list? Do I understand you to say that you have requested my services here for the duration?"

"You understand me completely, Captain. You said yourself, Captain, that you're not a ninety-day wonder. In that case you should know better than to disobey the orders of your commanding officer."

"I've obeyed every order you've ever given me."

"Every man in your company who's had more than two days of combat makes the sick-call formation more often than he makes retreat. I haven't gotten around to clocking your ten-mile hikes, but I'm reasonably sure they come closer to three-mile hikes. I've heard about your wonderful instruction in how to roll a light pack and make it look like a full field pack. I've noticed that no man in your company has ever been gigged at an inspection. You still think you obey my orders, Captain?"

"You have no right to keep me here, Sir."

"I repeat. I am the commanding officer of this post. You are under my command. I can keep you here until every other soldier in the ETO has spent his mustering out pay. I have a pretty good idea what you think of me, Captain. You are at least enough of a soldier to recognize that those two silver bars on your shoulder don't stand a chance against the silver eagle on mine. It works both ways. Those silver eagles keep me from telling you what I think of you—just as they keep you from telling me off."

"Shall we just take them off our shoulders, Colonel, and purge ourselves?"

"You'd like that, wouldn't you? It would fit into the

188

romantic mental picture you have of yourself, wouldn't it? There isn't a thing you could say, Captain, that every man in this mess hall hasn't already said to himself. Bully Boy Bronson, chicken colonel, tyrant, overbearing, arrogant, dirty no good S.O.B. Does that cover it, Captain?"

"It hits the high spots, Colonel. It doesn't quite cover it."

"And what about you, Captain? What do you want to be, the most popular boy in school? You don't know the first thing about commanding men."

"Do you, Sir?"

"You're damned right, I do."

The argument was getting out of hand. I recognized that frightening tone of voice that I heard when I asked Charley earlier in the day about Helen. I figured it was time to break it up before he pushed Grayson into doing something that would make him the star of a court-martial.

"Charley," I said, "isn't it about time to get back to the chess board?"

"Shut up, Cappy. Keep your nose out of this."

I suppose I should have gotten up from the table, picked up my musette bag and headed back for Paris. I didn't.

"Let me tell you one more thing, Captain," said Charley.

"By all means, Colonel."

"You wouldn't last six months in the peacetime army, Grayson. Captain? Don't make me laugh. You couldn't make corporal. You're a civilian. One of the field expedients we use. You have the gall to tell me I don't know how to command!"

"Colonel, there isn't a man in this camp and prob-

189

ably there isn't a man in the ETO that doesn't know your record and your reputation. Command? Sir, if I may, I'd like to add just one more description to that list you gave us a minute ago. It's a name that you carry around your neck like an albatross. 'Butcher Boy Bron son.' If you can't kill your men in combat, break theii spirits and destroy them in the rear echelon. Butcher Boy Bronson, Sir."

Charley got up from the table. His face was red and his hands were rolled up into a fist. The knuckles were white.

"Captain," he said, "I guarantee you, you'll spend the rest of this war right here. You'll make every fifteen-mile hike that's made. You will, by God, run your company the way I want you to run it."

He turned and walked out of the mess hall. I followed him.

I followed him because I didn't want to sit at the table with Grayson and the other officers after he left. I caught up with him in the hall and we walked down the hall to his room. Neither of us said a word.

The room was very attractive, with a huge canopy bed, a comfortable chaise longue, light, delicate chairs and tables, paintings, gilt-decorated mirrors, a tapestry and large terrace windows that overlooked the formal garden in the rear.

"Rank Has Its Privileges," I said. I said it to break the silence between us. It didn't work. Charley opened a commode beside the bed and pulled out a bottle of Scotch. He went into the bathroom. I heard him opening what sounded like a refrigerator door. He returned with a tray of ice cubes and a pitcher filled with water. I sat on the bed, took my shoes off and gravely accepted a

190

drink from him. He poured one for himself. It was a whopper.

"I'm sorry you were exposed to that scene at dinner," he said.

"Forget it."

"Sure. Will you?"

"It got pretty rough."

"If you don't mind, Cappy, I'd rather not go over it again. Can we not talk about it?"

"Whatever you say, Sir. After all, you are my commanding officer. I am, after all just a lousy little civilian in uniform."

"That pipsqueak bastard. 'Butcher Boy Bronson.' What the hell does he know about it?"

"I thought we weren't going to talk about it, Charley."

"We're not."

"You're right, you know. I could do a story on this place."

"I suppose you think that's amusing?"

"Not very. How about your Wac detachment, Charley? Any action there?"

"Nothing."

"By whose standards, yours or mine?"

"Even by your standards, Cappy. I picked them all personally. I'm not buying any of that kind of trouble. That's all I need, troops infiltrating the Wac compound."

"They're all dogs?"

"They look like the Notre Dame backfield." He started to laugh. "I think they were all professional wrestlers in civilian life," he said.

"Want to play some chess?"

"Not tonight, Cappy. I don't feel like it."

"He did get under your skin, didn't he?"

"Of course he did. What do you say we run up to Paris in the command car?"

"And find your little girl with the dirty saddle shoes?"

"I didn't say anything about that, did I?"

"Hadn't it occurred to you?"

"Go to hell."

He poured two more drinks.

"Charley, I'm going to get out of line again."

"I can't stop you, can I?"

"I don't think you can. You talk big about using things. About things having a certain utility. GI's are expendable. You have to use the material at hand. You don't practice that yourself, do you?"

"What does that mean?"

"What the hell is the symbol of the saddle shoes and the cardigan sweater, Charley? Now, wait a minute. I'm not a captain. You can't keep me off a shipping list. Those eagles on your shoulder don't mean a goddamned thing to me."

"As you said, Cappy, rank has its privileges. And you outrank hell out of me, you dirty civilian."

"Charley, you got yourself shot up. Forget for the moment, the military aspect of it. Stop trying to figure out whether you asked to get your ass shot up or whether you were being a smart-assed military genius. You got shot up. You wind up back in a hospital in Paris. You've taken an emotional beating. You go into Paris and you pick up a whore. Sure, she's clean and she wears saddle shoes and a white blouse, but she's a whore. Fine. But what do you do then? For some cockeyed reason you don't want her to be a whore. You try to turn her into something else, something she isn't. Something she can't be. And what do you accomplish? You confuse hell out of

192

her. She can't be what you want her to be. You won't allow her to be what she really is. You're not using the material at hand, Charley old boy. You're turning her into your daughter or the girl next door, or God knows what. But she isn't any of those things. And you take away from her her basic quality, the pride and instincts of a good whore. You turn her into a half-assed symbol of something. You treat her worse than a drunken GI who punches her off a wall."

"Now you're adding a new indictment. Bully Boy Bronson is unfair to the whores of Paris."

"You think you did her a favor by not sleeping with her? You didn't. You paid her to do nothing. At least that's the way she looked at it. She was an object of charity. You turned her into a different kind of a whore, Charley. A much worse kind. You didn't even let her have the satisfaction of thinking she earned her money."

"There isn't a one of you with that goddamned correspondent's patch on your arm that doesn't get delusions of Hemingway. By God, the hair is pushing right through the olive-drab shirt. You're men. You're virile. You shack up, you booze, you play poker. You're so goddamned tough, and the first time anybody doesn't fit into your pattern, you figure there's something queer about him."

"Get off my back, Colonel. We're not talking about me. We're talking about you."

"Who gave you permission to talk about me?"

"I don't need permission. I outrank you. Tell me the truth, Colonel. Didn't you want to climb into bed with her? Didn't you cop a feel? What made you immune?"

"Don't talk that way!"

He put his glass down. He was mad. I didn't give a damn. I figured he'd pulled rank on the captain when

193

the barbs got a little close. I figured I owed the captain a couple of good sharp barbs of my own.

"What makes you immune, Charley?"

"I told you to shut up."

I finished off my drink and poured another one. I poured one for him, too. We drank it in a gulp. I refilled the glasses. What the hell, there are worse things to do in a repple depple than get loaded.

"She's a whore, Charley. For God's sake, couldn't you show a little humanity and treat her like one?"

"Let me up."

"She was a whore, Charley. Why didn't you treat her like one?"

"She'd have gotten pregnant. We'd have had to do something about it. She'd have had an accident. God damn it, shut up, Cappy."

He threw his glass across the room. It smashed against the wall and shattered. He walked into the bathroom. When he came out, he was carrying another glass. He filled it methodically and sat down.

"I know, Cappy," he said quietly. "Whores don't get pregnant. And if they do, it's the hazards of the profession; it doesn't concern the customer."

"I'll drink to that. It's like the Magna Charta, one of the basic truths of our civilization."

"You know, Cappy. All you tough guys make too much out of the whole sex thing."

"Now you're setting up standards for the rest of the world. Who are you to tell me what my sex life should be like?"

"I'm only saying that I always thought it was overestimated. You want to know something? I've slept with only two women in my life. One was Margaret. I ruined the lives of both of the women by sleeping with them."

194

"How?"

"The first time it led to a tragedy. The second time it led to something that may even be worse, a kind of decay—disillusionment and destruction. In a way, Cappy, I killed both women—in bed."

I was getting pretty loaded by that time. I poured another drink. It was poured on the principle that all I needed was one more drink to clear the fogginess. It works that way sometimes. Charley was standing looking at me. I wanted him to shut up. I had the feeling that, if he kept talking, he'd say things that he couldn't face saying in the sober light of morning. I also had the feeling that nothing in the world could keep him from saying more.

"You're right about one thing, Cappy. I did intend to sleep with her."

"The saddle-shoed whore?"

"I wanted a woman very much. It was more than just wanting to sleep with her. I wanted to comfort her, to hold her in my arms and comfort her. I sat with Armstrong at that sidewalk café and watched them go by. They intimidated me. They were all so damn chic, so damn smart. They'd have laughed at me if I'd asked to hold them in my arms and comfort them. She didn't intimidate me. She looked young and fresh and almost innocent. I felt instinctively she wouldn't laugh. Then I found out that her name was Helene. That cinched it. I didn't even have to worry about saying the wrong name."

"Saying the wrong name?"

"I'd made that mistake once."

"You damn fool. You were paying her. You bought her. You could have called her Pontius Pilate if you wanted to."

"I'd bought the other one. I'd paid her, too."

"When was this?"

"Long time ago, Cappy. A long, long, long time ago. Forget it. It won't make any sense to you."

"How do you know it won't?"

"All right. O.K. Maybe it will. Make yourself another drink, Cappy. It's a long story."

I reached for the Scotch bottle. Just as I grabbed it, the door to the room opened. I looked up. Captain Grayson was standing in the doorway. He was very drunk. Charley turned and looked at him.

"What the hell do you want, Captain?"

Grayson put his hands across the doorjamb, as if to prevent anyone from pushing past him.

"I want to tell you a couple of other names that have occurred to me: 'Bastard.' 'Murderer.' 'Scum.' 'Son of a Bitch.' "

"Is that the best you can do, Captain? That's the trouble with you civilians. You don't even know any really good foul language."

"I'm warning you, Bronson, you better put my name on that shipping list tomorrow morning."

"You'll go on a shipping list after every German and Japanese soldier has received his pension and been mustered out of service. You'll go on a shipping list in time to celebrate your seventy-fifth birthday."

"I'm warning you, Bronson. I go on a shipping list tomorrow morning."

"Or what? You little punk! Or what?"

Grayson took one arm down off the doorjamb and reached into his pocket. He pulled out a .45. I saw that the safety catch was off, and hit the floor. I've seen the kind of a hole a forty-five slug can put in a man this

196

close. I hit the floor and rolled behind the chaise longue. Neither of them paid any attention to me.

"The captain has a gun. The warlike Captain Grayson has a gun. What do you know about that?"

"This is one ambush you're not going to walk away from alive, Butcher Boy. You either sit down at that desk and write out my shipping orders right now or——"

"Or what?"

"Or I'll put a hole through the middle of your lousy GI guts, that's what."

Charley started to laugh.

"For Christ's sake, Charley, write out his orders," I said. "He isn't kidding."

"Who isn't kidding?" said Charley. "Captain Grayson? Let's find out if he's kidding or not."

"For Christ's sake, Charley . . ." I said.

"Keep out of this, Cappy. . . . Now, Captain, let's see how much GI guts you have. I'm going to start to walk toward you and when I get close enough, I'm going to take that little gun away from you and beat hell out of you with it. Here I come."

Charley started to walk toward Grayson.

Grayson looked at him. He looked frightened. "Bronson, don't be a damned fool," he said. "All I want are my shipping orders out of here. Don't make me shoot you."

"You're not going to get anything, Captain—except a hell of a pistol whipping. You yellow little punk. Go ahead and shoot. Go ahead, shoot. Because if you don't, I'm going to beat the shit out of you."

Bronson started walking toward Grayson again. Suddenly the .45 in Grayson's hand went off. The impact shoved Charley halfway across the room. Grayson stood paralyzed, looking down at the pistol in his hand.

197

Charley shook his head and leaped on Grayson. He smashed his fist into his face. The blood spurted from Grayson's nose. I could hear the sound of the breaking bones. Grayson gave a kind of a moan and slipped to the floor. Bronson picked him up and held him against the wall and pounded his fist into his face. The blood was spattered down the front of his uniform. He methodically pounded the fist into Grayson's face—hard. Grayson gave several screams and then passed out. Bronson continued pounding and as he hit he screamed, "You lousy son of a bitch. You couldn't even shoot straight, could you? At ten feet you couldn't hit me in the gut with a forty-five. Goddamn you for that. Goddamn you. . . . Goddamn you. Why couldn't you hit me in the gut?"

I tried to pull him off, but it was useless. I grabbed the Scotch bottle off the table and advanced toward him. He was still pounding Grayson. Grayson's face was one mass of blood. The nose and the jaw were certainly broken and his mouth was one scarlet slash of mashed flesh. As I started to swing the bottle the door was broken open again and two MP's came in. Bronson released Grayson and he slid to the floor. I noticed for the first time that there was blood pouring out of a wound in Bronson's shoulder. He turned to the MP.

"Put this man under arrest," he said. "He's to be charged with attempted murder."

The MP's carried Grayson out. I picked up my musette bag and walked to the door.

"So long, Charley," I said. "It's been a very instructive session."

I walked out. I don't think he even heard me leave. He was standing in the middle of the room, the blood pouring out of his shoulder, crying.

198

La Guardia ☆ 1953

I pushed my way through the crowd on the field, looking for Margaret. The promenade decks behind and above us were jammed with people. The newsreel men were busy taking their stock shots of the crowd, panning up to the tower and taking close-ups of the twelve busloads of kids Buddy had arranged for. There was no sign of Margaret anywhere. I spotted Buddy talking to an NBC television cameraman and beckoned him over to me.

"What happened to Myrna Loy?" I asked him.

"She's gone back to the waiting room."

"Back to the Scotch bottle, you mean. Couldn't you sit on her until I got back?"

"I tried, Harry. She's a very determined woman."

"Yeah."

"She was very co-operative. She even cried a little."

"She's got reason to cry. How long ago did she leave?"

"Ten, fifteen minutes ago at the most. Don't worry about her, Harry. She looks fine."

"Sure."

"Harry, can I ask you something?"

"Sure, Buddy. Shoot."

"This dame swings, doesn't she?"

"What makes you think that?"

"Come on, Harry. This is Buddy, remember? She's a swinger, isn't she?"

"Like the man on the flying trapeze."

"I figured. You know, she's not bad-looking if you like the girdled type."

"She make a pass at you?"

"Are you kidding?"

"No, I'm asking. Did she make a pass at you?"

"Not a pass. I mean, somebody else wouldn't have even noticed it maybe. I got like an antenna for things like that. She was sending."

"Watch yourself, Buddy. She's got a very tough husband."

"How about filling me in on what gives with this bit, Harry?"

"What bit?"

"The returning-hero bit. You're an angle man, Harry. You're not out here for, like, a public service. What's the bit with the General?"

"No bit. It's a job. You're getting paid, aren't you?"

"Sure. Thanks. Like, I needed the job. But come on, Harry. What do we do with the general? Run him for President, maybe?"

"Maybe."

"I'm not kidding, Harry."

"So you're not kidding. I'll fill you in as soon as I know. Right now, you might say we're hitting opportunity targets. The way this guy's luck has been running, the plane will probably plough right into those twelve busloads of school kids. I'm going back and check on Mrs. Miniver. Keep everybody happy and you have my personal guarantee that our hero will arrive eventually."

I pushed my way through the waiting room, by-

200

passing the press bar. If the army didn't get Bronson here pretty soon, I was going to have a lot of drunken newspapermen on my hands. Margaret was sitting in the chair in the inner room. There was a full glass of Scotch in front of her.

I ignored the drink and sat down beside her.

"I hear you did a little crying for the newsreel boys?" I said.

"You should approve of anything that helps get the Scotch out of my system, Harry. I'm just replacing what I lost in the interest of public relations and the newsreel theatres of America."

She held her glass aloft. There was a note of challenge in her voice.

I ignored that, too.

"Harry, I have a great idea," she said. "Why don't we go back to the Waldorf and wait for Charley there. We've done our duty. The newsreels have pictures of me at the airport. Don't you think the Gen should greet his wife and his closest friend in the privacy of his tower apartment at the Waldorf?"

I didn't say anything. I fixed myself a drink.

"Or don't you?" she asked. . . . "You don't," she said. "It was just an idea."

"Margaret, what were Charley's politics?"

"Politics?"

"Was he a Republican, a Democrat or what?"

"Well, let's see. He hated Truman. He thought he handcuffed the army in the Korean War. He wasn't very impressed with Eisenhower. He thought he was a hack officer who got a lot of breaks. He didn't like Mac-Arthur much. To tell you the truth, I don't think he ever voted. Why?"

"Nothing in particular. I just wondered."

201

"You thinking of running him for President? That'd be great. It would be Charley Bronson's moment of triumph. He could do bigger and better things. He wouldn't have to settle for killing just individuals or platoons or companies. He could kill a whole country. I guarantee you, you put Charley Bronson in the White House and he'll start a war in two years. What a chance for Charley to take everybody with him."

"He has to do something. He could run for the Senate. Either party would be delighted to have a national hero on the ticket. It was just an idea."

"I'd be terrified to live in a world where Charley Bronson was making the decisions."

"It seems to me, Margaret, we're always living in a world where the Charley Bronsons are making the decisions. Sometimes they're the enemy, sometimes they're on our side."

"You're being pretty profound for a man who turns down an invitation to go back to the Waldorf."

"You haven't touched your drink, Margaret."

"I know. I really don't want it, Harry."

"Just like you really don't want to go back to the Waldorf. With me or anybody else."

"You are profound."

"You're using both of them as a prop, Margaret. It's a kind of reflex action, isn't it?"

"Is it?"

"Isn't it?"

"And what do I want?"

"Something so simple that it will make both of us laugh—or cry. You want that plane to come down with Charley. You want an uncomplicated Charley who takes you in his arms and says, 'I love you, Margaret. Not Helen or my memory of her. I love you.' You want all the

202

cliché finishes of all the cliché movies you've ever seen. You're really not so complicated at all, Margaret."

"Shut up," she said.

"It seems to me you or Charley are always telling me to shut up. You're feeling so goddamned sorry for yourself, aren't you, Margaret? You've spent your whole married life feeling sorry for yourself. You're on a high-calorie diet of self-pity."

"I suppose it was self-pity when he got drunk rather than face the reality of our wedding night? I suppose it was self-pity when he made love to me and called me by her name? I suppose it was self-pity when he couldn't bring himself to touch me?"

"You began to enjoy the hair shirt, didn't you, Margaret? It itched, but it kept you warm. That's the trouble with hair shirts. You get used to them. Oh, sure, you tried, didn't you? For six months you tried. Or was it a year?"

"Why don't you just shut up, Harry? Or better still, why don't you just walk out of here and leave both of us alone? Who asked for your friendship?"

"Both of you cry out for it. So far I haven't seen any other takers. So I'm afraid I'm it."

"You can talk plainer than that, Harry."

"Oh, we're back to tough old Margaret, are we? The original 'Who needs you?' girl. You're such a tough broad, aren't you? Listen, you want to know what I think?"

She didn't answer me.

"In that case I'll tell you. Sure, you had all the sympathy going for you. But you lost it, honey, when you outsmarted yourself and Charley. He didn't want you, he kept thinking of Helen when he was with you. You couldn't bear that. So you got yourself loaded every night

203

so he wouldn't be diverted by the fact that you were a woman, wouldn't try once more to see if he couldn't make love to you. You gave him his chance on your wedding night and when he booted it, you made sure he wouldn't make another attempt. That fed your self-pity, didn't it? Well . . . if he didn't want it, maybe somebody else did, so you started sleeping around. You didn't enjoy it one damn bit, did you, Margaret? As a matter of fact, it disgusted you, didn't it? But there was something more important than disgust, wasn't there? You were rubbing his nose in it. 'If you don't want it, somebody else does. If you don't like it, Charley, do something about it. Become a husband.' You wanted that more than anything else in the world, but you did the things that made it absolutely impossible for him to be a husband. If you didn't commit the crime, Margaret, you sure as hell were an accessory after the fact."

"All right, Harry. That's enough."

"Is it?"

"Yes. Please."

"O.K."

We didn't say anything for a while. I took a slug of my drink. Margaret sat looking at the glass in her hand. She reached over and put it on the table. It was still full.

"That's better," I said.

"It's a waste of time," she said.

"What is?"

"Figuring this time it's going to be any different. I've been through one hopeful home-coming, Harry."

"And?"

"That one didn't work out, either. It was a little different than this one. There weren't any bands or school kids with flags, or newsreel cameras or TV cameras, or official welcoming committees. I really tried that time,

204

Harry. He came home, whipped, with his tail between his legs, ripe for an understanding wife to console him. I was ready to do that."

"He's had a rough time, Margaret."

"I'm sick of hearing about what a rough time he had. Why did he have a rough time? Why? Because he killed a man. He didn't even use the Germans for an excuse this time. He beat him to death with his fists."

"After the man tried to shoot him. You're forgetting something. I was there. I saw the whole thing. The captain was drunk, pulled a forty-five on him, shot at him and tried to kill him. I testified for him at the Board of Inquiry."

"Fine, Harry. The captain took a shot at him. Fine. Charley took the gun away from him and hit him. How many times do you have to hit a man before he's harmless? You don't splatter his face all over the wall. You don't beat him to death with your fist."

"Sometimes you do."

"If you're Charley Bronson, you mean."

"I don't mean anything. I told you, I was there. Under the couch, but there. I was scared silly. Charley walked toward him and disarmed him."

"And beat him to death. If you were so damned proud of what he did, why did they have to drag you back from Paris to testify at the Board of Inquiry?"

"I had to be in Paris. I had work to do."

"You're a liar, Harry. You saw the Charley Bronson I've been living with all my life. You only saw it for a couple of minutes, but it scared you right out of the repple depple and back to Paris. It didn't fit in with your mental picture of brave old Charley, chess-playing Bronson, did it?"

"How do you know so much about it? I was there, you weren't."

"He told me all the details. He told me how he'd baited the captain. He told me how impossible it is to miss with a forty-five at that range. He told me how mad he was when the captain missed him. He told me how he held him up and hit him again and again."

"He told you?"

"He doesn't know he told me. He was telling it to himself."

"What does that mean?"

"What do you think it means? You're so smart. You're the world's leading expert on Charley Bronson. You're the official best friend, biographer, understander. Where were you when he came back with his tail between his legs?"

"He was cleared by the Board of Inquiry."

"Sure. You don't think the death of one drunken OCS captain is going to wash out one of the members of the club, do you? Sure, they cleared him. They also relieved him of his command within a month and sent him back to the States for reassignment. They cleared him all right. They cleared him right out of the European Theatre of Operations. You didn't hear about the 'Butcher Boy' signs that kept cropping up all over the place at the repple depple, did you? You didn't hear about the sitdown strike when the men refused to go out on ten-mile hikes and listen to lectures on map reading, did you? You didn't hear about the four GI's he put in the stockade in the middle of winter with no blankets, no shelter except a pup tent and a barbed-wire fence? You didn't hear about the silent treatment he was given by his officers who spoke to him only when they were spoken to? You didn't hear about the way he drove a command

206

car off a hill outside Paris? You didn't hear about the whore he brought back with him and moved into his billet at the repple depple? He went out with a blaze of glory, Harry. And they shipped him home on a Liberty Ship to sit out the war in some training camp somewhere in the red clay country of Texas or the dust of Georgia."

"I didn't know about any of those things, Margaret."

"I didn't, either, when I stood at the dock watching that Liberty Ship dock. All I knew was that Charley was coming home. I cried that day, Harry. Do you think all the things you just said to me come as news? Don't you think I told myself the same things? Don't you think I knew I was punishing myself and punishing Charley for something that I walked away from and ignored because I was hurt? I turned over the newest damn leaf you've ever seen. I was Myrna Loy that day for sure, standing on that dock. They had a terrible band from one of the port of embarkation units on the dock playing 'California, Here I Come.' I guess they didn't know 'Sidewalks of New York.' Some overage soprano was singing and there were three starlets who were lifted up for the photographers to kiss three GIs with their heads poking through the portholes. It was, I suppose, a routine return. The war in Europe was over and ships were pulling in with returned GI's. I'd done a lot of thinking, Harry. A lot of thinking about our life together. A lot of thinking about all the things you said off the top of your head a while ago. I stood there on the dock and cried like a baby. I was thinking that I had another chance to make our lives work. I was thinking I didn't need the liquor and the men any more. I was—well—you said it. I was the cliché ending to the cliché movie."

"And?"

"And what?"

"What happened?"

"I watched the reunions on the dock. I watched Pfcs, corporals, sergeants, lieutenants, captains and majors being reunited with their loved ones in the approved photogenic fashion. I watched the Red Cross girls hand out containers of milk and doughnuts. I watched soldiers come down the gangplank with German shepherds on the ends of pieces of rope. I checked with the transportation officer and found out that Charley was on the passenger list. He didn't show up. I tried to talk the T/O into letting me go on board the ship. He wouldn't let me, so I just stood there watching the gangplank, crying and waiting for Charley."

"And?"

"And finally a nice, clean-cut second lieutenant came over and asked me if I was Mrs. Bronson and was I waiting for Colonel Bronson. There would be a slight delay he said. Colonel Bronson was ill and wouldn't be leaving the ship until the next morning. No, he said, it wasn't anything serious. I guess he took pity on me because when the ship was emptied out, he came over and took me up the gangplank. Charley had a stateroom. Rank still had its privileges—even in disgrace. It wasn't anything serious, all right. He was cockeyed drunk. The second lieutenant was terribly embarrassed about it. 'I'm sorry to show you your husband this way, Ma'am,' he said. 'Just didn't want you to think it was anything more serious.'"

"What did you do then?"

"I left a note for Charley and went back to the hotel and got loaded. I went back to the ship the next morning and met him when he walked down the gangplank. We spent three days together in New York before going back to Fallview to visit our families on his leave."

"What were the three days like?"

"Like? I wasn't crying when he walked down the gangplank that second day. We were wary of each other. It was . . . I don't know. This will sound crazy, but we acted around each other the way you chew when you have an exposed nerve. Everytime you bite down you expect to feel a sharp pain and even if the pain doesn't come you don't really enjoy eating. We were very polite to each other. We went to the theatre, had dinner in expensive restaurants. We made love, too. That was part of home-coming, wasn't it? It was a little like the containers of milk and doughnuts at the dock. Part of the ritual. When it was over, Charley went in and took a long, hot shower, came out, kissed me on the cheek and climbed into the other bed and went to sleep immediately. He told me about the Board of Inquiry and being relieved of his command. Just the facts. A drunken captain had attacked him with a forty-five, he had defended himself and killed the captain. The Army felt that under the circumstances it was best to send him back to the States for reassignment. I was very good. I didn't have more than two drinks before dinner. I perfumed myself, made myself as attractive as possible. I made the effort to attract and arouse my husband, hoping, I suppose, that I'd be able to break through to him. Hoping, I suppose, to hear him say all those things you said I wanted him to say."

"He didn't say them?"

"He didn't say them. He started drinking in the morning on that second day. I don't think he was ever really sober while we were in New York. The third night he poured it all out, the whole story. He wasn't telling me. He sat on the bed, so drunk he couldn't see straight. I don't think he even knew I was with him. He told me

209

all about the ambush, all about the whore who looked like Helen. All about goading the captain into shooting him and his fury when it didn't work because the captain was too drunk or too bad a shot to carry out the execution. He told me about driving the command car at seventy miles an hour when he was drunk and turning it over on the side of a hill and walking away from the accident unhurt. The whole story. When he finished he stared at me without seeing me. Then he stood up and drove his fist into the wall and screamed 'Please kill me, somebody. Please, for God's sake . . . have some pity and kill me.' I undressed him and put him in bed. He never knew he'd told me any of it. Or maybe he did. We never talked about it."

"Did he continue drinking?"

"No. He got it out of his system in New York. By the time we got back to Fallview, he had the mask on again. We made the rounds of parties our old friends threw for us and Charley even addressed Rotary and the American Legion Post. I think he'd decided on his strategy. He pretended that none of the unpleasantness had happened. He was just a colonel who had done his share of the fighting and was home on leave. He had a chestful of ribbons, he got the Silver Star for that patrol you went on with him, and he hinted that his leave was only a temporary respite before going back into combat again in the Pacific. All this time he had orders in his pocket posting him to a basic-training camp in Texas. He made a lot of phone calls on that leave. He called every classmate who was now in the Pentagon, trying to get himself shipped to the Pacific. I think he realized it was useless. He could pose as the returned hero in front of the civilians but inside the Club, the West Point Protective Association, his goof-off in Europe was known and evalu-

210

ated. As far as he was concerned, the army had washed him out. He'd had his last responsible job with them. He was just another warm body. . . . Field-grade brass but a warm body. He'd go on for the rest of his career, filling in here, being assigned there but shut out of the top echelon forever. He knew that, but in the back of his head was the nagging thought that if he could just reach the right classmate or the right buddy, strings could be pulled."

"But he never reached the right classmate, did he?"

"He got to be a general, didn't he? He got to be a combat hero, didn't he?"

"I wondered about that. I mean, I wondered how he got himself off the hook, how he got cleared and back into the club."

"I think the worst thing that ever happened to him was the atomic bomb. It couldn't have been more of a catastrophe to him if he'd been underneath it at ground zero."

"How come?"

"He had the war in the Pacific figured out. Now that we were finished with the Germans, we were going to turn our attention to the Japs. It was going to be a tough war. A long war. He had charts showing how many casualties we would have to have to sustain a beachhead landing on the home islands of the Japanese. He had the feeling that time was in his favor. He had the feeling that they were going to chew up a lot of field-grade officers with combat experience, and when they began to reach into the bottom of the barrel, he'd be scooped up and sent back into combat. All he had to do was ingratiate himself with the brass at the Pentagon, do whatever job he was given to do as well as he could and be patient.

Sooner or later they'd have to use him. He had time on his side. Then they dropped the bomb."

"And he'd had it?"

"He'd had it. They'd called time on him. He knew that was it as far as the war in the Pacific was concerned. He knew too that the bomb had made his kind of war obsolete."

"Did his sucking around the Pentagon do him any good at all?"

"I don't know. I suppose so. He became a kind of permanent substitute. A kind of roving colonel, filling in where he was needed."

"What do you mean?"

"Well, if some colonel somewhere was moved up, promoted to brigadier or moved into a more important assignment, Charley was rushed in to take his place temporarily until a promising lieutenant colonel was promoted into the job. Charley was a frozen chicken. They couldn't demote him and therefore there weren't many jobs they could give him. They saved the good assignments for young officers on their way up. So Charley was a seat-warmer. He held down jobs in place of men who were moving up until he was replaced by men who were moving into that job in preparation for moving up themselves. He was frozen. He was a perpetual colonel. It's the West Point variation on Social Security. It's enough to live on but you don't get fat, famous or important that way. When they ran out of those assignments they sent him to school."

"To school?" I asked.

"To school. He studied jungle warfare in Panama. He went to the Command and General Staff School at Leavenworth and studied the principles of atomic warfare. He even spent six months at the language school in

212

Monterey learning Arabic. I sometimes think there must have been somebody at the Pentagon assigned to keeping Charley Bronson moving."

"What was happening between the two of you all this time?"

"Nothing. Nothing was happening. He knew the score. He knew what was happening to him. He knew he was the army version of the Flying Dutchman. But he didn't quit. In the back of his head was the idea that he was going to get off the merry-go-round. This was a penance that he felt he'd earned and he was, by God, going to take it. He took it all right. I didn't. I chickened out. I moved back with my family in Fallview. I even had an excuse. My father had had a stroke. I went back home to be with Mother for a while. But the while became permanent. Dad recovered as much as he was going to recover. He was going to live for five or ten years. There was no reason for me to stay on except a kind of tacit understanding with Charley that I'd leave him alone and let him work out his destiny by himself for a while. So I did. The army was very generous with him. Every time one of those assignments would wash out on him, they'd give him leave and he'd come home to Fallview. He got to be the army officer in residence. He made the speech at the Fourth of July picnic, addressed the Legion on Armistice Day, was made chairman of the community fund and the government bond drive. It must have been a terrible time for him."

"I wondered about him a lot after I walked out on him at the repple depple."

"You did walk out, didn't you?"

"Sure. Remember I'd been case-historied to death by Watson and Armstrong. Their picture of Charley Bronson didn't jibe with the man I knew. But hell, how well did I really know him? We went on that patrol. We played chess together. We liked each other. I liked him enough not to accept the head-shrinking talk of Armstrong and Watson on face value. Then at dinner I watched him needle that young captain. I watched a calculated cruelty that didn't square out with my chess partner. I think he must have sized that captain up pretty accurately. He was looking for an instrument, I guess. God knows how many others he had rejected. He pegged the captain right. Short-tempered, proud and tough. He knew that sooner or later he was going to put the captain in a position that he couldn't ignore or walk away from. He wasn't the least bit surprised when he found himself looking into the muzzle of a forty-five with the safety catch off. He was still in control of the situation. The captain was way out over his head. All he had to be given was the slightest opportunity to save face and he'd have put the gun back in his pocket. Charley wasn't letting that happen. He did everything but draw a target on his belly. He walked into the muzzle of that forty-five and then, when he discovered that his beautifully executed plan backfired, he got mad. His instrument of destruction had turned out to be faulty. There was no doubt in my mind when I left that repple depple that Armstrong and Watson were right about Charley's death wish."

"But you didn't give up on him, did you, Harry? You went back and testified for him at the Board of Inquiry."

"I knew what was going on. I was determined to sit it out. As far as I was concerned, Charley Bronson could get himself off the hook, pull his own chestnuts out of the fire. It was obvious from the beginning that they were going to clear him. I think I was glad. Charley is the kind of a guy you keep giving another mental chance to. You

214

should be the world's greatest authority on that, Margaret."

"I am. If I weren't, I wouldn't be here now, would I? Every time he lets me down, I tell myself that's it. I've learned my lesson, I've had it. But the next chance I get I'm waiting around for him, thinking it's finally going to be different. I feel that way now. Isn't that ridiculous?"

"No. It's not ridiculous at all. Why do you suppose I'm here?"

"You never did tell me, Harry."

"I know what you think of me. I'm a sharpshooter. An angle man. You're right, I am. And yet I don't have a single angle on this, a single axe to grind. The politics bit is so much hogwash. I don't think I could go through with it, knowing Charley Bronson the way I know him now. I don't think the country could survive him. We used to live in a simpler world. If the President was a chowder head, incapable of making decisions, out of touch with reality, insulated by a palace guard that kept unpleasantness away from him, it didn't make too much difference. Four years or eight years wasn't forever and we somehow went along without it making too much difference. It makes a hell of a difference now. We can't afford that kind of leadership any more. Sure . . . worship our heroes. Give them parades and pensions. Make movies about their lives. Put them in the history books, but don't give them the world to run. The fact that a man is a good general doesn't make him a statesman. Let's, for God's sake, stop making everybody a substitute father and relaxing because Father will take care of it, Father knows best. Father, a lot of the time is a god-damned fool to anyone over twelve years of age, who isn't related to him by blood. You're right, it would terrify me to live in a world where decisions affecting

215

life and death—the life and death of all of us—are made by the Charley Bronsons."

"What makes you think we're not living in that kind of a world right now?"

"Then for Christ's sake let's not make a dynasty out of it. Once we get out of the contract, let's breathe a sigh of relief and get down on our knees and thank God that we've survived it. So, scratch politics for Charley. There goes one angle. That leaves me without an angle to my name."

"You must feel naked."

"You know why I'm here, Margaret?"

"For the same reason I'm here."

"More or less. The Charley Bronsons of the world put a terrible burden of friendship on people who are caught by them. For instance, when the story broke about Korea, I hustled over to see you. I figured Charley had finally gotten his break. He was finally off the hook after a complete kicking around. I had no confidence that he wouldn't somehow manage to mess it up. This is something I know about, this hoopla, this puffing up something out of all proportion to its actual worth. I've done it for big bosomed broads, why not for Charley? So here I am, the angle man, naked of any ulterior motive."

"I think I knew that, Harry."

"Of course you knew it. You just went through the motions of being tough old Margaret with me. You lay a friendship claim on people too, Margaret."

"I suppose I do. I've never been aware of it before."

"Let me finish about Charley for a minute. You've filled in a lot of the gaps for me. Here is a poor guy carrying two very big burdens on his back. He's born with an obligation. He's lived all his life in a world he never made. He never had any free choice about anything. It

216

was all laid out for him when he was nine by his mother and the memory of his father. So he was going to be an army officer. In that case he'd be a damn good one. That means a successful one and in this game you're just a junior executive until you put a star on your shoulder. So he's been running after that star all his life. And he might have made it, too. He had all the equipment for it. Now add the second burden. Helen. Guilt. He couldn't shake either one of them off. He made the mistake of combining them—of trying to accomplish both ends with the same means. What Charley would have liked would be to have had himself killed in such a daring, brilliant way that he'd have been made a brigadier general posthumously. Guilt and obligation. Between them, they destroyed him."

"You know something, Harry. I don't even think he ever really missed Helen after she was killed. Missed her as a woman, I mean. I don't think he felt any great consuming loss. I don't mean that he wasn't in love with Helen. He was. But I think if she'd died of pneumonia or t.b. or something like that, he'd have been able to build an emotional life for himself. But feeling that he had killed her, he had that on his conscience and on his back all his life. It kept him from having a normal relationship with me. He'd have felt even more guilty about that. You know something?"

"What?"

"I think I can have a drink now. I've talked all the other alcohol out of my system."

"What happens with the drinking now, Margaret?"

"That depends on Charley. The drinking wasn't ever that important. It was a substitute. You see, Harry? I'm still convinced that this time things will be different. God, how many 'this times' there have been in my life!"

"The Korean War surprised him, didn't it, Margaret? He thought he'd run out of wars in his lifetime, didn't he?"

"I suppose he did. He gave up on getting himself killed. He went after that star on his shoulder another way. Maybe I was wrong, Harry. Maybe I was wrong to run out on him and run back to Fallview. I don't know. I'd had enough. He had to take it himself for a while."

She got some ice and freshened up the drink on the table next to her. She raised her glass in a mock salute and took a good healthy belt out of it. I raised my glass and did the same.

"Where the hell is that plane?" she asked.

"The weather's bad. They're probably flying around a storm front. He'll be here, don't worry about it."

"Who's worrying?"

"You mean besides you? Me, for one."

"What are you worrying about?"

"Charley and I haven't seen each other in five years. We weren't exactly blood brothers when we parted that time."

"Where did you meet him, Harry?"

"In New York. In a bar."

"Five years ago. There were so many assignments. I'm trying to figure out exactly when it was."

"You weren't with him. He was working out of Ninety Church Street, I think. It was a temporary assignment."

"They were all temporary assignments."

"I was startled to see him sitting at the bar. I didn't really think it was Charley. I remember thinking: That guy looks like Charley Bronson. He hadn't changed a bit."

"That's amazing isn't it, Harry?"

218

"What?"

"The fact that he hadn't changed. He never changed. He always looked like everybody's idea of a career army officer."

"It's funny, I don't think I'd thought about him at all after I testified in front of that Board of Inquiry. And yet when I saw him there, it was as if I'd seen him the night before. He looked exactly the same. All the years between the time I'd seen him last and the night in that bar just faded away."

"I know what you mean," said Margaret.

"Did he ever tell you about our meeting and what happened?"

"I wasn't with him much then. I was back in Fallview. He was on the road, like a traveling salesman, filling in."

"It was quite an evening."

New York ☆ 1948

I suppose everybody remembers exactly where he was on VE Day. I know I've listened to more drunks tell me in great detail where they were and what they were doing when they heard the news that the war in Europe was over. Somehow the fact that they heard it in the bathtub, while shaving or while tying their shoelaces gave it a kind of wonder. I remember one guy who told me he was lying on a table in an operating room. Just as the anesthetist lowered the nose cone with the ether, he said casually, 'I suppose you heard the war is over?' That was one of the few unique experiences I'd heard about. What ether-induced dreams that must have conjured up.

I heard about it during one of the most unpleasant periods of my life. When it became obvious that the war in Europe was coming to an end, I was ordered home by the paper. I boarded a Liberty Ship at Le Havre along with five hundred and seven GI's bound for the States for discharge or redeployment to the Pacific. Liberty ships may have won the war, but they are high on anybody's list of the most unpleasant way man has devised to cross an ocean. Expediency gives short shrift to comfort. The GI's were herded into the forward compartment of the ship. They slept on canvas hammocks sus-

220

pended in rows of six by steel chains attached to the steel upright poles that ran from floor to ceiling. It wasn't too bad during the day because all of us immediately upon rising headed for the open deck and the sunshine and fresh air. After a night in the hold that was only slightly more bearable than the Black Hole of Calcutta, fresh air —even the biting fresh air of the North Atlantic—was one of the few luxuries we had left. The chow lines started at dawn and snaked around the ship. Just about the time the last man had been fed breakfast, it was time to line up for lunch. Chow consisted of powdered eggs and scalding tasteless coffee for breakfast . . . creamed chipped beef and scalding, tasteless tea for lunch and a congealed mass that the army insisted was chili con carne and scalding, tasteless coffee, for dinner. The loudspeaker on the bridge blared music all day long. There were speakers all over the ship and it was impossible to escape the sound. After a while, escaping the sound became a major war aim. There was only one record in the ship's record library . . . a scratched platter of André Koste-lanetz's medley of hits from "Oklahoma." If the days were monotonous and irritating, the nights were worse. The ship reeled and pitched so hard that sleep was out of the question. Crap games went on in the aisles of the com-partment on a twenty-four-hour basis. Water was reason-ably scarce and the showers ran sea water.

Going dirty was the lesser of the two evils. And, of course, with the war still on, the ship was buttoned up tight at night. That meant five hundred and seven unwashed GIs in the compartment and "The Surrey with the Fringe on Top" making one more scratched voyage around the turntable. On board a Liberty Ship in 1945, war was undeniably hell!

The tenth day out the news of the unconditional

221

surrender was announced over the loudspeaker. The announcement came right between "Oh, What a Beautiful Morning" and "People Will Say We're in Love." There was a halfhearted cheer from the GI's. Those who were bound for a separation center and civilian life had long since given up any feeling of participating in the war. Those who were bound for the Pacific felt that they would wind up back in a fighting war sooner, now that all the attention was turned toward the defeat of Japan. My only feeling was one of relief that we no longer had to button up the ship at night and that it would be possible to get away from the Great Unwashed Soldiers of Democracy and sleep on deck. I might freeze to death, but at least I'd go with a pleasant smell in my nostrils. I suppose it was a fitting way to end the war. Any illusions about glamour and excitement went down the drain on that interminable voyage on the Liberty Ship.

It took me a while to get adjusted to civilian life. I suddenly realized how much freedom I'd had as a correspondent. I was at least an ocean away from a boss and as long as the copy kept coming in and was usable, I was free to move around as I pleased. It took a while getting used to having a city editor's beery breath on the back of my neck. I missed being able to pull up stakes when I wanted to. I was a working stiff again and the crowd around Bleeck's had had their fill of war stories and exploits. I requested a couple of months on general assignment, covering police headquarters, chasing fire engines and covering knifings in Harlem. It was a good bridge back to the normal life of being a reporter. Then I was assigned a special series. I did twenty-five pieces on Congressional Medal of Honor winners, where they were now, that kind of thing. In 1946 I wrote a book, sold it to the movies, took a leave of absence and went out to

222

the Coast to do the screenplay. When I got back from the Coast, I was assigned, on a temporary basis, to doing a column. I took to it right away. It was a license to steal. I was flooded with review copies of books, tickets to all the openings, cases of Scotch from night-club owners as Christmas presents and a due bill on everything that was happening in New York. Doing a column is the greatest thing in the world for the ego. Americans will do almost anything to get their name in a Broadway column. It's the closest thing to immortality the twentieth century has come up with. I learned all the tricks of the trade. A monthly mention of a restaurant took care of all my eating bills. Press agents fed me all sorts of scandal in exchange for a plug for a client. Somebody was always running a free junket to somewhere and it was like the war all over again. As a columnist, I was free to roam as I pleased as long as the copy kept flowing in. After a while it began to be a big bore. I think you have to be terribly frightened or terribly insecure or terribly ego-centric to continue writing a column for a living. The saturation point set in about a year after I started. Making the rounds of the night clubs stopped being fun and became a routine job. One night I dropped into a new bar in the Forties. I was paying the hat-check girl twenty bucks a week to feed me items. I had a fast drink at the bar, heard a couple of dirty stories from the bartender and got a fill-in from the hat-check broad on which Hollywood stallion was making time with which international tramp. I was finishing my drink when I looked into the mirror at the bar.

That guy in the blue suit looks like Charley Bronson, I thought. I turned to look at him, first hand. It was Charley Bronson. He saw me at the same moment and we just looked at each other. For a minute it looked as if neither of us would recognize the other and then suddenly he smiled that wonderfully warm smile of his, and started walking toward me. He took the stool next to me and put his hand out. We shook hands very solemnly.

"I thought it was you, Cappy. How are you?"

"Fine, Charley. What'd you do, quit the army?"

"Huh?"

"The civilian suit."

"Oh. No, I haven't quit. I just don't wear the uniform when I'm off duty."

"I can see how you wouldn't now that the Stage Door Canteen is closed."

"How are you, Cappy? I've wondered about you. Of course, I read the column, so I know what you're doing. I've almost called you a couple of times, but I wasn't sure you'd want to hear from me."

"Why not?"

"As I remember it, the last time I saw you, you weren't thinking of running me for President."

"I'm sorry about that whole thing, Charley. I was glad to hear that they cleared you."

"Were you?"

"Sure."

We didn't say anything for a couple of minutes. I ordered another drink for myself and a Scotch for Charley.

"How has it been?" I asked.

"Rough," he said. "Rough as a corn cob. Rough as Corn Cob Corridon. Remember him?"

"Sure."

"I'm assigned to Ninety Church, temporarily. I've been assigned to a lot of things temporarily lately, Cappy. The army's kept me moving. It's gotten to the point

224

where I don't even bother to unpack my suitcase any more."

"Margaret with you?"

"No. She's home in Fallview. Her father had a stroke."

"Still a colonel, Charley?"

"Still a colonel. How's your chess, Cappy?"

"I don't play much any more."

"Me either. I still have that set you gave me back at the repple depple."

"I have one just like it. I had the guy in Paris make one for me."

"Fine," he said.

"Yeah."

It seemed as if we'd suddenly run out of conversation. We drank our drinks and I slid off the bar stool. I was ready to turn around, shake hands, say it was great to run into him and I hoped we'd see each other again soon and take off. There were a lot of reunions like that in 1948. I turned and held my hand out.

"Don't go, Cappy. Please."

I sat back on the stool and signaled to the bartender for another drink.

"You don't have to be anywhere special, do you?"

"No," I said. "Nowhere special."

"I wanted to write you a letter, Cappy, when that whole thing was over. I know how you felt about it. I know how you felt about me and I wanted to thank you for what you said at the inquiry. You had a lot to do with clearing me."

"I just told them what happened."

"A lot of things happened that you didn't tell them, Cappy."

"They didn't ask for an analysis. At those prices, I

just tell what happened. I don't give them the benefit of my shrewd appraisal of human emotions and actions."

"How do you feel about me now?"

"To tell you the truth, Charley. I don't feel anything about you. I haven't even thought about you in the past two years. I'm glad to see you looking so well. Sorry the war blew up on you. Wars will do that. I assume you didn't get back into combat?"

"No. They bounced me all the way back to Fallview. I behaved myself pretty well. The A bomb took care of any more combat for me."

"Too bad, Charley. Too goddamned bad. They went and took your nice little war away from you. You'd have made such a nice general, too, wouldn't you?"

"I deserved that. I didn't mean it the way it sounded."

"The hell you didn't."

"The hell I didn't."

I felt nasty all of a sudden.

"Tell me something, Charley."

"What?"

"What kind of a funeral did they give that captain? What's the army protocol when a captain gets beaten to a pulp by a drunken colonel because he can't shoot straight? Do they sound taps over his grave? Do they fire a volley? Do they drape a flag over the coffin? Does he get a posthumous Purple Heart? Does his mother get a gold star to put in her window? Do they name an American Legion Post after him?"

Bronson got up from the stool and started to walk away. I grabbed his arm and turned him around.

"I'm sorry, Charley," I said. "I'm turning into a nasty drunk."

He sat down and finished his drink.

226

"They just bury them, Cappy. They pay off on the GI insurance, but they just bury them."

"Forget it, Charley. It's none of my business."

"I went to see his mother."

"And?"

"She had hysterics when I told her who I was. She screamed at me. . . . To hell with it. How are you?"

"You asked me that. A couple of times."

"I read your book and saw your movie. I liked both of them."

"Thanks."

"You suppose we could play chess again some time, Cappy?"

"Sure. What have they got you doing, Charley?"

"Errands. I'm the highest-paid errand boy in the world. As a taxpayer, Cappy, you should object to the way they're overpaying me. Actually this job is better than most of the ones I've had since the war. I work out of the public-relations office. I'm in charge of VIP's from Washington. I arrange for their hotel accommodations, get them tickets for the theatre, chaperone them around, do whatever little chores they want done."

"Sounds fine."

"Yeah. Fine."

"Why don't you quit?"

"And do what? I can retire in a couple of years and live off my pension. That's a laugh, isn't it? You know how much pension I'll get? . . . To hell with it."

"What're you doing here tonight? You turned into a pub crawler in your old days?"

"You'd be surprised. I know every headwaiter in town. I know where to get tickets for shows you can't get tickets for. I have phone numbers that are guaranteed to entertain the troops and get them out of the hot sun.

227

You'd be surprised the things I'm learning in the peacetime army. Tonight, Mr. Williams, I am the companion, friend and buddy of one of the nation's great heroes, General Holly Halloran. You have, I'm sure, heard of General Halloran?"

"No. That doesn't mean anything. I've never been as fascinated by generals as you were."

"General Holly Halloran is a fat-ass bungler who spent the war in Washington. We were classmates at the Point. But General Halloran managed to worm his way into the Pentagon inner circle. General Halloran managed to get that star on his shoulder without hearing a gun fired in anger. General Halloran happens to be in New York and I have been assigned to expedite his mission. As far as I can figure out, his mission is to get loaded and laid, as often as possible."

"The Armstrong Theory."

"Something like that. At any rate, any minute an overweight, playful puppy will come through that door, poke me in the ribs and say 'Where are the broads, Bronson?'"

"And where are the broads, Bronson?"

"On their way. They've been ordered."

"So the colonel is also a pimp, as well as an errand boy?"

"That's a very unpleasant way of putting it, Cappy. The colonel is operating as supply officer. Within a half hour we shall be a jolly little group of four. We shall start from here, go on to another, more expensive place for dinner, from there to a musical, from there to another night club, from there to the general's suite for fun and games. Or is it recreation and rehabilitation?"

"Is that really what you do, Charley?"

"That's really what I do. And two days from now,

228

General Halloran will go back to Washington and another general will be in with basically the same mission. It's quite a responsible job."

"You're back at the sidewalk café on the Grand Boulevard."

"Don't you think I'm earning that star, Cappy?"

"You're really still bugged on that, aren't you?"

"They owe it to me. I've taken every dirty assignment they've given me. I've done the job as well as I could. I've never once said, 'This is beneath me; this is a dirty deal,' or, 'How dare you.' I've done the job. And two years from now, when I apply for retirement, I'll get that star. It helps if you're wearing this ring, Cappy. When they retire you, they almost always automatically promote you, as a courtesy. And sitting on the promotion board will be a lot of guys who've had their ashes hauled through the courtesy of good old Charley Bronson who had the little black book with all those hot numbers in it."

"Sounds great, Charley. And where did you get all the numbers in the little black book? I thought it was spectator sport as far as you were concerned?"

"My predecessor willed it to me. And you'd be surprised how many new numbers you can pick up for a little black book if you're really trying. You're a big-shot columnist, Cappy. You know your way around, don't you? I'll bet I could take you on a tour of this town that would knock your hat off. I can take you to every after-hours joint in the five boroughs. I could take you to places that would make the old Sphinx in Paris look like a ladies' seminary. I can make one phone call and satisfy any vice that any visiting VIP might want to practice."

"When you do a job, you really do it, don't you, Charley?"

229

"It's a lousy way to end up, isn't it?"

"It beats going on patrol."

"Can you stick with us, Cappy? Come on, it might be good for some laughs for you."

"Laughs come harder these days, Charley."

"Please."

"Sure. Why not? How many girls do you have ordered?"

"Two. Young ones. Holly Halloran likes them young, blonde and cuddly. I can get another one for you, if you'd like."

"No thanks. I'll just come along, like you said, for laughs."

We had another drink and fifteen minutes later, almost to the minute a tall, red-faced man with a potbelly stood in the doorway looking over the room. He spotted Charley sitting at the bar and came up behind him. He put his arm around Charley's shoulder. "Where are the broads, Bronson?"

Charley put on a smile and turned around and hit the general on the shoulder.

"I was beginning to worry about you, Gen," he said. "I figured you were captured by a band of white slavers."

The general laughed. All of him.

"By God, that's a good one, Bronson. White slavers. I must remember that one. By God! That's a good one!"

"Gen, I want you to meet a friend of mine. This is Harry Williams. You've probably read his column."

"You bet I have. How are you, Williams?"

"Fine, General."

"This is Holly Halloran, Harry," said Charley.

"Harry?" I said.

"That's your name, isn't it?"

230

"Sure," I said. "That's my name. Glad to meet you, General."

"Make it Holly, Harry. No ceremony tonight. Well, Bronson, where are the broads?"

"They should be here any minute, Gen. What'll you have?"

"Two blondes and a brunette for a chaser. That's a good one, isn't it, Charley? Two blondes and a brunette." All of him laughed again.

"By God!" I said. "That's a good one. You don't mind if I use that in my column, do you, General?"

"What do you think, Bronson? You think it's all right?"

"I think it's all right, Gen. Harry will write it so everybody will know you were kidding."

"I don't know. You sure Sally will understand that it's a joke? My wife, Sal, Mr. Williams, reads your column every day. How about that 'Mr. Williams.' It just slipped out, Harry."

"That's all right, Holly. It just shows you were brought up properly."

"I guess it'd be all right if you use it like it was a kind of a joke."

"Thanks, Holly. That's real decent of you. It'll make the column and all the boys back at the paper will be so pleased."

Charley stepped on my foot and I decided, for his sake, to knock off on the sarcasm. I think he was being unjustifiably careful. Old Holly Halloran was immune to sarcasm.

"Did Charley tell you we were classmates at the Point?" asked Holly.

"Yes, I think he did," I said.

"He was right at the top of the class, first captain.

231

Weren't you, Charley? I was down in the bottom third. Just managed to get through. How about that? And here we are. I got the star on my shoulder and old First Captain Bronson is still a chicken colonel."

"That," I said, "is the way the old ball bounces."

"We're gonna get that star for Charley, don't you forget it. Old Holly Halloran is a good man to have on your side. I don't mind telling you, Harry, I pull a little weight down there at the Pentagon. One of these days Charley'll get that star."

"Does he really?" I whispered to Bronson.

Holly was busy telling the bartender how to mix a grasshopper. The bartender viewed the whole thing with a mixture of suspicion and disgust.

"Does he what?" asked Charley.

"Swing any weight? Can he get you the star?"

"He can get it for me. He won't though. Not until he has another one. It wouldn't do for old bottom-of-the-class Halloran to be a brigadier while First Captain Bronson is a Brigadier."

"I see what you mean," I said.

"Say," said Holly. "This bartender catches on real fast. This is a pretty good grasshopper."

"It looks it," I said.

At this point, the girls joined us. Charley had done his shopping carefully. If Halloran liked them young and blonde and cuddly, Charley had placed the right order. We were all introduced. The general immediately filed a claim on Joan, the youngest, blondest and cuddliest. Charley and I made conversation with Deedee. Deedee and I were old friends. If you cover the night-club beat the way I did, you get to know most of the call girls. I'd met Deedee first when she'd arrived in town from Columbus, Ohio, and went to work in the chorus of one

232

of the clubs. I watched her change from a bright, young, eager kid into the wise, hard-drinking café-society playmate into the hundred-dollar-a-night call girl. I don't know how many hundred-dollar-a-night call girls you know personally. I've always had a lot of respect for them. It isn't all El Morocco and silk sheets. A lot of wives could learn a lot of things from them. They're artists at flattering a man's ego. They laugh at his jokes, hang on his every word and take him arm protectively when they cross a street. When you consider the sheer boredom they must put up with every night in the week, you come to the conclusion that they're underpaid.

We had a couple of drinks at the bar. Holly Halloran took the bartender through the grasshopper course again and went into a long description of how the drink is made with the girls oh-ing and ah-ing as though he had just discovered penicillin. I stuck to Scotch. I was a little surprised to find Charley switching to grasshoppers and telling Holly how wonderful they were. There was a long discussion about where to go for dinner. The girls were plugging for a new French restaurant that had opened on the ground floor of a new apartment house on Lexington Avenue. I'd been there and knew that it would cost a fortune for the four of them, so I weighed in with the opinion that it was the only place to go. That settled it for Holly Halloran. I was delighted as I figured out how big a hole it was going to make in his bank roll. He insisted that I join them. I begged off.

"Please come, Cappy," said Charley.

"Does it matter to you?" I asked him.

"It matters a hell of a lot. I haven't seen you in a long time."

"I somehow don't think we're going to get much of a chance to talk about old times or play any chess."

"He likes you, Cappy. He's impressed with you."

"And that'll help you, won't it?"

"Sure."

"Fine. That's the old soldier, all right. Use whatever material comes to hand."

"Do you mind?"

"Why should I mind? Sure I'll have dinner with you on one condition."

"Which is?"

"If he's picking up the tab."

"He's picking up the tab all right."

"Good. I'll eat my head off. I think we can trust Joan and Deedee to ignore the right-hand side of the menu."

It didn't quite turn out that way. The manager of the restaurant recognized me and refused to give us a check. I made a note to mention his goddamned place in the column in the next week or ten days.

By the time dinner was over with, I was fed up to my ears with General Holly Halloran. He laughed loud and long at everything he said. Since he did most of the talking, that was a lot of laughter. He also told long, involved, unfunny, dirty jokes. He also belched. I was a little sore at Charley for the way he fawned over the general. He was servile and ingratiating. He really wanted that star bad and was trying to get it the hard way. They had tickets for "High Button Shoes." I didn't think I was up to Holly's reactions to the Mack Sennett Ballet, so I copped out when we left the restaurant. I promised to meet them afterwards at the Latin Quarter. [You know it was the Latin Quarter. You know it.]

I had no intention of showing up, but by twelve fifteen I had finished making the rounds. I had enough

234

notes in my pockets for the column and I found myself walking toward Forty-seventh Street.

I had no trouble finding them. The Latin Quarter is normally a pretty noisy place, but I'm sure I could have just stood at the door, closed my eyes and listened and horned in on the sound of Holly Halloran's laughter. He was, of course, laughing at his own jokes. Charley said he knew most of the headwaiters in town. He certainly knew this one because they had a ringside table. Of course, Charley may have had nothing to do with it. General Halloran had "Big Spender" written all over him. I threaded my way through the tables and pulled up a chair and joined them. . . .

"Where have you been, Harry? We're a couple of bottles of champagne ahead of you," said Holly.

"I'm not even going to try to catch up," I said.

"Fine," said Holly. He turned to Joan and put his arm around her. She smiled. It was reflex action.

"You know this guy is a big-shot Broadway columnist, honey? I mean, I read him over breakfast every morning. How about that?"

Joan smiled at me.

"Listen, Harry," said Holly, taking his arm from around Joan and putting it on my shoulder. "Listen, Harry. I want you to put it in your column. This girl here has one damn fine singing voice. Now don't be embarrassed, Honey, you can use the plug. You could say: 'Deedee Marshall has the sweetest singing voice these tired old ears of mine have heard in many a moon.' How's that?"

"Let me get that down," I said. " 'Tired old ears.' My God, Holly, you have a brilliant talent for imagery. 'In many a moon.' You know that's almost poetry."

General Holly Halloran beamed. He turned to Joan

again. "And you can say that Joan—Honey, what did you say your last name was?"

"Marshall," she said.

"Marshall. You mean you and Deedee are sisters?"

"Mother and daughter," I said.

"Really?" said Holly. "I'll be damned. . . . Oh. . . . You're kidding. That's a good one all right, mother and daughter. That's a real good one."

"I thought so," I said.

Charley looked at me and pleaded with his eyes.

"You can say," continued Holly, "that Miss Joan Marshall is the greatest—what is it you do, honey?"

I didn't say a word.

"I'm a model," said Joan.

"That Miss Joan Marshall is the world's greatest model. You know, maybe you could give her an orchid or a bravo or whatever it is those fellows do in the columns."

"I think I'll just say they both have General Holly Halloran's seal of approval. Like *Good Housekeeping*, only more rigid."

"That's a good one," said Holly. "More rigid."

"Harry's only kidding, Gen," said Charley.

"What do you mean kidding? What the hell's wrong with Holly Halloran's rigid seal of approval?" He went into gales of laughter again.

"Holly, you said yourself you read Harry's column at breakfast," said Charley.

"Sure I did. Be a damned big improvement to have my name in it. Right, girls?"

The girls laughed on cue.

"Who reads it with you, Holly?" asked Charley.

"Oh," said Holly. "I get you now. You mean Sal? What Charley's trying to say, Harry, is that he's not sure

236

my wife Sal would understand. Hell, Sal's pretty broad-minded."

A big laugh started in his belly. I steadied myself.

"Sal may be broad-minded," he said between guffaws. "But she's not anywhere near as *broad*-minded as I am. That's a good one, Harry. Get it? *Broad*-minded? Get it?"

"I got it."

"Say, Harry. You oughta put in a good word about that show we saw tonight, I mean it deserves it. I mean you could say, 'General Holly Halloran puts his rigid approval on 'High Button Shoes.' It's a damned fine show. A jim-dandy."

"I'll do that, Holly. Now if you'll all excuse me, I think I'd better get back home. I have a column to write."

"Now you just sit still, Harry," said Holly. "You stick with us, boy, and we'll give you enough material to fill your column for six weeks. Won't we, girls?"

"I'm sure of it," I said. "Excuse me for a minute. I have to make a phone call."

I got up from the table and headed for the lobby. Charley came along with me. I went into the men's room and he followed me.

"Pretty grim," he said.

"Charley," I said. "If you feel a homicidal tendency coming over you, you have my permission to give it free rein."

"You're not really leaving, are you, Cappy?"

"You're damned right, I'm leaving. And listen, Charley, if you have any compassion in you for the poor overworked call girls of New York, you'll keep pouring that domestic champagne into Friend Holly so that Deedee and Joan can get home free."

237

"He's pretty awful, isn't he?"

"Your Gen friend is the greatest anti-war argument I've ever seen. One evening with General Holly Halloran and I'm willing to fold an umbrella and go to Munich. Anything to keep from putting him in command of anything except a couple of paid-for blondes."

"He let something slip tonight."

"His lid?"

"He's getting another star."

"The military mind passeth all understanding."

"You know what that means, Cappy?"

"No, Charley, what does it mean?"

"It means that he can push for my star if he wants to."

"And if he has a good time tonight, he's going to want to."

"And he's impressed by you. How about it?"

"Why the hell do people do what you want them to do? I want to get the hell out of here and go home. I don't want to spend two more consecutive minutes in the vicinity of General Holly Halloran. But because it may just do you some good, I'm going back to rejoin him at the table and slap my thigh everytime he opens his mouth."

"And you're even going to put his name in your column tomorrow morning."

"Now wait a minute, Charley. Enough is enough. . . ."

"It's going to hurt to say that he's in town on a special hush-hush mission."

I smiled.

"That's a good one," I said. "A real good one. A jim-dandy. Damned fine."

"How about it?"

238

"Sure. Holly Halloran isn't the first bore that's made the column."

We went back to the table and sat through the show. Holly co-starred with the comic, throwing the punch lines before the comic could deliver them. That gives you some idea of the comic's material. The gen finished two more bottles of champagne personally and did a fair shimmy with the chorus line. He got a big hand from the rest of the drunks scattered around the night club and, as an encore, he did a very creditable Charleston. Charley did his best to head the party out after the show, but old Holly wasn't having any of that. He ordered more champagne and got to his feet.

"Excuse me," he said. "I have to go to the head."

He leaned over, put his arm around my shoulder and screamed in my ear. "That's navy talk for the latrine," he said and roared with laughter. Still laughing, he lurched across the floor and headed for the men's room.

"You're in luck," I said to Deedee. "You're with Charley here."

"That's what you think. Old lobster claws has big plans for both of us. He filled me in on the whole picture."

"Now's your chance to beat it."

"Thanks," said Deedee. "I'll stick. I signed on for the duration."

"That's the old American spirit that won the war," I said.

"Listen," said Joan. "We spent two hours in the library reading up about West Point, the army and Washington."

"You what?" asked Charley.

"You heard me. We always do that. When we have

239

an assignment, we prepare for it. Like last week when the Hardware Convention was in town, we had dates all week with hardware dealers. Between us we knew more about the hardware business than Sears or Roebuck."

"You really do that?" asked Charley.

"Certainly," said Deedee. "The customers we get like to talk about themselves. We're a service, so if a man wants to talk about himself it helps if you know what he's talking about. It flatters him if you ask him the right questions. You'd be surprised some of the information we've picked up in our line of work."

"Frankly," I said, "I doubt that old Holly is going to want to talk about Flirtation Walk or the Office of Strategic Services. And speaking of our departed friend— what do you suppose happened to him?"

"Nothing happened to him," said Charley. "Nothing ever happens to the Holly Hallorans of the world."

"Listen," I said, "why don't we just get up while he's gone and meet him in the lobby and get him out of here before he's aware of what we're doing?"

"Good idea," said Charley.

I signaled for the waiter.

He came over to the table. "There'll be no check, Mr. Williams. You and your party are the guests of the management."

"No," I said. "Please. I'd rather you didn't."

"I'm sorry, Sir," said the waiter. "I'm just obeying orders."

So I overtipped him. So far Holly had had a pretty cheap evening. I wondered if Deedee and Joan were going to give him a due bill for a mention in the column. I took out the notebook while I thought of it and reminded myself to drop in a mention of the "Jim dandy show at the Latin Quarter."

240

When we got to the lobby, the girls excused themselves and headed for the ladies' room. There was no sign of the general, so we went into the men's room. He was standing on top of a toilet bowl calling out close-order drill commands. The attendant was executing about faces, right turns and to-the-rear marches. I broke it up.

"You don't have to break it up on my account," said the attendant. "Your friend has had a little bit too much. He thinks he's a general. I don't mind. He's paying me a quarter for every time I do the right thing. I'm seven bucks into him now."

I gave him a ten-dollar bill. "You owe the general twelve about faces," I said.

"Yessir."

The world's greatest living general was rather noisily sick. The attendant stuck Holly's head under the cold-water faucet, dried him off and combed his hair.

"Damned fine noncom material," said Holly.

"Yessir," said the attendant. "Next time you come here, General, I pay you those twelve about faces."

"That's all right," said Holly. "Keep it as a tip."

"Thank you, Sir."

By the time we got him into the lobby he was feeling better. Joan and Deedee were waiting for us. He advanced on them, put his arms around both of their waists and shouted, "Let's get these troops out of the hot sun. Smoke if you got 'em. Sir, she walks, she talks, she's full of chalk, the lacteal fluid extracted from the female of the bovine species is highly prolific to the nth degree."

A look of great joy came over Deedee's face. "Holly, baby," she said, "how are they all?"

"They are all fickle but one, Sir," said Holly.

Joan got into the act. "How many lights in Cullum Hall?" she asked.

"Three hundred and forty lights, Sir." Holly looked at both of them. "I'll be damned," he said. "You," he said, pointing to Deedee, "what do plebes rank?"

Deedee snapped to attention and saluted. "Sir," she said, "the superintendent's dog, the commandant's cat, the waiters in the mess hall, the hell cats and all the admirals in the whole blamed navy."

"I'll be damned," said Holly. "I'll be damned. Aren't you a pair of jim-dandy girls!"

Between us, we managed to get the jim-dandy girls and the general into a cab. Charley gave the driver the address of Halloran's hotel. He was having none of that.

"We are not going back to the hotel," he said. "Not yet. Dammit, Bronson, is this the way you take care of your superior officer? I am the highest-ranking officer present and I shall give the order of march. We are not going back to the hotel."

Charley looked at me and shrugged his shoulders.

"Beat Navy," I said.

We went to an after-hours joint in the East Eighties. Fortunately they didn't know me there, so Halloran got stuck for the tab, which was a whopper. From there the five of us went back to Holly Halloran's hotel. He opened a bottle of Scotch and bribed the elevator operator to get him a carton of ice. He lurched into the bedroom. "Be right back," he said.

"OK, Charley," I said. "I've done my duty. I'm cutting out."

"Thanks, Cappy," he said. "I'm very grateful to you. Strange as it seems that slob can really help me."

"Sure," I said. "Any slob that can help you is a

friend, indeed. Like good old chess-playing, honest-witness Williams."

I was sorry I said it as soon as it was out. But what the hell! I figured Charley had one coming to him after the evening he'd put me through.

"You really going to put our names in your column, Harry?" asked Deedee.

"Sure," I said. "I may do a whole column on our gala evening together."

Holly came running back into the room. He was holding a Polaroid camera. They were brand-new that year. They'd just come out for the Christmas trade.

"I wanted to show you what I bought old Sal for Christmas. How about this thing. You take a picture and a minute later, it's all developed. Isn't that a jim-dandy?"

We all agreed it was a jim-dandy. He attached the flash holder and took pictures of all of us. I took a picture of him kissing Deedee and then, for a change of pace, took a picture of him kissing Joan. They came out fine, sharp and clear.

"Won't old Sal just about bust a gut when she sees this?" he asked.

"It'll be the sensation of the bridge games," said Charley.

"Sal plays a damn fine game of bridge," said Holly. "Don't you forget it."

"I think bridge is a wonderful game," said Joan.

"Wonderful," said Deedee. "We play it all the time."

"Never play it myself," said Holly. "I'm glad you girls like card games."

"We love them," said Deedee.

243

"That's just fine," said Holly. "What do you say to a little poker?"

"Any special kind?" I asked, feeding him his cue.

"Well," said Holly. "Since we're all such good friends, we might just as well get comfortable. How about a nice friendly game of strip poker?"

The girls giggled.

I made a mental agreement with myself that if either of them blushed, I'd double their fee personally. They didn't. They evidently figured giggling was enough. Holly Halloran was too loaded to notice a subtle nuance like a blush.

"I don't think I know how to play," said Deedee.

"Me neither," said Joan.

"It's simple," said Holly. "You just play it like regular poker, except that, instead of betting money or chips, you bet something you're wearing. You just take it off and throw it into the pot. If you win the pot, you get to put back on whatever you bet."

Deedee giggled again. "It sounds like fun," she said.

"It is," said Holly.

"I'll bet Sal's a great poker player," I said.

"Oh, no," said Holly. "Bridge is her game."

"Gen," said Charley, "why don't you and the girls play? I have to be at the office in a couple of hours. I'll just have one more drink and take off."

"You'll stay," said Holly.

There was no mistaking the voice of command and no mistaking the fact that this wasn't a suggestion. It was an order.

"Sure, Gen," said Charley. "I didn't mean I'd leave right now. You know what they say, three's company, five's a crowd."

"Say that's a good one," said Holly. "A damned

good one. Did you get that down for your column, Harry? Three's company, five's a crowd. I don't think old Charley here would mind if you gave me credit for it, would you, Charley?"

"I think it'd be a shame to waste you on the column, Holly," I said. "What I have in mind is maybe doing a full-length piece on you for the *Reader's Digest*. 'The Most Unforgettable Character I Ever Met.' "

"That's a jim-dandy idea," he said. "Me and Sal read the *Reader's Digest* every month. They certainly do have some bang-up articles."

"Bang up," I said.

"I'll tell you what," said Holly. "Let's all have a couple of drinks and dance a little. We have plenty of time for that poker game. Sal always says I'm like a little boy: as long as I know I'm going to get dessert, I don't care how long the rest of the meal takes."

He mixed five heavy Scotches, handed them out and turned on the radio. He took turns dancing with Deedee and Joan. Charley and I sat on the couch and watched.

"Do you get the feeling," I said, "that you're a chaperone at the class-day dance at a cat house?"

"Something like that," said Charley.

"You certainly lead an interesting life, Colonel."

"This is one of the dull evenings. Holly's just a normal, fun-loving American boy. You should see some of the other characters I inherit."

We watched Deedee and Halloran for a minute.

"You know," said Charley, "I always thought that a madame must have a cynical, jaundiced view of life. I know about that now."

"Listen, Charley. I really have to get out of here. The copy boy will be at my apartment to pick up the

245

column at nine thirty this morning. I have to get to work on it. Even with all those gems from the fearless leader, I still have a couple of hours' work ahead of me."

"Cappy, thanks."

"Anytime. I'm available for private parties, bar mitzvahs, patrols and Board of Inquiry hearings. Never too busy to say hello."

"Can we have dinner tonight, Cappy? Just the two of us?"

"Sure. When are you going to get some sleep?"

"I'll cut out of here soon and go home and go to bed. I have an apartment down on Grove Street. I'll show up at the office around four. They're used to that. Where do you want to meet?"

"Why don't you come over to my place around seven?"

I gave him the address and he wrote it down and tucked the piece of paper into his little black book. I was flattered. I was in distinguished company.

"I hate good-byes," I said. "I'll just slip out while the Gen is busy with the troops."

It was easy. I think I could have moved the entire Barnum and Bailey circus through that suite and General Holly Halloran would never have noticed it. When I got to the door, I turned and took a final look. I suppose, to be entirely accurate, you'd have to describe what I saw as a "Halloran Sandwich." The general was standing between Deedee and Joan and they were giggling, tickling and dancing. Charley Bronson was standing at the bar with his back to them, mixing himself a drink. He didn't see me standing there and, when he turned, with the drink in his hand, he looked at the three figures with a look of such intense loathing that I felt sure they must have felt the force of it. For a quick

246

second I had one of those flashes of understanding. I saw a whole succession of evenings like the one I'd gone through. I saw Charley Bronson, who was not a play-boy, a lush or a lecher, doing a job that may have been a hell of a lot more difficult for him than leading a patrol or commanding a repple depple. I left with a kind of grudging respect for him. God! If he wanted the pro-motion that bad, he was certainly earning it. When I got down to the lobby I gave in to an impulse. I went over to the house phone and picked up the receiver.

"Listen," I said. "I'm a guest with a room on the twelfth floor. There's a terribly noisy party going on in Suite Twelve C. Will you please do something about it?"

"But, Sir," said the operator, "you're calling from the lobby."

"I know it, dammit," I said. "It's the only place in the hotel I can get away from the noise."

I hung up, grabbed a cab on the waiting line out-side the hotel and headed for home, feeling a lot better about the whole thing.

The column came easy. I was finished by eight thirty and by the time the boy came to pick up the copy I'd had breakfast and showered and was ready to hit the sack. I wondered how things were in Suite 12 C. I'd taken care of all my obligations in the column. I put in a healthy plug for the French restaurant and the Latin Quarter. I said that the newest singing sensation in the saloon set might well be socialite, Deedee Marshall, who was about to embark on a career as a chantoosy with-out the approval of her veddy social, veddy wealthy Back Bay family. I said that one of the great wits I'd run into around town was Washington Biggie, General Holly

247

Halloran, in town briefly on an important hush-hush assignment. It was a good night's work.

At five thirty, the switchboard called to wake me up, and fifteen minutes later room service delivered my breakfast and all the morning and afternoon papers. I spent twenty-five minutes on the phone with my secretary downtown at the paper and she went through the mail with me. I dictated answers to any letters that needed answering. I normally don't eat dinner until ten thirty or eleven at night and I try to combine it with work by choosing a place like Sardi's or El Morocco or the Sert Room, where I can pick up some items along with the nourishment. I also like to stay three or four columns ahead so that I can take an occasional night off, but when you're writing the kind of three-dot, spot-gossip stuff I was writing, you can't get very far ahead of yourself. Once in a while, for a change of pace, I do a full column of blind items without names, using the stuff I couldn't use with names without turning into a shill for Reno. It isn't a bad life. You eat well, you become the most overentertained man of your generation and you long for a nice quiet evening with your in-laws in Queens, talking about baseball and the plumbing bills. The paper I worked for made it a policy of never keeping a man on a column assignment more than three years. They figured by that time he'd be so bored that some of the dullness he was exposed to rubbed off on the column. But being a columnist is a fatal disease. I've never known an ex-columnist who didn't resent every penny he had to pay to buy a book, a meal, a ticket to a play or a movie or a bar bill. Once you live your life on a due bill, you're ruined.

Charley Bronson showed up at seven fifteen. I made drinks and we sat down and talked.

"I'm glad you're doing so well, Cappy," he said.

"I'm doing all right, Charley. I figure I'll be off this column beat in a couple of years."

"You must have made a lot of dough out of the book and the movie job."

"Most of the book money went for income tax. Most of the money from the movie job went to real-estate agents and bartenders. What the hell! The success of the book was a freak and since I got a free ride to the Coast, I figured I might just as well live it up a little. You'd be surprised how a swimming pool and a couple of starlets can eat into your bank account. How's the world's greatest general this morning?"

"I put him on a plane two hours ago. He wasn't feeling too well."

"Did you stick around long after I left?"

"Somebody complained about the noise and the house detective arrived. That took care of the dancing. In case you're interested, the gen won the strip poker game."

"It figured," I said.

"Where do you want to eat, Cappy?"

"I don't know. If you'd like, we can order from room service and spend the evening talking and playing chess."

"That sounds like a wonderful idea. Are you due anywhere?"

"I have to go to an opening-night party about midnight. It won't last long. The play is a dog and by one o'clock, when the reviews come out, nobody's going to feel much like celebrating. You want to come along?"

"No thanks. I'll go home to bed when you leave for your party."

"Has it really been rough, Charley?"

249

"It's been very rough. After they sent me home from Europe, I thought seriously about retiring."

"Why didn't you?"

"What would I do? This is the only trade I know, Cappy. It's a little late to start as an office boy. There aren't many jobs floating around for colonels who resign after being kicked in the rump by a Board of Inquiry. I couldn't pull any strings for anybody at the Pentagon like some of the retired generals that are always getting seventy-five thousand dollars a year as chairman of somebody's board. Even if all that wasn't true, Cappy, I couldn't quit. It would be like walking out on a play in the middle of the second act. You may think you know how it's going to end, but there's always the chance that the playwright has a couple of surprises up his sleeve in the third act."

"How about Margaret?"

"What do you mean, how about Margaret?"

"How does she feel about the whole thing?"

"I really don't know, Cappy. Margaret and I have long since given up confiding in each other. I really don't know what she thinks or feels or wants any more."

"That's too bad."

"I suppose it is. And I suppose, looked at objectively, it's a failure as a marriage. If it is, the fault is mine."

"If that's true, Charley, why don't you do something about it?"

"I think the time has passed when anybody can do anything about it."

"That's too bad," I said.

"Yes, I suppose it is. I don't know, Cappy. I've always felt that, once I make general, I can turn my attention to living my life and straightening it out."

"It may be too late then."

"You think I have an obsession about promotion, don't you?"

"Don't you?"

"I suppose so. It's more than an obsession, Cappy. It's something they owe me. I've worked hard at my trade all my life. Even now. You saw me last night. I even work hard"—he paused and lit a cigarette—"You were right, Cappy," he continued. "You were right when you said I'd do anything to get the star. I have. I'll use anything that comes to my hand, use anybody and never stop to examine the ethics of the morality involved."

"What does that mean?"

"Something I did. Last night."

"What'd you do, feed Holly Halloran a poisoned call girl?"

"I'll tell you about it later. I don't think you're going to like it much and I'd just as soon tell you after we've had a chance to talk and eat and drink together."

"You're pretty mysterious for a chicken colonel."

"Sure," he said. "Sure. How about some chess?"

"Fine," I said. I went to the sideboard and got out the chessboard and the carved set that was the duplicate of the one I'd given him at the repple depple.

He fingered the pieces and started to laugh.

"What's so funny?" I asked.

"I was just thinking of the set we could have made for Holly Halloran."

"You couldn't send it through the mail," I said. "But I'd sure like to be there when Sal opened the package."

"To hell with it. Let's play chess."

I think if you toted up all the time Charley and I have spent together in our lives almost half of it was

251

spent across the chessboard. I hadn't played in a long time and, in the middle of the second game, I suddenly realized how much I was enjoying myself. We took a break there, had dinner sent up, on a whim ordered some German beer and went back to the chessboard and played until eleven fifteen. I started to get dressed for the party. Charley sat on the bed and watched me in silence.

"You have something on your mind," I said. "Go ahead, shoot."

"Before I tell you about it, Cappy, I'd like to say something."

"What's all the mystery about? What's on your mind, Charley?"

"Will you let me tell you my own way?"

"Go ahead."

"You mind if I mix myself a drink?"

"This must really be something."

"It is."

"Go ahead. Mix one for me while you're at it. I don't think it would be wise to show up completely sober at the wake."

I finished dressing and came out into the sitting room. Charley had the drinks in his hand.

I took one and sat facing him. "O.K. You may fire when ready."

"I'm very fond of you, Cappy. It's a little silly to say that I suppose, when you think of how little time we've actually spent together and how casually we know each other, but I have the feeling that you're fond of me, too. You may not always approve of what I do or how I do it, but you have a kind of compassion and understanding."

252

"You're really backing into this one, aren't you?" I asked.

"I'm what you'd call a loner," he said. "You know what I mean? I haven't made any real friends . . . not since my second year at the Point. As a matter of fact, I guess you could say that you're the only friend I have in the world."

"Get to the commercial, Charley," I said.

"Don't be so damn flip and sophisticated, Cappy."

"I'm sorry, Charley. I feel pretty much the same way about you."

Charley reached into his pocket and pulled out an envelope. He tossed it across to me. "Take a look at these," he said.

I opened the envelope. Inside were pictures taken with Holly Halloran's Polaroid camera. The first five were the ones that we'd taken while I was still there. There were also pictures of the strip-poker game at various stages of its development and finally a series of pictures co-starring Holly, Deedee and Joan. They were very sharp and very clear.

"Well?" asked Charley.

"General Holly Halloran in the nude is a rather staggering sight. It isn't something you'd be apt to see on a recruiting poster."

"I told you I was ruthless, Cappy. I told you I'd do anything to get that star on my shoulder."

"Maybe you'd just better begin at the beginning, Charley."

He took a long slug at his drink.

"The idea came to me when we got back to his suite last night and he showed us the camera. He was very proud of the camera, so there was no problem taking the pictures of the poker game."

"How about the others?"

"He was too drunk or too engrossed to notice or care."

"O.K. So you tried a little blackmail on Holly Halloran."

"No, I didn't."

"Wait a minute, Charley. You've lost me. Holly Halloran could pull enough wires to get you that promotion. You wound up with a collection of snapshots that might be worth quite a bit to a sober, Sal-bound Holly Halloran. What do you mean, you didn't try any blackmail? What did you take them for, your memory book or your twenty-fifth reunion at the Point?"

"If I'd tried blackmailing him, Cappy, it would have cooked my goose good. A few words in the right quarter to wearers of the ring and I'd have been quietly bounced out on my ear with no way of tying Holly to the bouncing. And no matter what the provocation, no West Pointer ever blackmails another. I think it's in the articles of war."

"So?"

"So I want that promotion. I said that, when an officer retires, they almost always, as a gesture, promote him one rank so he can retire on a higher pension. I said almost. Not always. In my case I think they would probably have passed up that nice little social amenity. I'd already used up whatever consideration and favors were owed to me as a member of the club when they cleared me at the Board of Inquiry."

"I repeat. So?"

"So I couldn't blackmail Holly."

"But I could. Is that what you're trying to say, Charley?"

"That's what I'm trying to say."

"Go ahead, give me all of it."

"The gen wasn't feeling very good when I woke him up. He was hung over and he was certain that he had something in excess of four hundred dollars when he got back to the hotel this morning. His wallet was empty."

"Deedee and Joan rolled him."

"Personally I think they earned it."

"After looking at those pictures, Charley, I know they earned it. Go on."

"I fed him breakfast and packed for him. I loaned him a couple of hundred bucks to take care of his hotel bill, tips and taxi fare to the airport and then I sat down and had a heart-to-heart talk with him."

"That's when you flashed the pictures?"

"That's when."

"It must have been a memorable moment."

"It was. He had no memory of the picture-taking at all. You like a little piece of ironic humor?"

"Sure," I said.

"He kept saying, over and over, 'And he took these horrible pictures with Sal's Christmas present!' I apologized for having introduced you to him. I said I didn't know much about you, that we'd met casually during the war when you were a correspondent, but I discovered that the column was only a side line with you. I told him that your real business was blackmail."

"Thanks a lot."

"I told him you'd been to see me this morning with a whole collection of pictures. I told him that the ones I'd shown him were only a few of the less sensational ones you had. I told him you wanted twenty-five thousand dollars in cash or you were going to deliver them personally to Sal and his superior officer at the Pentagon."

"How did he take this interesting piece of news?"

"He got sick."

"You mean like I'm going to get sick in a minute?"

"Cappy, I had to do it."

"Like you had to badger that captain and beat him to death with your fists? You mean like you had to walk into that trap in the Siegfried and lose two companies?"

"God damn you. You have no right to talk to me that way."

"I have every right in the world to talk to you. I bought that right, Colonel. I have the right to pound you off a couple of walls if I want to. What right do you have to use me the way you've used me since I met you? Who the hell are you, Colonel Bronson? I don't recognize the divinity in that class ring of yours. I don't belong to your goddamned club."

"I deserve that, Cappy."

"Don't get humble on me, Charley. If there's one thing I can't stand, it's a humble heel. You'll forgive me if I don't think the world is coming to an end if you don't make buck general."

"You want to hear the rest of it, or don't you?"

"You bet I want to hear the rest of it."

"Where was I?"

"General Holly Halloran was getting sick. You had just happened to mention that I was a blackmailer and old Sal was going to get a private showing of some rather interesting pictures. I think you also mentioned that I planned to give a chalk talk on them to his superior officer at the Pentagon."

"I told him you wanted twenty-five thousand dollars. I told him that I thought I could pull some strings and apply some pressure on you and get the pictures back and shut you up."

"How did you tell him you were going to do that?"

"I told him I knew where a couple of bodies were buried."

"You sure do."

Charley looked at me. He flushed and he tightened his fingers into a fist.

"That gets to you, doesn't it, Charley? That hits you where you live? You think you have the patent on cruelty?"

"I told him I had an in with the publisher of your paper and that you wouldn't want to take a chance on losing the column which was the source of all your information for a lousy twenty-five thousand dollars. I told him I was very sure that I could get the pictures back and shut you up."

"He must have been grateful."

"He was. He said, if I could do that, he'd never forget it."

"And you drove in over left tackle after he gave you that opening?"

"I told him that, if I did it, I'd depend on his being grateful. He said, if I got those pictures back, he'd do anything I wanted him to do. I told him I wanted a promotion. I told him to go back to Washington and work on that and I'd stay here and work on you."

"You mean you're going to keep him dangling for a while?"

"The army kept me dangling for a long time, Cappy. It might even do Holly a little good. It might even sweat some of that potbelly off him."

"You are a sadist."

"Yes, I suppose I am."

"You're full of fine talk about how I'm the only friend you have and how important that is to you. You're

257

a loner all right. So were Bruno Hauptmann and John Dillinger."

"Come on, Cappy. It isn't that bad, is it?"

"You don't think it's that bad? You don't see anything immoral and dishonest in what you did?"

"To Holly Halloran?"

"No dammit, not to Holly Halloran. To me. To me."

"Does it really matter that much to you that a fool like Holly Halloran thinks you're a blackmailer? What do you care what Holly Halloran thinks of you?"

"That's not the point, Colonel. That is not even close to the point."

"And what is the point?"

"The point is that you are so obsessed by that star on your shoulder that friendship doesn't mean a damn thing to you. You'd steam-roller anybody that got in your way and that includes the German army, me or your wife."

"Margaret has nothing to do with this. I'm sorry you feel that way about it, Cappy."

"How would you expect me to feel?"

"I'd expect you to understand that it must be something I want very much or I wouldn't do what I had to do to get it."

"Why don't you just get the hell out of here, Charley. Why don't you just get to work on that second star. Hell, who wants to be a buck general when he has friends he hasn't even used."

Charley got up and went over to the chair and picked up his hat and coat. He put them on and walked to the door.

"Someday you may understand the whole thing, Cappy."

258

"I understand it just fine now."

He opened the door and paused in the doorway. "So long, Cappy," he said.

"So long, Gen."

La Guardia ☆ 1953

"Did he ever tell you about our meeting and what happened?" I asked.

"I wasn't with him much then," said Margaret. "I was back in Fallview. He was on the road, like a traveling salesman, filling in."

"It was quite an evening."

"In what way, Harry?"

"Did you ever meet Holly Halloran? Big man, potbellied. One star general. Maybe two when you met him. Red-faced. Had a wife named Sal."

"Always laughed at his own jokes?"

"That's the boy."

"Jim-dandy, we used to call him. I remember him. We saw a lot of him while we were in Washington. He was in Charley's class at the Point, I think. Why?"

"I met him that night with Charley in that bar in New York. He never told you about that?"

"No. Should he have told me?"

"I don't know. It seemed important to me at the time. Maybe it wasn't so important after all."

"Charley had that New York assignment for almost a year. Then suddenly he got orders for Washington, was permanently assigned to the Pentagon and got his promotion."

260

"When was that?"

"In March or April of 1949."

"That late?"

"I'm sure it was either March or April. I remember it started getting hot in Washington a month or so after we arrived. We had a house in Georgetown. It was an old carriage house on one of those cobblestone streets. I loved it."

"You're sure it wasn't around Christmas of 1948 or early January?"

"I'm very sure. Charley came home for Christmas that year. He seemed changed."

"How?"

"Different. He was very nice to Pop and we went away together for ten days up to Canada to ski. He said there was a chance that his promotion would be coming through and that he'd get some sort of a permanent assignment. I'd heard that before. He went back to New York in the middle of January and I didn't see him again until he came to Fallview with his orders and asked me to go on ahead to Washington and find a house."

"Did he ever tell you how he got the promotion? How he got the Washington assignment?"

"No. I never asked him. I know he was trying to pull strings with old classmates. Is that why you brought up Holly Halloran? Did he get the promotion for Charley?"

"I don't know. I just wondered. Was it any different in Washington?"

"For a while it was. I stopped drinking and acting like a tramp. I told you, I'm the world's number one 'This time it'll be different' discipline."

"Was it?"

"Well . . . Washington wasn't like an army post. We had, as I said, a house in Georgetown. Charley left for the

Pentagon in the morning like any other husband who was off for work. I made a lot of friends and there were things to do. The kind of things you don't find around army camps, things like concerts and plays and formal dinners where the conversation wasn't restricted to army shoptalk. If we weren't the slick magazine's ideal of a married couple, there were enough distractions to take our minds off that. I think the only army people we saw at all were Holly Halloran and Sal. I don't know how I pulled a blank on his name before. How could you forget Holly Halloran or Sal for that matter?"

"I met him only once, but I could draw him from memory."

"Oh God! It all comes back. I remember Charley kept including them in every dinner party we had."

"I think he owed Holly at least a couple of meals. I think it's a safe guess that without Holly Halloran your husband would still be floating around army camps in this country filling in instead of being on the receiving end of a hero's welcome."

"Fate chooses rather strange vehicles for its purpose, doesn't it?"

"Are you talking about Holly or Charley?"

"Both. The wife of a hero, how about that, Harry?"

"A pretty unlikely piece of casting. Almost as strange as casting me as the one and only friend of the hero."

"Would you tell me something, just between the two of us?"

"Sure."

"What Charley did in Korea wasn't too much different from what he did in the Siegfried Line. He got surrounded, sucked in and clobbered. In one case they bounce him out of the combat area and in the other they

262

turn him into the biggest thing since Lindbergh. How come?"

"There was a big difference, Margaret. In Germany he walked into a trap, disobeyed orders and lost ninety per cent of his men. In Korea the whole army was retreating in the face of the Chinese Communist troops. They were pulling back, 'bugging out' they called it. They were trying to pull back with as many men and as much equipment as they could until they got back to a defensible line. You know, Margaret, in spite of myself, in spite of knowing Charley, in spite of having spent most of my life in a profession that makes a specialty of looking for the clay in the feet instead of the gold in the halo, I'm impressed as hell. When I really think about what he did I get goose flesh down my back. Do you really know what he did, Margaret?"

"I read the stories in the papers."

"To hell with his motives. To hell with why he did it. He did something magnificent. When you read about it in the history books, it won't matter a hoot in hell who Charley Bronson was or why he did what he did or how many head doctors claim he had a death wish. What will matter is that he held up the whole damned forward wall of the Chinese army at one vitally vulnerable point long enough to allow a division of men to escape. In a way, you know, it was a kind of cockeyed example of military genius."

"Genius?"

"Yes."

"Come on, Harry. I know you're a member of the Charley Bronson fan club, but that's a little heavy isn't it? Where was the genius in turning yourself into a sitting duck?"

"But he did more than turn himself into a sitting

duck, Margaret. You know, for all your talk about bridge games and the boredom of being an army wife, I think you're pretty uninformed about your husband's business."

"Go ahead, Harry," she said. "Tell it good."

"All right. The Chinese came pouring through and the whole damned army started to pull back. Do you have any idea of what it's like to be involved in a retreat? All the things you take for granted disappear. Communications get to be pretty primitive when you pull out wires and take off. Nobody knows where anybody else is. Everybody is so hell-bent on getting back safely that he doesn't give a damn for anyone else. You never really know where the enemy is or when he's suddenly going to come bouncing in on your flank or attack you from behind. It's a pretty wild and frightening feeling to be part of a retreating army."

"You really have a kind of boy scout view of war, don't you, Harry?"

"Everybody does, deep down. It's an ambivalent thing. I hate war. Intellectually, that is. All the time I was on the line in World War Two I hated it. I saw a lot of friends blown to pieces or shot down. I knew how filthy and dirty it was. I knew about the lice and the trench feet and the fear and the futility. And yet—I admit it— it was exciting. It was damned exciting. If you live through it, it's important to you as a man to know that you took the big gamble, you played for the big stakes. At least once you put your life up for grabs."

"You ought to go in for recruiting. You'd be great at it."

"Let me get back to Charley for a minute. Back to what was happening in Korea. He had one of the roughest jobs in the world, trying to pull back a whole division with limited supplies, no intelligence reports to guide him and the kind of panic that retreat breeds. He took a calculated risk. He stopped the division and dug them in. He halted the crazy pell-mell rush back to the rear. He had to find out what was behind him and what was in front of him. He sent patrols out and he found out. He found out that they were pouring in on him from all sides. He knew that not only was he going to get massacred, but his area was the end of the funnel, and the whole damned Chinese army was going to pour through and overrun the others who were just blindly running back. He kept one battalion with him and sent the rest of the division back. He used that battalion to build up a defensive position. He rimmed his position with deep trenches. He set up a circular defense. To hell with M-1's. He set up the light and the heavy machine guns and the mortars around the perimeter of his position in a three-hundred-and-sixty degree arc and he kept one company with him to man them. He had only one crazy, unrealistic plan, to hit the Reds with every piece of heavy armament he had when they attacked; to make them feel, by committing everything he had, that he had a lot more, and maybe to stall them while they made plans for storming a position that they thought was much more heavily defended than it was. He was fighting for the one thing that offered any hope—time. Now comes the genius part. He hooked up all the guns with a crazy arrangement of wires to one central control point. In other words, Margaret, one man in a hole could sit and fire the machine guns all around that defense perimeter. And then when the Chinese did attack, he pulled another crazy stunt. He had the men in that one company that stayed behind with him take off for the rear one man at a time. It was a military version of the Haydn Farewell Symphony

265

where the musicians disappear one at a time. And as the men took off, he took over that gun by remote control. Finally there was nobody left on that hill but good old Charley Bronson. He sat there alone and pulled those wires and fired those guns until he ran out of ammunition. And dammit, it worked. It stopped the Reds cold. They regrouped for a counterattack and when they did come, there was nothing to stop them but a lot of empty guns and one shot-up buck general."

"It *was* something, wasn't it, Harry?"

"Something! The newspapers threw around a lot of talk about his saving the retreat and being responsible for getting the bulk of the American army safely through that sector. I don't know about that. Maybe all he did was slow them up for a couple of hours. What is important is that it was one hell of an awesome thing to do. As far as I'm concerned, Charley Bronson evened the score with everybody on that hill in Korea. He paid off for everything he ever did to any of us."

I smiled at Margaret a little sheepishly. I'd gotten carried away by my oratory. I mixed myself a drink and offered her one. She shook her head.

"Only one thing went wrong with his plan, Margaret," I said. "When the Reds overran his position he was unconscious. He had two slugs in his legs and one in his back. Instead of being able to rush at them in a final suicidal gesture of defiance, he was out cold and helpless and they took him prisoner."

"How do you know he was going to do that? What makes you so damned sure?"

"It figures, off past performance, doesn't it?"

"Off past performance it figures, all right, but that doesn't make it a fact."

' "Anyway, they carted him off to a prison and the

266

army sat on the story of Charley Bronson until they were able to arrange to have him exchanged. A couple of weeks in a hospital in Seoul and they have a great big fat Korean War Hero on their hands."

The door opened and Buddy came in.

"He's about five minutes out, Harry," he said. "They just contacted the tower for landing instructions. The jets should be flying over any minute. The newsreel and TV people are asking for Mrs. Bronson."

"Right, Buddy, we'll be right out."

Buddy went out and closed the door behind him.

"Ready?" I asked.

"As ready as I'm going to be."

"I don't know about you, Margaret, but I, for one, will be damned glad to see him."

"I'm always glad to see him." She smiled at me and reached for my drink. "Can I have a sip? I'm scared silly."

"Maybe this is time for a small act of faith, Margaret. Why don't you try it without the booze?"

There was a loud roar as a formation of jets swooped over the field.

"I'm afraid, Harry."

"Come on. You're a big girl now."

She was crying quietly.

"I've done this once too often. I cannot go out there and meet Charley again with the nagging hope in the back of my head that it's really going to be different this time."

"Then try it the other way. It isn't going to be different. You know damned well it won't be any different."

"I'm not sure this time, Harry. It could be."

She reached into her pocket and pulled out a letter. She handed it to me. "I've been holding out on you, Harry. I keep downgrading it in my mind. That's why I

267

didn't say anything to you about it. If it turned out to be unimportant, it wouldn't make any difference. He wrote it in the hospital in Seoul."

"And?"

"I won't be suckered again, Harry. I won't run to him like a faithful dog, expecting a pat and getting a slap. I've done it too often. At first I wasn't going to come at all. I had to. I knew that. I owed him that. Then I started to drink again to bring back what you call 'tough old Margaret.' That didn't work, either. In spite of everything, there was the old familiar feeling that maybe it was going to be different this time. Only this time I had something a little more tangible to base it on than my own hopes."

"The letter?"

"Read it."

I opened the letter. The first two pages told her about the prison camp and kept repeating that he was all right. On page two there was a paragraph that I read twice.

"I told the newspapermen that I was unconscious when the Chinese troops overran the position," it said. "That wasn't true. I'd been shot in the legs and had a shrapnel wound in my back, but I was still able to walk. I suppose to be accurate, I should say hobble. My plan was to run, screaming, toward the first Commie soldier I saw, and have him shoot me down. But suddenly, alone on that hill waiting for them to come, I realized a lot of things. I realized what I had done to you. I realized that finally I had earned that star on my shoulder. I realized that Helen was really dead. Most important of all, I realized that I wanted to live. I wanted to live. Not to die. I put my hands over my head and sat in that hole in the ground, crying. I was crying for Helen and for you and a little bit for myself. It's ironic, Margaret, but that general's star on my shoulder saved my life. Even a Chinese Communist GI has an awe for the star. If I'd been anything less than a general, I'm sure they'd have shot me down. But troops don't go shooting generals down. They're very valuable for information and hostage purposes. So they put me on a litter, carried me to the rear and I became a prisoner of war. I'm telling you all this very badly, but I'm doing it because I want you to know that your husband is coming home. Not Helen's fiancé, or General Bronson or the man you married. Your husband."

"You see?" asked Margaret, when I'd finished reading the letter.

"Yes, Margaret. I see. And I think maybe he does, too."

"I'm ready," she said.

"Good."

"A regular Myrna Loy."

We went out through the waiting room. The bar was empty. A policeman spotted us just outside the gate where the plane was due to unload and made an opening through the crowd for us. The band, the school children and an assortment of army brass were in place. The newspaper men and the photographers were out on the field. The TV camera was sweeping across the crowd on the promenade deck. I spotted an army plane coming in for a landing.

"There it is," I said.

"Where?" asked Margaret.

I pointed the plane out to her and she watched it come in and touch down. Her eyes were never off it while it taxied across the field. It finally swung around, the motors died and attendants rushed out and pushed the portable steps into place. The detachment of soldiers that were standing with the honor guard were called to attention and presented arms. The band began playing "The Corps" and I was amazed to discover that I was crying. I've always been a sucker for bands, parades and "America, the Beautiful."

The door of the plane opened and Charley Bronson stepped out. A great cheer went up from the crowd and we were pushed forward by the crush of the photographers and reporters behind us. I found myself standing next to Margaret at the foot of the ramp. I looked up at Charley and smiled and he smiled back. He looked the same . . . a little thinner, a little grayer, but the same. He saw Margaret and he ran down the stairs and took her in his arms. They held on to each other and I could see that they were both crying.

"I'm home, Margaret," he said. "I'm home and I love you very much. . . ."

I pushed my way through the crowd, into the passenger shed, out into the main rotunda and down to the taxi stand. A cab pulled up and I climbed in. "The Waldorf," I said.

There was a newspaper on the back seat of the cab and I picked it up.

"Bronson Home," it said.

You know, for once they were right.

He really was.

For the first time.